Death

The Hex Next Door

Witches of Moondale: Book One

By: Lou Wilham

Death

Midnight Tide

praise for the hex next door

"Hex has it all... Charming characters with deadly pasts, a sassy bewitched house beside a graveyard, and a mystery that digs its claws in and drags you into the afterlife."

   - **H.R. Truelove**, Author of *Alter*

"Once again, Wilham brings together a collection of unique characters who create a beautiful landscape of representation and individuality. The Hex Next Door is a lovely picture of family being more than just blood, and reminds us that those who truly love us, will always find a way to be there for us."

   - **Christis Christie**, Author of *Ephesus*

"If The Ex-Hex and Practical Magic had a sapphic baby, it would be The Hex Next Door. A wickedly charming second chance HFN romance wrapped in a snarky, Cozy Witch package."

   - **Justin Arnold**, Author of *Wicked Little Things*

"An eloquently imaginative read with an intriguing plot line and creative setting. [The Hex Next Door] is a brilliantly magical start to a bright new series."

   - **Nicole Northwood**, Author of *The Devil You Know*

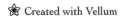 Created with Vellum

To those of you looking for home.
Sometimes it's right where you left it.

Emily

Always believe in

your own magic! ✦

Lou Willa

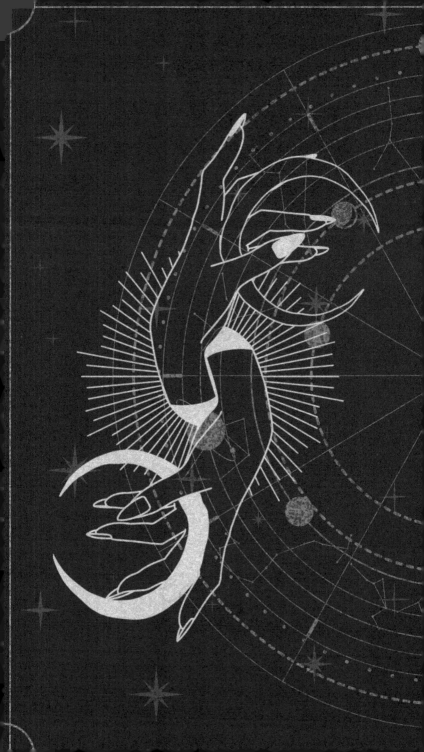

1

"WHAT THE FUCK," Rus muttered, her gaze fixed on the Moondale town sign. She'd said she'd never come back to this place. But that was the thing about where you grew up: it had the power to drag you back like the fucking Bermuda Triangle. And Rus would know—she'd been to the Bermuda Triangle four or five times in the years since she'd left Moondale behind. The particulars weren't important. What was important was that Rus was sure she'd wind up there four or five more times before she died.

"Rus?" Nesta tilted their head, a piece of floppy black hair falling into their eyes. They looked just how Rus remembered them, and she still wasn't sure how to feel about that. But she'd likely beg for Nesta's skin care regime before the day was done.

"Nothing. Let's just get this over with." Rus shook herself and jerked her gaze back to the view through the windshield.

Moondale looked different and yet the same. It had sprawled out past the little dot on the coast where its founders had originally settled, up into the mountain beyond to include a ski lodge and even a few big-name hotels. Of that Rus was grateful; she didn't think she could stay in one of the inns in town with the kids. Not if she wanted to keep the Board of Magic off her ass for more than a week.

Nesta was still glancing at her from the driver's seat. Rus could feel those cunning eyes looking for . . . something. Maybe some sign of what Rus was thinking. They wouldn't find anything. More than a decade spanned between them, and Rus had learned long ago to keep her thoughts tucked away where they couldn't be used against her.

"I just can't believe you became a realtor." Rus tilted her head, letting a teasing smile tug up the corners of her mouth. It would hopefully be enough to keep Nesta from asking inconvenient questions.

Nesta shrugged, turning down one of the side roads off Main Street. They were headed toward the older part of town, the buildings around them changing from relatively modern retail to small suburban homes to Gothic-style houses that would make the Addams family jealous.

"How did your parents take it?" Rus pressed. Anything to ignore the way her stomach was writhing with nerves. She hoped she wouldn't see anyone else she knew, not before she was settled. But in a town that hardly had more than a few thousand residents to boast, that was likely impossible. At least *she'd* be at work, so Rus could avoid that particular awkward encounter. "I mean . . . a cupid not becoming a matchmaker for the board? That's—"

"I told them I didn't think the board would be using matchmakers much longer," Nesta said, and they sounded smug about it. Like they'd realized a new hairstyle would be trending long before anyone else could.

"And?" Rus had to know, because she could just

imagine old man Holyore absolutely losing his shit at his child chucking tradition out the proverbial window. He might quiver right out of his beard.

"And they didn't agree . . ." Nesta's mouth twisted up into a knowing smirk, their eyes still firmly on the road. "At first."

Well. That sounded like a story and a half. One they probably didn't have time for, and it would likely require wine. Lots of wine. Rus snorted, rolling her eyes. "Okay, but a realtor though?"

"Why not? The same principles apply. It's all about listening to harmonizing energies. And this house?" Nesta put the car in park outside of yet another Gothic-style house perched on the far end of one of Moondale's more ancient-looking cemeteries. "It wants you, Rus."

"Ew. Don't make it sound creepy." Rus huffed, her hand twitching to give Nesta a fond shove, but she resisted the urge. They weren't friends like that, not anymore. So instead, she turned her attention to the house.

Rus blinked up at it. It looked like something out of Hansel and Gretel, with a small porch, three walk-out balconies off the rooms upstairs, and a legit tower. Or . . . maybe *tower* wasn't the word for whatever that was, but Rus imagined the room on the first floor would be the perfect place to put a reading and playroom for the girls, and the second an ideal shrine for their parents' tablets. The only thing was —

"Nesta, you are aware that this house is . . . *pink*, right?" Rus cocked her head. It wasn't unbearably pink. It didn't reek of Barbie Dreamhouse. But it was most definitely a shade of pastel that Rus was sure she'd never worn in her entire life.

"Lilac, actually. And what's that saying about not judging a house by its siding color?"

"I'm pretty sure that's not a thing."

"You ready to see inside, or what?" Nesta asked, already reaching for the door to climb out.

Rus nodded dumbly, scrambling from the car to follow them through the little wrought iron gate and up the walk. The door opened onto a small foyer bedecked in black walls, and a little gray bench off to the side with hooks hanging above it for coats.

Nesta was saying something about the history of the house, and the remodeling, and something about all the furnishings coming with the place if that's what she wanted, but Rus had largely stopped listening. Because the house— 157 Mourning Moore—was exactly what Rus had always imagined when she'd thought of a home for herself. The walls were all black, but there was enough natural lighting about the place that it didn't feel dark and gloomy. And there were pops of color here and there: A throw pillow on the bench in the foyer. Silver birch tree wallpaper in the study. A collection of velvet pillows in the strange round room of the tower that Rus had decided would make a great study and playroom. It was—

"Who's watching the kids?"

"Huh?" Rus shook herself, tearing her eyes away from the frankly spectacular nursery. Aihuan was a little old for a crib, but that was an easy enough fix. She'd love the brightly painted forest critters on the black wallpaper. "Oh. Their Uncle Fernando. But I can't leave them with him long, or by the time I get back they'll have given him a makeover. Buzzcut included. Meiling is a menace."

"Fernando?"

"Yeah. He's one of the witches I met online. Good kid. Little awkward, but who isn't these days? He'll be moving in with us for a bit until we're settled in and we can find him his own place." Rus paced to the window. The view from the nursery was of Moondale, and not the cemetery. She'd have to check to make sure Meiling's window didn't overlook it either. Neither of her girls needed to see the spirits that were standing on the edge of the property looking up at the house. Even now, Rus could feel their gaze on her, making the hair on the back of her neck stand on end. Really, she'd thought the board had Rules about letting spirits languish without rest like that. But then . . . maybe they hadn't had another medium in town since she'd left. And if those spirits weren't doing anything other than just floating around, no one would notice them outside of a medium.

"Is he your . . . ?" Nesta drifted off, their perfectly plucked brows turning down to wrinkle in the middle.

Rus laughed. "Goddess no. We're just friends. He's good with the girls, though."

"I see. Well. There's still the attic." Nesta gestured to the narrow stairs that led up to the last room in the house.

"Lead the way." Rus gestured for Nesta to go first and followed them when they turned on their heel to head upstairs. She'd have to set wards to make sure the girls didn't leave the house without her knowing if she wasn't on the same floor as them. But what was magic for if not to keep her girls safe?

The little door at the top of the steps opened to a large bedroom with stripe charcoal on black wallpapered walls, an awkwardly cut ceiling, and a heavy-looking fourposter bed. In the one little nook in front of a window that overlooked the cemetery was a small desk, which would be perfect for Rus's more . . . unsavory experiments. And opposite that was a small bathroom with a clawfoot tub, two tiny stand sinks, a toilet, and a plant in front of a window that would definitely not live to see the end of the week if Rus had anything to say about it.

"Okay. You're right." Rus laughed a little to herself as she turned to tip an imaginary hat to Nesta. "Me and this house are soulmates."

"I hate to say I told you so—"

"No, you don't."

"I'll go grab the paperwork out of the car. Meet me on the back porch. And feel free to look around the yard."

"Is it screened in?"

"Would I show you a house with a porch that wasn't?" Nesta winked, and then disappeared down the steps.

Rus went back into the bedroom and turned on her heel, looking around. It would need some personalization, but she could see herself being quite happy there. "Well," she said to the house because places, like people, liked to be acknowledged. "I hope you'll take good care of me and my girls."

The house didn't respond. They never did. But when Rus made her way past the nursery again, the crib had been swapped out for a little gray loft bed with a slide and a toy chest underneath. And, she supposed, that was enough of an answer.

The yard abutted two sides of the old cemetery, which seemed to have been built around the house instead of vice versa. Rus exhaled loudly, her breath pushing strands of chin-length bright pink hair out of her face.

"I'm going to have to do something about you, aren't I?" she said more to herself than to the spirits toeing the line between the yard and the cemetery. There was no fence to distinguish one from the other, but it was clear where her yard ended and the graveyard began because the spirits wouldn't cross the property line. "The worst part is, the board probably won't even give me credit for it. They'll attribute the lowered negative energy to like . . . their attempts to promote unity through more frequent clan and coven meetings or some shit." Rus snorted, rolling her eyes.

"It's warded." Nesta slapped a manila folder down onto the back porch table.

"Hm?"

"The whole property is warded against malignant energies. That's one of the selling points."

"Who did the wards?" Rus sat in one of the wrought iron chairs and started flipping through the contract, pretending to read it. They both knew that was bullshit; Rus had never read paperwork a day in her life. But she liked to pretend she was an adult who considered big commitments like a house carefully.

"Crimson Tide Coven."

"Of fucking course it was them." Rus huffed. "You think Greer will be super pissed if I take them all down and put up my own?"

"Probably. But when was the last time you cared what Evander Greer thought? Plus, if you sign here"—Nesta tapped the paper with one neatly rounded fingernail—"it'll be your property and there's nothing anyone can say about it, not even the sheriff."

"Doesn't mean the board won't try," Rus grumbled, grabbing the pen to start signing her life away. "Wait." She stopped halfway through the fourth page. "Did you just say *sheriff*?"

"Yeah. Sheriff Evander Greer." Nesta tilted their head, but their mouth was twitching up at the corners.

Rus groaned, dropping forward to smack her head on the table. It hurt. But likely not as much as a run-in with *Sheriff Greer* would. "Remind me to stay out of his way for the next like . . . hundred years or so."

"Oh, don't be silly. I'm sure he's not still holding a grudge because of the time you—"

Rus lifted her head just enough to raise one brow at Nesta.

"Well, maybe he is. But either way, you'll be fine. I mean, you've got your girls, and the house, and the business. There won't be time for you to stir up trouble."

Rus continued to stare at them with the same brow lifted.

"I won't tell him you're back in town, and maybe he'll never find out?" Nesta sagged.

"That's all you had to say." Rus sat up and went back to signing the papers. "Maybe I shouldn't have come back, though. We could have gone . . . somewhere else."

"Why *did* you come back?" Nesta pulled out a chair to sit across from her, their face suddenly open with curiosity.

"Moondale's got a good school system for witches." The lie slipped easily off her tongue. It wasn't even really a lie — Moondale did have an excellent magical school system. But she was sure she could have found someplace equally as good in Europe if she'd wanted to. Or even taught the girls herself. But there was safety in a place as steeped in magic as Moondale was. The very earth the place was built on would give off enough ambient energy to hide Rus and her children. Or so she hoped.

"Fine. Keep your secrets." Nesta leaned over to watch Rus scrawl her untidy signature across page after page of legalese.

Rus lifted the pen to shake out her hand where it had started to cramp when she finally got to the last page.

"So, are you going to see Azure?"

Rus's hand jerked, the pen skittering and leaving a nasty mark across the page that she was sure Nesta would need to reprint. "What?"

"Azure Elwood. Are you going to go see her? Does she even know you're moving back?"

"I'm pretty sure Az hates me," Rus said, instead of telling Nesta that *no, Az did not know she was moving back to Moondale.* She finished the final signature with a flourish then pushed the folder over to Nesta for them to sign.

"*Hate* isn't the word I'd use." Nesta closed the folder with a snap.

"What?" Rus frowned.

"What?" Nesta tilted their head, their nose crinkling up in an expression of innocence that no one who knew anything about Nesta Holyore would ever believe. "You can start moving in tomorrow. You're keeping the furniture, right?"

"Yeah. I mean, I don't have any of my own, so." Rus stood, stretching out her neck from side to side where it had grown stiff from being hunched over the papers.

"All right then. I'll have my crew come by and help out if you need it?"

"That'd be great. I have to finish opening up the shop tomorrow, and Fernando needs to be there to help wrangle the kids while we work."

"You know, I never asked." Nesta headed back through the house toward their car. "How old are your kids?"

"Aihuan will be four in October. And Meiling just turned thirteen. I've already got her signed up over at Moondale High."

"Ah, so they're . . ." Nesta drifted off, looking like they expected Rus to fill in the blank of what they were trying to say. But Rus had spent the last six months filling in the blank for people, and she wasn't about to do that. Not here. Not anymore.

"They're amazing," Rus said. It didn't matter if they weren't hers biologically—they were hers in every way that counted.

"Right. Well, you can stay the night here if you want."

Nesta pulled a key from their pocket to hold out to Rus. "I'm sure the bedding is clean. The house generally takes care of all that."

"Before you go, can you tell me what happened to the previous owners? I mean . . . it's so well-behaved, I can't imagine a magical family just up and leaving it."

"Well," Nesta said, a little smile crinkling their eyes as they looked back to the house. "It's got a bit of a sassy streak. I guess the previous owners didn't find that amusing. But I'm sure you'll get along with it just fine."

"A sassy streak?"

"You'll see." Nesta winked, and then they climbed into their car and pulled away from the curb without another word.

Rus crossed her arms over her chest and turned back to the house. The little cherry blossom out front was swaying gently, its orange and red leaves falling to the ground in a hush.

"You're not going to give me any trouble, are you?" she asked the house.

The house didn't respond.

"Didn't think so." She pulled her phone from her pocket and dialed Fernando. "Hey. You can bring the kids to the house. I'll send over the address."

"Do we need to bring the truck?" Fernando's voice was soft on the other side of the line, but Rus could hear Aihuan squealing at something and Meiling talking probably too loud for the small hotel room.

"No. Nesta said they'll send by movers to help us. We'll deal with all that tomorrow. For tonight I'll just order us a pizza, and we can rest. Do you need me to come help get them in the car?" A crow cawed, its black body swooping low over the cemetery to better assess the threat levels before Darcy came to rest on Rus's shoulder, his talons digging into her thick hoodie. "Cause if not, I've got some cleaning up I need to do around here."

"I don't think so." Fernando was smiling into the phone; Rus could hear it. "I think I've finally figured out Aihuan's car seat."

"If you need help, just ask Meiling. She knows what to do. I'll have dinner waiting for you guys when you get here."

"Is that Aunt Rus?" Meiling asked in the background.

"Yes." Fernando pulled his face away from the phone, and Rus could imagine him turning the full softness of his smile onto Meiling.

"Did she get us a house?"

"Yes! I got you a house!" Rus shouted into the phone, her excitement unseating Darcy, who cast her an annoyed glance that she shrugged off. "The perfect house! You're going to love it, A-Ling!"

"YEEEEEEEEES!" Meiling cheered. "Huaner! We have a house!"

"We have a house! We have a house! We have a house!" Aihuan shouted, feeding off her big sister's excitement. It sounded like Fernando had put Rus on speaker.

"But that means you two need to help Uncle Nando get packed up and get over here so you can see your rooms." Rus felt her cheeks aching from the smile that split her own face.

"Okay!" Meiling called, and then Rus could hear some commotion on the other end as she presumably got to work picking up all of Aihuan's toys or maybe just shoving stuff into the oversized duffle Rus had left on the floor by the door.

"You sure you don't need me to come help herd the cats?" Rus asked with a little laugh.

"No. I've got it covered." Fernando's shirt rustled against the phone as he too began to help packing. "I think you managed to get all the really important stuff into the car before you left."

"Toys are important!" Aihuan shouted.

"Right, sorry, of course, Huaner. Anyway, we'll see you there." Then he hung up, and Rus was left standing on the porch of her new house, listening to the silence of it. Darcy settled on her shoulder again, giving his witch an affectionate nip to her ear. A gentle reminder.

Movement out of the corner of her eye made her turn her head, and she saw the restless spirits on the edge of the graveyard again, turned milky in the fading light of early evening. "Right. Got to deal with them real quick before the girls get here."

She tucked her phone into her back pocket and strode across the yard.

2

IT WAS a morning like any other Azure had experienced. She woke with her alarm in enough time to go for a short run down the trail behind her house, shower, feed Lizzie, and eat breakfast before she needed to leave home for work. Really, the whole routine was like clockwork. Violet often joked that she could set her watch by her little sister's morning.

Except . . .

Someone was moving into the house down the street.

Azure stopped on the sidewalk, her routine carefully slipping away as the ten-minute walk into town turned into eleven, then twelve, then fifteen.

Someone was moving into the house down the street. The house that had called to Azure since she was five years old, newly orphaned, and moving in with Aunt Carmine. *Her* house. With the lilac siding and lavender accents. The one that she'd always known she would one day buy. She'd dreamed of it so often when she was a little girl that she'd almost started to think it had actually happened in another life. That she had bought that house, and moved into it with the person she loved, and lived happily ever after.

Except . . .

Except someone else was moving into it now. Someone with a child, maybe two, if the boxes labelled toys were anything to go by.

Aunt Maureen would want to stop by later with something to welcome the new neighbors. A cake. Or a lasagna perhaps. It was the polite thing to do. Indigo could go with her. It should be Azure, since she was the oldest sibling still living with their aunts, but she'd refuse. Courtesy be damned.

"Hey, can you read the handwriting on this box?" one of the movers called, his arms weighed down with a cardboard box almost bigger than his torso.

Another of the movers came over, tilting her head this way and that as she tried to figure out what it said on the label. She shrugged. "No idea. Just put it in the living room with the other miscellaneous stuff. The owners can sort it out when they get home."

He nodded and headed inside with the box. Azure shook herself, turning back to the sidewalk that would lead into town. She forced her thoughts away from the new inhabitants of her house and toward work, running through the short mental opening checklist she'd compiled from the previous evening's close.

Restock the planner section—they had run low because of school starting up.

Log in the shipment from the weekend.

Check the stock on tarot cards.

Reorganize the—

Wait. She stopped in front of the shop, her eyes narrowing on the reflection in the glass of the window from across the street. Azure turned, frowning.

The coffee shop seemed to have appeared overnight as things were wont to do sometimes in a town so steeped in magic. Like a dead mouse or a new sprout on one's plant. Not there one minute, and suddenly there the next.

The exterior had been painted black all around the big open windows and double doors. And on the big blank space where a sign usually went on shops in Moondale rested the word *Necromancer's* in a distinctly boney-looking script. As Azure stared up at it, the bone-white skull sitting against the black backdrop in the place of the *o* seemed to wink back at her.

She rolled her eyes and wished the joke were lost on her. It wasn't. She saw how it might be funny. In a tactless, macabre way. And maybe if she was in a better mood, she would have spared it a chuckle. After all, it seemed the kind of joke—

No. Azure huffed, forcing herself to turn away and head into the little occult bookshop run by the Elwood family. There was much to be done before she opened for the day; she couldn't waste time feeling nostalgic. And that's all nostalgia was: a waste of time. The wanting for something that was long gone and would never be again.

The gentle consistency of a morning at the shop lulled Azure back into her routine and pushed thoughts of the house and the new coffee shop across the way from her mind. With the register pointed away from the door, and shelves to stock, she didn't even have to look at the decidedly stupid sign if she didn't want to.

And she didn't until around lunchtime when Mrs. Doughtery sidled into the shop, her reusable grocery bags tucked under her arm. Azure took a moment to let her eyes slip over the older woman. There was a bit of crumpled paper clutched in one hand, and if Azure closed her eyes and held her breath, she could slow down the world around her and walk through the space unhindered to read it.

A car stopped in the middle of the street outside, windows down to let the warm early-autumn air in. The leaves stopped drifting downward from the trees out on the sidewalks. And Mrs. Doughtery's list said that she needed some sage, orange candles, and the latest Gwydion Derwyn novel. Although why she needed to write down that particular bit to remember it, Azure didn't know.

When she opened her eyes, the world started spinning again.

"The latest crop of romance novels is on the end cap in the romance section. I'll get your candles and sage while you browse," Azure said, already stepping from behind the counter to head down the short hall off to the right. They kept actual supplies in an adjoining retail space that could only be reached from the main shop. It was not always so. At one point, everything had been lumped in together. But when the bookstore down the block closed up, the nice elderly couple that ran it retiring to Florida, the Elwoods had risen up to fill in the gap.

Azure thought she heard Mrs. Doughtery call a quick "thank you" over her shoulder, but she didn't pay it any mind. When she returned to the register with the items Mrs. Doughtery needed, the older woman was still puzzling over the romance display in the back. Azure sighed.

"Do you need help finding it?"

"No. No. I was just thinking maybe I'll read this new author too. Cecil . . . something. How does he pronounce his last name?" Mrs. Doughtery made her way back to the register with no less than five paperbacks stacked in her arms, and Azure sent up a thanks to the Goddess that at least this one customer didn't actively need her help to find things.

"Beauchamp."

"Right. Thank you." Mrs. Doughtery slid the books onto the counter and pulled out her wallet as Azure started ringing them up. "Has your aunt read anything by him? I always trust Maureen's recommendations more than anyone else's."

"I haven't asked." Azure found that most customers would talk themselves out without much prompting. She didn't need to be overly friendly or have a customer service smile, whatever Aunt Maureen might think. She just needed to make a noncommittal comment here and there, and usually they'd do all the talking. Which was better, because Azure fucking hated talking to people. If she had things her way, she'd lock herself away in a library or a lab somewhere and spend her days fiddling with spell creation until she was old and gray.

"Ah, well. I'll just have to give her a call myself. How are your aunts? And your siblings?"

"Everyone is doing well." She took the bag Mrs. Doughtery offered and loaded her purchases carefully into it.

"Good. That's good." Mrs. Doughtery held out her credit card, a little smile on her face. "Oh. Did you see the new place across the way? It's a coffee shop, I think? Or maybe they sell tea? I'm not really sure. I heard they're doing a soft opening, but they plan to have a grand opening in a week or so."

Azure nodded, then handed Mrs. Doughtery back her card and her receipt.

"You should pop in and try it. Maybe they'll want to do some kind of collaboration with you. I mean, books and tea go together like . . . well . . . books and tea!" Mrs. Doughtery laughed.

"I will discuss it with my aunt."

"Good. Good." Mrs. Doughtery took her bag and offered Azure a too-wide smile. "It was nice talking to you. I'll call Maureen about that book."

"Please do."

And then Mrs. Doughtery left the shop, the little bell over the door ringing merrily, and Azure's shoulders relaxed. She leaned for a moment on the counter before pushing herself back to her feet.

"Tea," she said to the room at large and disappeared into the back room to start the kettle. The bell over the door chimed just as she was pouring it into a cup to steep, and she resisted the urge to groan before returning to the front of the shop. It was a small gaggle of teenagers, likely on break for lunch from the high school. And they had no idea what they wanted, other than to be loud and annoying to someone. Azure was glad Indigo had grown out of that phase rather quickly.

By the time they left, she had a headache and over-steeped, cold tea, and they had bought exactly nothing but somehow managed to completely disorganize the fiction section. Azure took one look at the selection of Discworld books all out of order and turned around.

"Tea." She flipped the sign to the "be back soon" side—which was really the "closed" side magicked to say "be back soon"—and strode across the street without bothering to look to make sure there was no traffic.

The door to Necromancer's was propped open, and too-loud rock music drifted through the space and out onto the sidewalk that sounded like it was coming from an actual record player, of all things. Azure wrinkled her nose but headed inside. There was a small line at the register, and someone was screaming along to "Love is a Battlefield" behind the steamer. Off to the side, at a booth close to the pick-up window, was a toddler babbling along to the song as she colored, and a young teen with earbuds in reading what looked like a textbook.

Azure shook herself and looked up at the menu. By the time she'd gotten to the front of the line, she'd decided on a simple chai.

The awkward boy at the register gave her a tentative smile and said, "Hi. Thanks for visiting Necromancer's. What can I get for you?"

"Just a large chai, please, with a little milk."

And then she turned to see the person making the drinks, and it was like using her sight: the whole world slowed to a crawl, and everything became so sharply focused it hurt. Because there, behind the counter, her fingers glowing with magic as she settled the lid of a cup into place, was Icarus Ashthorne. Rus.

Goddess, it had been so long. It had been . . . ten? Eleven years? Azure had lost count. Or, at least, she liked to lie to herself and say that she had. Because the truth was if she really thought about it, she could probably tell anyone who asked exactly how many hours it had been since she'd last seen Rus. She ignored that errant thought and instead focused on the magic glowing at Rus's fingertips.

"You can't just charm every cup of coffee you serve," Azure said instead of hello as she approached the pick-up counter. Her hand tightened around the strap of her purse, the leather creaking under her fingers.

Rus looked up at her for a moment, shock clearly written in those gray eyes before she smiled, brushing strands of bright pink hair back from her face. "Why not? There are no board rules against it."

Azure pressed her lips together hard enough that her jaw ached and didn't say, *Because you'll wear yourself out, you beautiful imbecile.* Because it was no longer her place to say such things. She had forfeited that right over a decade ago when she'd let Rus leave Moondale without forcing her to explain what the *fuck* was going on. Azure forced herself to not notice how Rus was still achingly beautiful. How the years had thinned her out to the point where she practically swam in her well-worn long-sleeve black T-shirt. How her eyes were tired, but her smile was bright. How the bright pink of her hair made her freckles all the more noticeable.

"Even if there were . . ." Rus continued as if she didn't notice the stricken look on Azure's face. She probably didn't; she'd always been blatantly unobservant when it was convenient to her. " . . . the rules were made to be broken, Az."

"I am fairly sure that's *not* why the rules were made." Azure didn't even have to think about the words. They flew from her lips like they'd been waiting to be spoken for the last decade. Like she could just fall right back into the teasing push and pull of a conversation with Rus. She couldn't. She shouldn't. But she also seemed unable to stop it. Or unwilling maybe.

"How would you know? Were you there?" Rus winked and poured a splash of oat milk into Azure's chai, just how she liked it. Because even a decade later, Rus knew her. It made something jolt in Azure's chest, but she swallowed that down.

Instead of responding, she stared at Rus until the other woman handed over her tea, tanned fingers brushing Azure's brown fingertips a little too much to be coincidental.

"You haven't really changed at all, have you?" Rus's head tilted to the side so that a few strands of hair fell loose from her short ponytail to brush her cheek. "You know," she said quietly like she'd almost forgotten where they were and that the people around them might overhear. And then she shook herself, cleared her throat, and offered Azure a customer service smile that didn't wrinkle her moonlit eyes. "We should get together and catch up."

"We should." Azure nodded, ignoring the way it made something in her stomach clench. She wondered idly if this was one of those times where people said that, where they made vague plans, but where they ultimately never spoke again. But no . . . Rus was right across the street now. Azure could come by and "catch up" whenever she wanted. And that made something strange like anxiety and embarrassment and excitement and relief, all rolled into one, buzz under her skin. "I'll let you get back to work."

"Right. Bye!" Rus waved.

BUT RUS'S EYES FOLLOWED AZ OUT THE DOOR. BECAUSE Az looked the same. No. Not the *same*. That wasn't right. Her eyes were the same. That barely there look of annoyance that she kept hidden under layers and layers of politeness, *that* was the same. But the rest of Az was different. Very different. She'd traded her boxy cardigans and hand-me-down zip-up sweatshirt from Violet for a pale seafoam-green leather jacket that fit like a glove. It was probably vegan, knowing Az.

A sharp undercut peeked out just over one ear loaded in piercings, and she'd pushed her sleeves up to her forearms, likely because it was warmer in Necromancer's than it was out on the street. Her brown forearm was a spiral of twisting, growing flowers and vines all the way down to her wrist where a single fallen cherry blossom petal had settled onto the bone just off to the side that Did Things to Rus. Rus wanted to nip at that bone, and then proceed to trace the flow of petals and vines all the way up Az's arm with her lips about it. She wouldn't. She wasn't that girl anymore. She wasn't the lovable little gremlin who Az looked at with a soft, indulgent expression. That much was proven by the look of casual contempt Az had given her as she'd taken her tea. But Goddess, how Rus wanted to. Practically ached with it.

"Boss?" Fernando asked, his tone hesitant as he reached for the metal cup she'd been using to steam milk to run it under the tap. "Are you okay? Do you need a break?"

"How many times do I have to tell you not to call me that?" Rus huffed, snatching the cup back. "I'm fine." It wasn't totally the truth. Her knees were starting to ache a little, even with the deeply cushioned mat under her feet, but it wasn't anything she hadn't powered through before. Besides, they'd be closing up soon.

"Boss! Boss! Boss!" Aihuan shouted from her booth.

"Shush, you," Rus scolded with a little laugh. "You have artwork to create. I will not have our fridge empty for more than a week. Do you understand me, little miss?"

"Yes, boss," Aihuan said with a little smirk. "I'll make all the arts."

"That's my girl." Rus shook her head and turned back to Fernando. "Did you want something?"

"Oh . . . yeah, I was just wondering who that was? The one with the . . ." Fernando hesitated, his nose wrinkling up as he tried to think of a kind way to put whatever was going on in that adorable little head of his. "The one who ordered the chai with milk."

"That's Azure Elwood. Az." Rus started on the next order. It was harder to force the customer service smile on her face after seeing Az and her heart lodging somewhere in her throat. But she'd manage. "She was . . . We were . . ." Rus let out a breath, pinching her eyes shut for a moment to breathe. "She's my ex-girlfriend. From before I left Moondale."

"Ooooooh. *That* Az." Fernando nodded slowly like he could see the whole interaction in a different light now. And he probably could. Rus had told him enough about Az to paint a clear picture of what Az had meant to her. Of how Az had meant *everything* to her.

"Yeah. That Az." Rus shook herself. Now wasn't the time to think about that. She didn't know when the time to think about that would come, but now wasn't it. "Can you watch the girls for a bit after we close up? I've got a friend coming over to help with the wards on the house, and I don't want Huaner under foot."

"Yeah, I think I can handle that. Are you gonna be good for Uncle Nando tonight, Huaner?"

"Yeah!" Aihuan's fists flew up into the air with her cry.

Fernando chuckled, turning back to the register to help their next customer.

"That's my girl." Rus smiled to herself and let the excited babble of Aihuan, the soft hum of the steamer, and the gentle buzz of the café lull her back into the safety of this space. Tucked away from the world. They were okay. They'd be okay. She just had to keep her nose clean and the board from jumping down her throat for something stupid. She could do this.

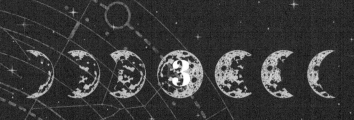

3

THE KIDS WERE TUCKED AWAY inside when Cagney arrived on her bicycle, her long red hair in a messy bun, with a bandana holding any loose strands back from her face. She looked exactly as Rus remembered her, not a day older, and Rus was beginning to wonder if it was something in the water. If maybe the key to avoiding crow's feet, and the couple of gray hairs she'd covered up with her obnoxiously pink hair dye, was right there in Moondale. Maybe that's why their ancestors had settled there—maybe it's where the fountain of youth was. She shook herself and waved.

"Show back up in town, and I'm the *second* person you call?" Cagney accused, her arms already crossed over her chest as she headed up the walk toward where Rus had sprawled across the front steps.

"I had to call Nesta first. I needed a house!" Rus bit back a smile, hiding how pleased she was that it didn't seem like anything had changed between herself and Cagney. At least that was one person she didn't have to worry about.

"Needed a house, my ass." Cagney swatted her on the

arm before sitting down beside her, one leg pressing loosely against Rus's. And it was as good as Cagney saying, "I missed you" but without all the throat-clenching agony of actual Emotions. This was why Rus loved her. "Nice place you got here. You going to show me around?"

"After we deal with the wards." Rus pushed herself to her feet, biting back a soft groan when her knees protested. "Then you can meet the girls."

Cagney's lip twitched into a little smile. "Have they gotten bigger since the last time you sent me pictures?"

"Oh definitely." Rus's laugh was a little clipped, a little short, as she focused her attention on walking normally. She didn't need Cagney prying into the mess that was her body these days.

"You okay, old lady?" Cagney walked beside her, a teasing note to her tone, but Rus could feel those keen green eyes dragging over her body, assessing, calculating, trying to understand. *Fuck.*

"Yeah, just not used to standing still behind a counter for six hours serving coffee snobs yet. I'll adjust." The lie slid easily from her tongue, and it *was* a lie. Because she knew deep down, she'd never adjust. No amount of time would make standing like that not leave her aching all over. But she could pretend, at least for the time being, that it was the newness of the activity that was hurting her, not the strain of it. She'd have to tell Cagney everything eventually, but the longer she could put it off . . . the better. Not that she didn't trust Cagney. Rus trusted Cagney with her life. But the less people who knew, well, the less likely the board would find out.

Cagney gave her another once over, her nose wrinkling up in the center, but she didn't say anything else. She had heard the lie, and she was going to let it slide, for now. Rus nearly sagged in her gratitude. They made their way across the yard to a little stone no bigger than Rus's fist. It looked a little like a hide-a-key if a hide-a-key was an unpolished, roughly cut piece of black tourmaline. Really, as far as hide-a-keys went it stuck out like a sore thumb, but then no one who wasn't magical would know what it was.

"Bit on the nose." Cagney squatted next to the stone, poking at it with her neatly trimmed fingernail.

"Yeah, well . . . Crimson Tide never was the subtle type." Rus settled beside her, hoping Cagney didn't hear the way her knees crackled at the movement. "If it'd been me—"

"You'd have just done it directly into the earth." Cagney hummed in agreement. "A little more difficult but—"

"Safer." Rus turned the rock over to look at the runes that had been scratched into the underside of it. Powerful magic ran through it and the lines the Crimson Tide Coven had drawn beneath, but they wouldn't be enough. Not for what Rus needed them to do.

"So. On a scale of one to ten, how pissed do you think the board is going to be when they find out you took down the wards on your house?" Cagney asked, standing up and brushing off the knees of her jeans as if she'd been kneeling in the grass. She hadn't, but Rus recognized it for the nervous gesture it was. She was just as worried about the board and their bullshit as Rus was. Which was fair. They were notoriously a pain in the ass.

"If they find out."

"When they find out."

"I'm not taking them down. I'll leave the tide's shitty little fence in place. I just want to put up my own." Rus shrugged. That much was true. Mainly because she knew if she took down the wards already in place, someone would be alerted. And fuck if Rus wanted a visit from *Sheriff*

Greer. Honestly, if she could avoid seeing his smug-ass face for at least a month, she'd be thrilled.

Cagney raised an eyebrow, the accusation not spoken but definitely there. Rus let out a long breath, brushing her fingers through her tangled pink hair.

"Look. Cags," she said, shoving her hands into her back pockets where Cagney wouldn't see the way she wanted to fidget under the scrutiny. "The wards the Crimson Tide Coven put up suck. You know it. I know it. Any witch worth their salt knows it. They're catch-alls for any vaguely negative force within a small radius. And I have some very . . ." She paused, licking her lips as she thought of how to put this lightly. "*Specific* things I need to arm us against."

"Right." Cagney's green eyes had narrowed, and Rus fought the urge to hunch in on herself like she was fifteen again and Cagney had just caught her smoking weed in her shed. Not that Cagney had cared, she'd just been pissed it made the place smell like skunk for a full week after. "And those specific things are?"

"Are you going to help me or not?" Rus set her jaw and met Cagney's searching gaze head on. Because that was the only way to deal with a nosey druid. Otherwise, they'd walk all over you.

"Am I actually being given a choice?" Cagney tilted her head, one stray wavy piece of red hair falling loose from her bandana.

"Not really. But I find that with the girls, sometimes the illusion of choice is enough to get them to behave." Rus shrugged, a knowing grin tugging up her lips.

Cagney just blinked at her; red painted lips parted a little in awe.

"What?"

"You're scary now that you're a mom."

"Uh . . . thanks?" Rus toed the stone with her scuffed

boots, not really sure how to take something like that from Cagney.

"That wasn't a compliment," Cagney said flatly, her lips twitching up into a smirk.

"Yeah, it was."

"Yeah, it was." Cagney laughed. "Fine. What do you need me for?"

"Right!" Rus clapped her hands together, bouncing on her toes in her excitement. "So, see the big old oak back there?" She pointed to the gigantic tree on the back corner of the property, its gangly limbs stretching out across her lawn. It wasn't even technically hers, she was sure, as half of it was in the cemetery. Which meant that was likely where it had been planted to begin with. Or had maybe grown from an acorn forever ago.

"The root system on that thing . . ." Cagney's voice was soft, reverent. Rus couldn't see it, but she knew that her friend's toes were curling in her trendy fall boots, itching to kick them off and run barefoot over the grass.

"It probably spans most of the yard," Rus finished for her, her feet already turning to lead them toward the tree. It'd make a great climbing tree for the girls. And she was sure if Aihuan pouted enough, they could get Fernando to hang a tire swing from it. But that would be a project for later. For now, she needed to focus on protecting them. "I figure if we mirror the runes from the Crimson Tide's wards, we can hack into that power and build on it. It'll make the whole thing easier."

"And a druid was your best bet for convincing a tree to do your dirty work."

"Well, if I want it to let me use its ecosystem as a power source, yeah. I probably could have asked one of the elementals but . . ." Rus shuffled to the tree, leaning against it to look up through the branches at the slowly changing leaves. "Well, why bother when I've got a druid?"

"Especially a druid who isn't going to run back to the board and tell them all your dirty little secrets." Cagney snorted. But she was already kicking off her boots and shucking off her socks where she sat at the base of the tree, her back to it. "You know you're going to owe me *big* for this. Especially with winter on its way."

"I know."

"I want first dibs." Cagney folded her legs over one another in a lotus pose, her hands moving to rest on her knees as she closed her eyes.

"First dibs on what?"

"Anything you create now that you're back," Cagney said without opening her eyes. "I know you've got at least five inventions stewing in that brain of yours now that you've perfected your digital grimoire. I want first dibs on anything new."

Rus barked a laugh, shaking her head. "You've got a deal."

"Delightful. Now go make me some green tea, and get the fuck out of my hair while I work."

"Yes, ma'am." Rus did an awkward little curtsey, which Cagney didn't even bother opening her eyes to witness, and then headed back to the house. The back door opened to the kitchen, and Rus smiled a little when she saw the tea pot already sitting next to the sink. "Thank you," she called to the house before moving to fill it.

With the kettle on the stove, she went in search of the girls. They had sprawled themselves and their things out across the living room floor where Fernando had kindly pushed aside the coffee table. Fernando was lying on his stomach across from Aihuan, building a little tower out of blocks, and Meiling had her back against the couch, taking notes from one of her textbooks. She hadn't started school yet, but she'd insisted she get her books so she could be caught up when she did.

"Who's that?" Meiling asked, her face lifting from her book to narrow dark brown eyes on Rus for a moment before they flicked out the window to stare at Cagney's bicycle.

"That's Aunt Cagney. She's one of my friends from college. She's a druid."

Meiling let out a little gasp, her head jerking back to stare at Rus with eyes so wide they practically ate up her round face. It wouldn't be round much longer; puberty would rob her of those cute chubby cheeks, but Rus would cling to them as long as she could. "She's a druid?"

"Yeah." Rus flopped onto the couch, kicking her feet up over the arm lazily. "You can meet her when she's done dealing with the wards."

"I want to watch."

"Watch what? She's just sitting out there meditating." Rus frowned.

"No. She's talking to the earth. Pleeeeease, Aunt Rus. Let me watch."

Rus narrowed her eyes on Meiling for a moment, and the girl's lower lip puffed out in a truly impressive puppy dog pout that Rus was ashamed to say she'd taught her, and worked every fucking time. "All right. When her tea's done, we'll all head out to watch. But you two have to be quiet, all right?"

Meiling nodded firmly, her lips pressed into a resolute line.

"Why?" Aihuan asked. She'd abandoned her block tower to shuffle over to the edge of the couch, holding onto the plush velvet cushion tight enough that Rus could hear the seams creak.

"What do you mean, why?" Meiling snorted, rolling her eyes.

"Don't be mean to your sister, A-Ling," Rus chided and was gratified to receive a muttered "sorry" from the errant teen.

"Why do we have to be quiet?" Aihuan continued as if she hadn't heard Meiling. She was very good at ignoring her sister, especially when Meiling was being a brat, which was about sixty percent of the time these days.

"Because, little monster," Rus said, pulling her legs off the arm of the couch so she could bend down to scoop Aihuan up into her arms and hold her close. "The earth is very very shy and only knows how to talk very very softly. So if we're too loud, Auntie Cags won't be able to hear it."

"Ooooooh." Aihuan nodded, her whole body bobbing with the movement.

"Can you be quiet so Auntie Cags can still hear the earth?"

"Mm-hmm! I can be the most quiet." Aihuan grinned up at Rus.

The kettle started whistling just then, and Rus set Aihuan back on her little feet. "Go find your shoes and a jacket. It's chilly out there."

"Not cold."

"And I didn't ask." Rus eyed the little girl for a moment, wondering if Aihuan would pull a stubborn streak now of all times. But she just huffed and went off to the front door to find her jacket and shoes with Meiling scurrying along behind her. "Do you want some tea, Fernando?"

"Yes, please." Fernando rose from the carpet to follow her into the kitchen, his socked feet soft on the hardwood floors.

"You may as well come out with us and have a look.

We'll both need to wind our own magic into the wards once Cagney has them set up to keep them charged."

Fernando stilled where he'd been pulling the box of tea bags from the cabinet by the sink. "Are you sure you ought to —"

"There isn't a choice," Rus said, not looking up from where she was pouring steaming water into mugs. "With the winter coming, the earth will need a little help keeping them charged. Not much, but a little. Plus, if we're connected to it, we'll know when they've been tripped. I'm not taking any chances. Not with this place." *Not again* went unsaid, but Fernando seemed to sense it anyway. His shoulders hunched forward a little. "Green for Cagney."

Fernando wordlessly dropped tea bags into each mug.

"Don't do that." Rus sighed, her shoulders sagging.

"I'm not doing anything."

"You are, and you know you are." She watched him out of the corner of her eye, saw how his posture had sunk in on itself. How he'd tried to make himself smaller. Always trying to make himself smaller. "I'm not mad at you. It wasn't your fault. It just —"

"Aunt Rus, we're ready!" Meiling called, her voice bright as she came up behind them. When Rus spun, she found the girls hand in hand. Meiling had managed to wrangle Aihuan into a scarf, even though Aihuan looked like she'd like nothing more than to rip it off and use it as a jump rope instead. Not that Rus could blame her; she'd never been the scarf type herself. She'd always run too warm, until she didn't anymore.

"Perfect. Now, Huaner, do you think you can get down the stairs with just A-Ling to help? They're a little steep. Or should I have Uncle Nando carry all the tea and I'll carry you down?"

"I can do it." Aihuan puffed out her cheeks, looking stubborn. "I'm a big girl."

"Of course, you are." Rus smiled, reaching out to ruffle her short brown hair. Her eyes flicked to Meiling to make sure she could handle this, and Meiling nodded. "All right then, girls, let's go see what this druid thing is all about, yeah?"

"Yeah!" Aihuan and Meiling cheered and scrambled out the back door before Rus could turn to pick up her mug of tea. Shaking her head, Rus chuckled, and she and Fernando followed closely behind. Once out on the grass, both girls stopped, their eyes wide as they watched Cagney work her magic. The druid hadn't moved an inch, but she was emanating a softly glowing green aura now, her lips moving quickly with words they couldn't hear.

Meiling took one look at her and dropped down onto the grass just as she was, ripping off her own tennis shoes and socks to curl her legs up into a lotus pose. Aihuan followed a second later, her own movements clumsy, and her legs more just bending at the knees a little than folding properly. Still, it was adorable, and Rus resisted the squeal on her tongue as she pulled out her phone and snapped several pictures while their eyes were closed.

Rus settled onto the back steps with Fernando beside her, sipping his tea. Her fingers sketched a charm over Cagney's to keep it warm, and Darcy came to land on the banister, his head cocking as he watched the whole scene with vague interest. Rus let herself settle into the peace of the moment.

That . . . didn't last long. Unsurprisingly.

Because eventually Aihuan got bored and started racing around the yard, her steps a little clumsy. Rus's eyes followed her, not really worried about her causing trouble as she explored. The quiet stretched, and Rus found herself drifting into a lazy daze, just letting the magic flow and hum around them in the safety of their yard. It wasn't perfect yet, but it would be soon. Once the wards were up and they'd finished unpacking, this place would be good for the girls. Not home, no, but good.

"Rus," Cagney said, suddenly in front of them, taking the tea from where it sat on the step beside Rus. "Why are beetles following your little girl around?"

Rus's head jerked back to where Aihuan was still pacing around the yard, her eyes flicking down when something reflected off the house lights in the grass. Darcy cawed and swooped off the banister to eat whatever it was, but before he could get there Aihuan spun around, crossed her arms in irritation, and shouted a firm, "No!"

Darcy cawed in question, wings flapping hard to hover in front of the tiny three-year-old now giving him the stink eye.

"I said no," Aihuan repeated. "Friends, not food."

Darcy cocked his head, letting out another disgruntled sound.

"Darcy, no."

The crow seemed to huff, and then spun in the air and flew back up to the eaves of the house where it glared at the little girl sullenly.

Cagney, who had been watching the whole exchange, let out a strangled sound. "Are those—"

"Toddlers, am I right?" Rus asked with a laugh, and before Cagney could finish that thought, she was on her feet and scooping Aihuan into her arms, her feet scattering the little carrion beetles in her hurry. Aihuan let out a squawk of upset. "You can play with your friends later, Huaner. Now, I think it's time for supper. You staying, Cags?"

Cagney's grip on her coffee mug had gone tight enough to push the color from her fingers, but she nodded, her eyes narrowed on Rus in a very we'll-be-talking-about-this-later type of way.

"Wonderful! Come on, girls. Let's get washed up for supper," Rus said, perhaps too shrilly as she led the way into the house with Cagney hot on her heels, and Meiling and Fernando bringing up the rear. She didn't have to look back to know that they had exchanged worried looks. It was better she didn't see those anyway—there would be time to worry about their worry later.

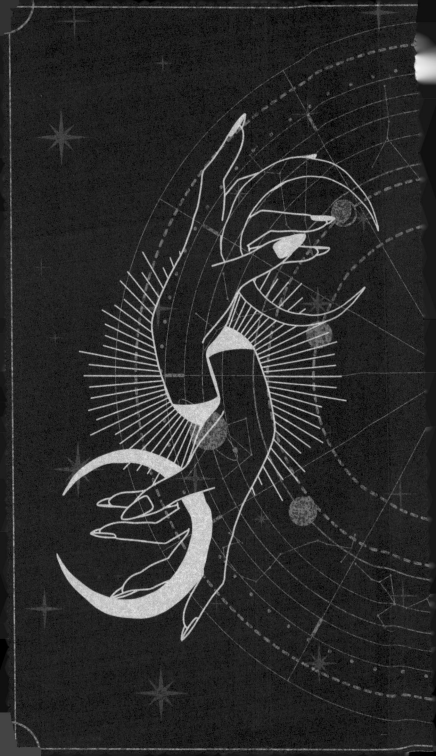

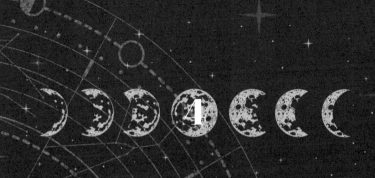

AZURE DIDN'T HATE Evander Greer. She felt it was important to clarify this, even in her own mind. She didn't hate him. But she didn't *like* the man that the board had chosen to be her match when she'd turned twenty-one either. He was loud, brash, and arrogant by turns. But it wasn't those things that she didn't like about him, because admittedly those were the things that had always attracted her to Rus, and then to . . . every other person she'd been with since. She had a type, so sue her. No, it was the simple fact that someone else had chosen him *for* her. Picked him out of all the eligible witches in Moondale when they knew *damn* well she was already with Rus. Had been with Rus for two fucking *years* at that point. Was planning to *propose* to Rus after graduation.

And although they'd come to an understanding—an understanding that neither of them would ever want the other and they both said fuck it to the board—he still showed up at the shop every couple of weeks and hung around like they were *friends*. Azure supposed being able to be adults, talk about the fact that they didn't want to marry, and come to some kind of amicable agreement meant that they were kind of friends. Or, at the very least, partners in pissing off the elders. Which, Azure acknowledged, Rus would have probably found deeply amusing. If she'd been there. If she'd known. If she'd stuck around long enough to fucking see what would happen.

But she hadn't. And now she was back. And Azure was . . . Goddess above, she was as in love with Rus as she'd ever been. The image of the engagement ring she'd chosen all those years ago, sitting in her jewelry box at home, settled into her mind and made her palms itch. It would be terrifyingly easy to go home, get it, and knock on Rus's door. To fall down onto her knees and beg for Rus to take her back. But . . . Well, she didn't know but what, but she knew there *was* a but.

"Are you even listening to me?" Evander grumbled like a dog who had been forced to wait too long for its owner to just throw the damn ball. Azure didn't much like dogs either. She didn't hate them, just like she didn't hate Evander Greer. But she'd always been more of a cat person.

"Yes. Sorry. You were saying something about . . ." She let the words drift off, knowing full well that she hadn't been listening but if she responded exactly this way, Evander would scoff it off and continue on whatever tirade he was on. Great Gaia, when would his fucking break be over? She could tell him that *no, she wasn't listening, and he should go back to work because they both had a fucking job to do*. But honestly, the headache that would come from his bitching just wasn't worth the pleasure of telling him off like the errant child that he was.

"About Rus modifying the board-approved wards we put on her house."

"What?" Well, that caught Azure's attention. Her eyes flicked from where she'd been staring out the window, pretending she was enjoying the fall colors when she was actually watching the door to Necromancer's open and close periodically. She'd wondered if she'd get to see Rus, but so far no luck. Azure's focus narrowed down to a point, the point at which she was getting the first information she'd gotten about Rus in the two weeks since she'd moved in down the street. Rus Ashthorne had been strangely quiet since moving back to Moondale, and it was unsettling. The Rus Azure knew wasn't quiet. Ever.

"You heard me right. She modified them! Had Cagney go out there and tie them to that old oak in the cemetery. That oak isn't even her fucking tree, it belongs to the cemetery. But does that matter to Icarus Ashthorne? Nooooo."

"I'm sure she has her reasons." Although those reasons may have just been to piss the board and Crimson Tide off, because that seemed Rus's speed. But Azure wasn't anyone to judge; she'd done a lot of pissing off the board herself in the last decade or so. And refusing to marry the match they'd chosen for her was probably the least of it.

Evander scoffed, his tongue clicking noisily against the roof of his mouth, and Azure thought, not for the first time, that if it weren't for the fact that Azure disliked him on principle, they probably would have gotten along swimmingly. They were both the exact same kind of bitch, after all.

"Did you speak to her about it?" Azure asked. *Instead of making wild assumptions and running around town bitching like a teenager whose mother took away their cell phone*, went unsaid. That probably wasn't fair. Azure wouldn't have spoken to the person who pissed her off either. She would have bottled it up and made vaguely scathing remarks at them until either they or she died from the toxicity seeping from her pores. Whichever came first. But she also didn't run around making her pissy mood everyone else's problem. Except, you know, when she did.

Evander barked a laugh, and that was answer enough. "What's there to say?"

And that was the crux of this whole shitstorm really, Azure realized. Rus was back, and what was there to say? Rus was back, modifying wards, running a coffee shop, reaching out to her old friends, and what was there to *say*? The buzzing under Azure's skin that had been there since she'd seen Rus a couple of weeks ago seemed to crank up to an eleven, making the hair on her arms stand on end. Azure looked out the window, blinking when she saw Rus's bright pink head duck back into her shop across the way, and her stomach gave a sick twist. Fuck. She needed to get this over with, didn't she?

Evander had taken her silence for agreement, or maybe he didn't even need agreement, because he was going off again. His rant devolved into mumbling expletives and grumbles about the time Rus had convinced him to try some potion or other and he'd lost all of his hair. They had been thirteen. It had grown back. He should be fucking over it already. But he wasn't.

And Azure was done listening. She tuned him out until his radio crackled to life, and he left with a muttered, "Shit, break's over. See you later."

It took every ounce of self-control for Azure not to say, *I'd really rather not*. Because being rude to the sheriff would ultimately be more trouble than it was worth. Azure leaned heavily against the counter, hanging her head, her dark purple hair falling forward and blocking out the light from the store.

She really needed to bite the hex and get it over with. There was no way she could continue to avoid Rus. Moondale was too damn small, there was only one occult store, and eventually they'd run into each other. Azure wasn't sure how yet, but they lived down the street from each other, and worked across the street from each other, for fuck's sake. It was bound to happen!

Azure's phone dinged, drawing her attention from the sulk she'd thrown herself headfirst into, and she pulled it from under the counter to glance at the notification. She hissed, the brightness too high in contrast with the dimmed store lights, making her eyes ache.

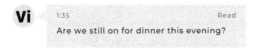

Vi   1:35   Read

Are we still on for dinner this evening?

Azure let out a groan, pushing her hair back from her face and straightening. She'd completely forgotten about the monthly Elwood bonding night, a tradition that had started shortly after Violet had gotten married and moved out.

Sent   1:36   **Az**

Yes. It's Indigo's turn to cook. So be ready for takeout.

Vi   1:36   Read

Sounds lovely. I'll bring the wine.

Well. She'd just have to get her shit straight before she saw Violet. Because she was *not* hashing whatever this was out with her elder sister. And if she didn't get it settled before then, Violet would see it on her face, and there would be all manner of poking and prodding until she gave in.

Azure took a breath and set herself to the task of untangling the emotional knot in her chest.

WHICH APPARENTLY DIDN'T FUCKING MATTER. NONE OF the work she'd done to deal with her shit fucking mattered at all. Because as they were sitting down to eat, the aunties blissfully out on their regular date night, a half a glass of wine warming Azure's empty belly, Violet looked over at her and said, "I heard Icarus Ashthorne is back in town."

Indigo nearly choked on a noodle, just barely managing to gulp several mouthfuls of water before he could cough half-chewed low mein back onto his plate. "What?"

"She is," Azure said, not missing a beat as she dumped spicy tofu onto her rice. Her eyebrow twitched, but she did *not* let her eyes flick over Violet's shoulder to the window where she could just see the corner of Rus's yard outside. If Violet knew Rus was back, then she knew where Rus lived, and worked, and anything else someone could hope to know about a person who had just moved to town. Violet's wife, Taryn, was terribly good at finding shit like that out. Probably because she worked at city hall, but that didn't change how annoying it was.

"Since when?" Indigo's voice was still a little scratchy from when he'd nearly died violently by way of Chinese takeout. Azure didn't turn her head to look at him. She kept her eyes almost disinterestedly on Violet, hoping she gave nothing away.

"Two weeks ago." Violet was staring back, her dark eyes looking for any change in her sister's demeanor. She'd find none. Azure was a vault. Azure was a tightly sealed compound. Azure was—"She has two kids."

Azure was deeply fucked. Damn it.

Indigo made a sound like a wounded animal. Like he'd rather be anywhere but at the table sitting between his two elder sisters as they tried to stare each other down. Poor kid. If Azure had any attention to spare, she'd dismiss him from sibling bonding night and tell him to go lock himself in his room and work on whatever his latest pet project was instead of dealing with what was going on between herself and Violet.

She didn't, though—have any attention to spare. It was all taken up by the slamming of her heart against her ribs. She hadn't made the connection. She'd known Rus had moved into the house down the street. She'd seen the boxes of toys. She'd seen the two girls sitting at Necromancer's. But she hadn't made the connection. Why the *fuck* didn't she make the connection?

"How old?" Azure asked, picking up her glass to take a sip of wine for something to do.

"Thirteen and three."

Thirteen. Well . . . one of them couldn't have been Rus's, that was a relief. Although, Azure wasn't really sure why. It wouldn't have mattered. Rus could have gone off and had five kids, and come back with a minivan packed full, and Azure would still have wanted her. She'd have been more than happy to help raise them, and teach them magic, and make them dinner, and—

"She and her partner brought them by the office the other day so we could get their records moved here."

"Her partner?" Azure felt her grip tighten on the wine glass enough that Indigo reached over to take it from her fingers and set it back on the table. Bless Indigo. He was the only one who came to this week's sibling bonding night not looking to throw Azure's life into the fucking woodchipper. This is why he was her favorite.

"A younger witch," Violet said, like that answered Azure's question. It didn't. They both knew it didn't. And their food was getting cold between them at that point, but Azure couldn't give less of a fuck. "I think his name was Fernando. He seemed nice."

"I see." She didn't. Not really. Because Azure couldn't imagine Rus with anyone but herself. She couldn't imagine Rus running off, having two kids, and showing back up in Moondale with a boyfriend in tow. No. It just wasn't . . . it wasn't Rus. But then, what the fuck did Azure know? She hadn't spoken to Rus in a decade or better.

"I'm not telling you this to hurt you." Violet sighed. And that at least sounded like she meant it. Although Azure hadn't thought she was doing it to hurt her. What she was trying to do, Azure wasn't sure, but she knew her sister better than that, and Violet couldn't hurt a fly. In fact, she refused to do certain types of ritual magic because they involved sacrifice. She was the witch equivalent of a vegan. It didn't do her any favors, but Violet didn't want anyone or anything else to suffer for her power, and Azure had always admired that about her. Until right now when her tone sounded more condescending than caring.

"Of course not." The words felt robotic in her throat. Trite. Like they weren't her own. Like she'd read them in a script somewhere and then repeated them so many times they didn't even make sense anymore.

"All I'm saying is . . ." Violet took a breath, like she was preparing herself to say something that was going to bring the world down around their ears. Maybe she was—Azure certainly felt like her world was about two breaths from shattering. "Maybe it's time you moved on."

Azure bit her tongue so hard she could taste thick metallic blood coat the inside of her mouth, replacing any hint of food or wine that might have been lingering. It was the only way to keep herself from asking Violet what that would look like. How anyone could just *move on* from Icarus Ashthorne? It seemed impossible even in the abstract. But saying that would reveal too much about herself, and she wasn't ready to lay herself bare on the kitchen table at *sibling bonding night*.

"Give Greer another chance. Or maybe . . . I don't know, maybe find someone else? I mean . . . Azure, you could do so much better."

And that was it. That was the straw that broke the broomstick. Azure narrowed her eyes on her sister, scooped up her plate, grabbed the wine bottle, and stormed off to her room without so much as a word. She slammed her door behind her loud enough that the windows rattled. She settled onto the thick purple quilt of her bed, her legs curled up under her.

Lizzie lifted her head, pale blue eyes wide and questioning.

"Don't."

The fluffy white cat nodded, then she set her head back down on her paws and promptly went back to sleep.

Azure jerked her head at the curtains on her window, and they twitched out of the way so she could look at the lavender house down the street. A beat-up blue sedan was parked out front, and most of the lights were on inside. But she couldn't see into the windows to see where Rus was, or what she was doing.

INDIGO WAITED UNTIL VIOLET HAD DRIVEN HER expensive silver hybrid down the street and out of view before he bothered knocking on Azure's door. Azure grunted. She hadn't moved from her spot leaning against the headboard, but she had set aside her empty plate, and the empty wine bottle, on the nightstand.

The door opened a crack, and Indigo stuck his gangly arm through to wiggle a full bottle of wine at her. "I come bearing gifts."

"Is that meant to be a peace offering or a flag of surrender?" Azure asked, but there was no bite to the words. She wasn't mad at her brother. She wasn't even really mad at her sister. If she was mad at anyone, it was herself, and maybe a little bit at Rus, and maybe a lot a bit at the situation.

"Can't it be both?" Indigo nudged the door open a little more to fix her with a wide, toothy smile.

"Fine. But if you get drunk, I'm not hiding it from Aunt Carmine again."

"Pft. I'll be legal in like . . ." Indigo drifted off, counting months on his fingers as he came to sit beside her on the bed.

"Two years, Indigo. You're nineteen."

"Shhhh. It sounds better if we say I'll be twenty-one in like sixteen months or something."

"Twenty."

"I said shhhh." He took a sip from the open bottle, then passed it over to her. Indigo's dark gaze had fixed on the house down the street. "Vi's wrong. You know that, right?"

Azure swallowed down another mouthful of wine.

There was a pleasant tingle in her fingertips and just behind her eyes that she was loath to give up. Not yet. "About what?"

"About Rus." Indigo didn't take his eyes off the house, but Azure could feel him watching her still. Conscious of every movement she made. Every shift in her breath.

Azure took another swig from the bottle. If Aunt Maureen saw her drinking wine like that, she'd probably scream loudly enough to shatter every pane of glass in the greenhouse. Not because it was rude, or gross, but because the grapes deserved more respect than that. Azure took a breath in the space and the silence between herself and her little brother.

The pair of them had always been closer than she and Violet had been, in spite of the fact that she and Violet were related by blood. But Violet remembered their parents. She remembered what it was like to not be an orphan living with her aunties. She knew what the words *mommy* and *daddy* felt like on her tongue. And Azure and Indigo didn't.

Azure had been fifteen when Indigo's parents, some distant relatives of Aunt Maureen's, had died in a car accident and Indigo had come to live with them. And Azure vividly remembered looking down at the baby, his chubby fists tight around her finger, and thinking, *This is it, this is my best friend*. And she'd been right. Even with the age difference. Indigo had somehow always understood Azure. Azure had been the first one he came out to when he realized he was trans. She'd been the one to help him shop for his tux for prom. And he'd been the one to eat junk food and rewatch *Pride and Prejudice* with her over and over after Rus had left until they were both sick of the sight of Colin Firth.

Indigo was family.

"It's not time to move on. Not yet," he said like he had read her thoughts back in the kitchen. Like he knew every corner of her heart. He probably did.

"Honestly," Azure said, setting the bottle down on the bed between her legs so it didn't tip over. "I don't even know what that would look like, Indie. Like . . . what would my life be without a Rus-shaped hole in the middle of it?"

"I don't think you're going to have to find out." Indigo still hadn't looked at her. He was watching as the lights in the house down the street turned off one by one. Rus putting her little family to bed.

"Why not?" Hope crept in like an uninvited guest at a séance, settling over her insides where it likely didn't belong. But if Indigo thought there was hope . . . Fuck . . . Azure was going to cling to it.

Indigo shrugged like he didn't really want to answer. But she knew he would. He always did. They were honest with each other—that was the only rule. They had to be honest. They could be as bitchy and spiteful and brutal as they wanted with one another, but they had to be honest. And he'd be honest with her now. He wouldn't give her hope if there wasn't some to be had.

"I went by Necromancer's on my way to school the other day." Indigo wiggled on the bed, lifting his hips to dig around in his too-deep pockets. Honestly, why the fuck did men get such deep pockets? It wasn't fair. "And saw Rus just sitting there, staring out the window at the shop like some lovesick lobster," he muttered, grunting a little when he dumped everything from his pockets onto his lap. "Ah, there it is." He grinned, triumphantly holding up a bit of wrinkled receipt paper. "This," he said, setting the paper on Azure's knee, "is Rus's new number. You should text her."

"How did you get this?" Azure narrowed her eyes

suspiciously, but she snatched the paper up before he could think to take it back.

"Vi isn't the only one who knows how to find things out in this place." Indigo took the bottle from her and took another swig. "And those kids? They're adopted. Whatever conclusion Vi jumped to was way off base. Rus didn't run off and get pregnant right after she left Moondale."

"I didn't think that she had." Azure ran her fingers over the chicken-scratched numbers. She almost couldn't tell if one of them was meant to be a five or a six, but she figured she'd take the gamble anyway.

"No. I don't suppose you did. You, unlike our darling sister, who I don't know how she got into medical school let's be honest, can do basic math." Indigo grinned at her. "Anyway, I'll leave you to that. Just, you know . . . don't wait too long. Or better yet, give me your phone."

"What?"

But Indigo didn't wait. He'd already snatched it off the charger on her nightstand, unlocked it, and sent off a text to the number on the receipt. Then he grabbed the bottle of wine, hoisted himself off the bed, and tossed her phone down beside her. He ambled out of the room, his familiar — a calico cat named Emma — swishing her speckled tail in satisfaction as she followed behind. Azure hadn't even noticed Emma come in.

When the door clicked shut behind them, she finally looked down at her phone and let out a long breath that sounded like a whistle.

> 7:30 **Az**
>
> Hi Rus! This is Az. You said we should catch up. I'm free around two on Sunday. I can swing by your place, if you want.

It didn't sound like her. Rus would know it wasn't her, surely. But . . . a moment later, a response came through.

Ru 7:31   Read
Sure! That'd be great! We'll just be here
unpacking. Here's the address.

So . . . clearly, she hadn't realized. And now Azure had no choice but to go. *Fuck*.

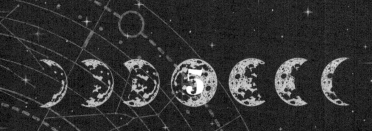

5

AZURE WAS POSSESSED, that was the only explanation. She'd been possessed by some perky '50s housewife with two and a half children and a white picket fence. Really, that was the only way to explain the fugue state she'd gone into upon getting up that morning that resulted in the ludicrous amount of baked goods now perched precariously on every surface of her aunties' kitchen. She hadn't even known how to make beignets until about an hour ago. What the fuck?

"Oh. You stress baked again," Aunt Maureen said, her light brown eyes widening as she took in the mess that was their kitchen. Peaches, Aunt Maureen's orange tabby familiar, sat across her shoulders, his tail twitching in curiosity. And her pixie cut hair was still a mess from having just woken up. "Please tell me this was stress baking, and not like . . . a sudden urge to open a bakery? You're not having a quarter life crisis, are you?"

"I made blueberry lemon scones."

"Ah." Aunt Maureen nodded as if that were answer enough. "So it is stress baking then."

Azure turned to pull a tray of pumpkin muffins from the oven instead of answering. She looked around for a place to set the tray down until Aunt Maureen moved a round pan of cinnamon rolls out of the way.

"This is about Icarus, isn't it?" Aunt Maureen set the cinnamon buns down on the kitchen table, somehow miraculously finding space among the other pans and trays there. Azure could practically see her mentally tallying up how many had been used, and likely concluding that Azure had had to conjure an extra pan or two. They were Violet's. And she wasn't going to return them until Violet noticed they were missing. Which might be never.

"I made coffee." Azure dropped her oven mitts onto the counter and grabbed a fresh mug for her aunt.

Aunt Maureen accepted the mug, taking a sip and grabbing a scone from the tray perched precariously close to the sink. She leaned against the counter, her head tilted. Peaches let out a soft chirp of curiosity. "Do you want to talk about it?"

Azure stilled where she'd been making herself busy refilling the coffee pot and dumping out what was left of her own stale mug. It was nice to be given the choice to talk. To be asked if that's what she wanted. Not to be forced into it like Violet would do. She let out a long, slow breath, her shoulders untensing a little. "Not particularly."

"All right then. I'll go find one of Carmine's fancy trays so you can take some of these when you go visit, and then we'll figure out *something* to do with the rest of them. Maybe Indigo can take them in for some of his friends. Or we can wrap them up and sell them at the shop? I don't know. I'll think of something."

"Aunt Carmine is going to be pissed when she finds out I used all of the flour again." Azure fiddled with the ties on her frilly pink apron.

"Did you put chocolate chips in the pumpkin muffins?"

Azure blinked at her for a moment, offended at the insinuation that she *wouldn't* put chocolate chips in the pumpkin muffins. "Obviously."

"Then she'll be fine. Just make sure you save her some."

Hanging the apron on its hook in the pantry, Azure went to pour herself her third cup of coffee for the morning. She was starting to get a little jittery with it. But she couldn't seem to stop. She needed something to do with her hands, and there really wasn't any flour left. Although she supposed she could make a flourless —

"Did it help at least?" Aunt Maureen's voice drew Azure's gaze back to where she'd polished off her scone and was watching Azure keenly.

"Not really." Azure slumped back against the counter, her eyes flicking over the messy kitchen. Fuck, it was going to take forever to clean up. And where would they store everything once she was done? She really hadn't thought through this particular spree.

"Ah well. I guess not everything can be solved by pastry." Aunt Maureen finished off her coffee. "When do you plan on returning Vi's pans to her?"

Azure looked back up to meet her aunt's gaze, eyes narrowed and lips pursed.

Aunt Maureen laughed. "That's fair, I suppose. Well, let's get to work. It'd be better if Carmine didn't see this."

Peaches jumped down from her shoulders to join Lizzie on the giant pillow in the corner, and they set to work. They were interrupted a few minutes later by Indigo joining them, his dark hair sticking up all over the place.

He took one look at the still overfull counter tops and kitchen table, and let out a low laugh. "Damn, Az. You really outdid yourself this time. Is there even any flour left in Moondale?"

Azure cut him a dirty look and went back to cleaning.

HOURS LATER, WITH ONE OF AUNT CARMINE'S VINTAGE trays tucked under her arm, crinkling with plastic wrap, she headed up the walk to 157 Mourning Moore. A crow sat on the round ball at the bottom of the banister, eyeing her wearily.

"Darcy," Azure greeted him, offering him a respectful bow.

Darcy cocked his head, giving her a dissatisfied gurgle.

"I'm not here to pick a fight." Azure's fingers tightened around the edge of the tray, getting far too close to squishing one of the croissants.

Darcy cawed right in her face. Because he was now, and always had been, a petty little bitch. Honestly, she didn't know why Rus had chosen him out of all the familiars available to them after high school. But Rus had taken one look at the ornery crow and said, *That one.* as if it were the most logical thing in the world. It wasn't.

"No, these aren't for you. Yes, I did make them myself. And I'll fuck you very much not to talk about how ugly they are, you pissy little blighter." Azure's jaw ticked in her irritation. There was really only one creature on the planet that could annoy her enough into cursing out loud, and it was this fucking crow. Honestly. Who did he think he *was*, insulting her that way?

Darcy hopped a little, flapping his wings in contempt. Like an utter bastard.

Azure bit the inside of her cheek, her teeth grinding as she walked past the damn animal and up the steps. He wouldn't stop her. He never had. He'd just continue to be a little shit about things he knew absolutely nothing about. Because he was an asshole.

The door opened before she'd even had time to knock, and there, staring up at her, were the narrowed green eyes of a pissed-off druid. Because that's what she needed after a night of little to no sleep. Honestly, it was like the Goddess was testing her. Wanting to see how much irritation she'd put up with in the name of seeing Rus again. Well, joke's on you, Hecate, Azure had a patience streak a mile wide when it came to Rus and Rus's little family.

"Oh. It's you." Cagney's lip pulled back in a sneer. Because she, like Darcy, had no qualms about showing how much she disliked someone. Azure had to respect her for that. Cagney had never hidden her contempt under the layers of stifling cordiality Azure always had to. And for that, she envied the druid. How nice it must be to have the freedom to be exactly as you were.

"Cagney." Azure went for polite, but she knew it came off stiff, even as she ducked her head to show her respect to the other woman. There was a loud shriek from somewhere in the house and Cagney stepped out, shutting the door behind her, effectively blocking Azure's way. Because of course she did. Azure ignored the urge to fidget under the druid's knowing stare. "Can I help you?"

"You're not going to go in there and fuck with her head again," Cagney said, every word dripping with venom. The smell of damp, musty earth drifted through the air. A threat, if Azure had ever seen one from a druid. No . . . not a threat. A promise. A promise that if Azure so much as put one toe out of line, Cagney would have the earth swallow her whole and there wouldn't even be bones for her family to find by the time the ground spat her back out. Delightful.

"I don't intend to." She'd never intended to. Whatever

had happened between Azure and Rus, she'd never meant to hurt Rus. She'd never meant to . . . Azure shook herself.

"You'd better not drive her away again. You're not the only one who missed her, you know."

Azure did know. She knew better than anyone that Moondale itself had a Rus-shaped hole in the middle of it. A place where the spritely medium had been and no longer was. A place that Azure wondered if she'd fit back into like a puzzle piece. Or maybe Rus had changed so much that the shape of her would be entirely different, and Moondale would have to rework itself to fit this new version of her. Azure thought she might like that.

"No," Azure agreed. "But I am the only one she did not see fit to keep in touch with." Azure meant for the words to sound equally annoyed, but they came out a little broken, a little strained. Like they'd been dragged over broken glass.

Cagney opened her mouth to say something else, but the door flew open before she could.

"What're you two standing out here for? It's cold! Come inside!" Rus laughed, her cheeks a little flushed from whatever she'd been doing before opening the door. Maybe chasing around her toddler. She turned on her heel as if expecting them to follow.

Azure didn't wait for Cagney to stop her again; she strode past her and into the house. She stopped in the foyer, her eyes falling on the basket of shoes, particularly the tiny neon green Chucks.

"And this is the foyer," Rus said as if Azure couldn't see that. Her gray eyes were bright, and her pink hair had fallen into her eyes. "Here, let me take that so you can get your boots off." She reached out and took the tray without waiting for Azure to agree, and let out a soft, strangled noise. "You umm . . . you stress baked again, huh?"

"Aunt Maureen is hosting book club this week and

asked me to provide the snacks." Or that had been the lie Indigo had thought up for Azure to tell, anyway. What would Azure do without her little brother? Die of embarrassment, probably.

"Ah. Of course!" Rus laughed, the sound high and bright where it settled into Azure's bones. "So, you still live with your aunts then?" Rus asked, and Azure knew she didn't mean it that way, but it sounded like, *Are you single?*

"The Elwoods have always stayed at home until they marry," Azure said, and she hoped Rus heard it for the *I've been waiting a decade for you, you beautiful fucking idiot* that it was.

"Right. Of course." Rus cleared her throat, looking anywhere but at Azure. "Well, come on back to the kitchen. I just put the kettle on." Then she was bounding through the house again, socked feet skidding on the dark stained hardwood. "That's the office. And that's the living room." She motioned to the room where Azure could hear soft whispered voices from beyond the couch. "Girls! Come meet Miss Azure! She brought . . . well, a whole lot of everything."

"I wasn't sure what they'd like," Azure murmured, ignoring the way she could feel Cagney's eyes on her as they made their way back to the kitchen. Why in the name of the Goddess was everyone and their mother in Rus's house?

"What kind of everything?" a voice drawled, and Azure looked over to see a young girl leaning against the back of the couch. She had her arms crossed in front of her, her long dark hair plaited into a messy fishtail braid, and a truly unimpressed expression on her face.

This must be the teenager.

"Are there cupcakes? Cupcakes are Huaner's favorite!" another voice shouted, putting hard emphasis on the T in favorite, and Azure barely had a moment to process the slapping of bare feet on hardwood before a tiny body barreled into her legs.

Azure blinked down at the little girl. Huaner had big round eyes, the irises almost dark enough to blend in with her pupils, chubby cheeks, and a wild mass of curling black hair on top of her head.

"Nope. I don't see any cupcakes. But I do see muffins! How about we try a muffin and see where that gets us?" Rus laughed, setting the tray down in the middle of the table, already unwrapping the plastic wrap. "Oh, I think these are pumpkin, Huaner. You know what that means?"

"No. What?" Huaner tilted her head, listening to Rus, but she was still looking up at Azure, her little fists tight on Azure's long black skirt Aunt Maureen had picked out for her when she'd gotten too overwhelmed to choose an outfit.

"That means chocolate chips! Az always puts chocolate chips in her pumpkin muffins."

Huaner let out a loud gasp, dropped Azure's skirt, and scrambled down the rest of the hall and into the kitchen without looking back. Azure's shoulders relaxed in relief as she followed the sound of her feet to the back of the house. The teenager had moved to look over the plethora of pastries with a critical eye before picking a lemon blueberry scone.

"Okay, so introductions," Rus said, her hands deftly peeling the wrapper away from a muffin, and not looking one bit bothered as Huaner took a bite from it, dropping crumbs all over the kitchen floor. Cagney rolled her eyes and grabbed the broom from the closet. "This little monster is Aihuan. Say hi, Huaner."

"Hi!" Aihuan mumbled through a full mouth, showing Azure an impressive amount of half-chewed muffin.

"Ew! Huaner! Finish chewing and swallowing before

you talk," the teenager huffed, her own half-eaten scone making a crumbly mess of her black hoodie.

Aihuan stuck her tongue out and then went back for another bite with a happy murmur.

"And that's Meiling." Rus nodded to the teenager, who gave a halfhearted wave. "I'd introduce you to Fernando too, but he's at the shop. We got a shipment in today, and he volunteered to unload everything. Sweet kid."

"All right, girls," Cagney said, clapping her hands like a schoolteacher trying to get twenty-or-so children to pay attention. "Now that we've got snacks and you've met Azure, it's time to get back to our studies. Right?" She cut her eyes to Rus.

"Oh. Right." Rus nodded eagerly, wiping her hands off on her faded black jeans after tossing the wrapper from the muffin into the bin. "Go on. Back to your lessons." She shooed them.

And though the girls made a show of groaning about it, they let Cagney herd them back into a big round room off the study that looked like it was full of brightly colored pillows and plants.

"How are your sisters?" Rus asked without missing a beat, already moving to pour them two mugs of water and drop tea bags into them. "Is Violet still a fucking Disney princess? And fuck . . . Peri—"

"Indigo," Azure corrected gently as she sat at the kitchen table. She should eat something; she hadn't eaten anything since dinner the previous night. But her stomach was still roiling in anxiety, so she nudged the tray a little farther from herself. "My little brother, Indigo, goes to the university. He loves it. He's currently studying to be a stitch witch, but that seems to change every other semester."

"Indigo." Rus repeated the name as if she needed to say it herself to remember, then she nodded. "Cool. I bet whatever he does, he'll be great. You Elwoods are always so fucking talented. And Vi?"

"You visited her office the other day. She's a pediatrician."

"Oooooh. She was *that* Dr. Elwood." Rus laughed, sliding a teacup over to Azure and setting a container of sugar down beside it. "So, even more of a Disney princess then."

Azure bit the inside of her cheek to keep from snickering and spooned some sugar into her tea. She knew Violet hated that comparison because, *I don't talk to animals, Icarus. Stop acting like mice made my dress!* It was still an apt comparison, though.

"What about you?" Azure asked, taking a sip from her tea. "How is your . . . family?" It felt weird to say it, because Rus had never considered herself to have a *family* before she left. Sure, she had friends as close as sisters. She had Azure, who loved her more than breathing. But she was an orphan through and through; it was what they had bonded over first when Azure had moved to Moondale. But they weren't the same because Azure had her aunts, and Rus had no one.

"They're good. Really good. I feel like everyone is settling in really well." Rus smiled, her eyes flicking over Azure's shoulder—likely to check on the girls in the other room. "But that's not what you're asking, is it?"

Azure wasn't sure what she was asking. She wasn't asking anything, if she was being honest. She was just trying to prolong this conversation as much as possible. She wanted to know anything and everything that Rus felt comfortable with sharing. And if she thought that—

"You want to know how I adopted them."

Well . . . if she was going to say it, who was Azure to disagree? Azure nodded. "If you don't mind."

"Well. You know how it is when you're traveling." Rus shrugged, her hands moving to wrap around her mug.

Azure didn't know. She'd never left Moondale once she'd come there, apart from conferences. Rus knew that. But Azure bit her tongue and didn't interrupt.

"Sometimes you meet this family, and you get along so well you start traveling together. And then the wife has a baby and you're kind of there for that. And they say, "Hey, you wanna be our kids' moonmother?" And you're like sure! What's the worst that can happen? Thinking you'll just be the cool vodka aunt who teaches them cuss words, and how to con their parents out of extra sweets before dinner. And then the worst that can happen happens, and suddenly you're the guardian to a precocious pre-teen and a canny toddler with a nose for trouble. These things just sort of happen. You know?"

They didn't, but Azure nodded anyway. She could see where these things might just sort of happen to someone like Rus who was so open, and honest, and lovable. "And they didn't have anyone else?"

"No." Rus frowned, sipping from her mug. "But it's all right, they've got me."

"They're lucky to have you." Azure offered her a soft smile.

"I'm lucky to have *them*." Rus shrugged, reaching forward to grab a scone. "Thanks for these, by the way. They'll keep us in breakfast for at least a week. You really didn't have to."

"Aunt Carmine taught us to never go anyplace empty handed."

"Ah, the Elwood manners. I've missed those." Rus smiled, a soft, vulnerable thing. And Azure felt it all the way down to her toes. She needed to get out of there before she did something intolerably stupid. Like ask what else Rus had missed. Or propose. Or kiss Rus. Or decide to plant roots in the kitchen floor so no one could ever make her leave again. Damn it.

"So, Fernando?" she asked, instead of leaving like she knew she should. Because Rus wasn't the only idiot between the pair of them.

"Oh! Fernando is my business partner. I met him in one of the covenless forums online, and we got to being friends. He's a sweet kid, great with the girls. And when I told him I was moving back to Moondale, he said he'd be happy to come along to help me out."

The word *covenless* made Azure's insides ache, but she didn't say as much. Instead, she nodded and said, "Tell me about your girls."

And then she spent the better part of an hour listening to Rus go on and on about how brilliant her girls were. How Aihuan was already doing some low-level spells. How Meiling's first quiz at school had come back with one hundred percent on it. And Azure, the masochist that she was, let herself daydream about how she'd fit into the little family that Rus had built for herself.

RUS COULD TALK FOR HOURS ABOUT HER GIRLS. SHE'D only been their legal guardian for six months, but she'd been a part of their lives for so much longer that it felt like they had always been a part of hers. But eventually she looked up at the clock in the kitchen and frowned.

"You should probably head out. I'm sure you've got more important things to do on a Sunday." Rus smiled, her fingers twitching against her mug as she resisted the urge to reach out and pat Az's hand. With anyone else she wouldn't have hesitated, but Az had never liked it when people touched her, and Rus wasn't about to invade her personal bubble now.

"Yes. I probably should." Az nodded, but she made no move to stand. She didn't even grab the mug that she'd abandoned halfway through their talk. She just sat there, looking at Rus, and Rus painted herself a mental picture of this moment. Of Az sitting in her kitchen, their tea long gone cold. Of the soft murmur of the girls in the other room. Of the smell of sugar and dough coming off the tray still on the table between them.

It was almost funny that Rus had been given the title of *crow witch*. Ironic, even. Considering her tendency to hoard away bits and pieces of a happy life like a crow did shiny things. The soft, clean cotton smell of Az's magic. The sound of Cagney's barely there laugh. The rush of riding down the spiraling banister in the Jade Waters coven house, Az waiting at the bottom, her eyes crinkled with amusement but her tone disapproving. It was always almost enough—almost—to build a cozy little nest out of. But like a crow, Rus's nest would never be complete. Because shiny things weren't all that a person needed for a happy life.

After what felt like too long, Aihuan squealed loudly in the other room, shattering whatever moment they'd been sharing, and Azure nodded. "I'll stop by Necromancer's tomorrow for a chai around lunch."

"Oh. All right." Rus nodded, her smile crawling up her cheeks without any permission from her brain. "I'll walk you out."

"Thank you."

And that was that. Rus walked Az to the door. Az put on her shoes. Az left, walking back down the street to Carmine and Maureen's house. It wasn't until Rus heard

Cagney clear her throat behind her that she realized she'd been watching Az the whole way.

"She was flirting with you," Cagney said over her shoulder, already heading back to the kitchen to start pulling out ingredients for dinner.

"What?" Rus squeaked, following her. "She's not flirting with me. Fu—" she looked over at where Aihuan had set herself up at the kitchen table, coloring. "Fudge off."

"See?" Cagney lifted the tray of baked goods, moving them to a counter so she could package them away. "This is why we can't have nice things."

"Because Az brought us pastries?"

"Because you're stupid. Come help me make dinner. We're not ordering take out again."

"Don't you have your own kitchen to cook in? Your own house to terrorize?" Rus pouted impressively.

"I like it when Aunt Cags cooks," Aihuan volunteered, like a traitor. And Cagney looked so victorious, letting out one of those soft barely there huffs of laughter, that Rus couldn't say no after that.

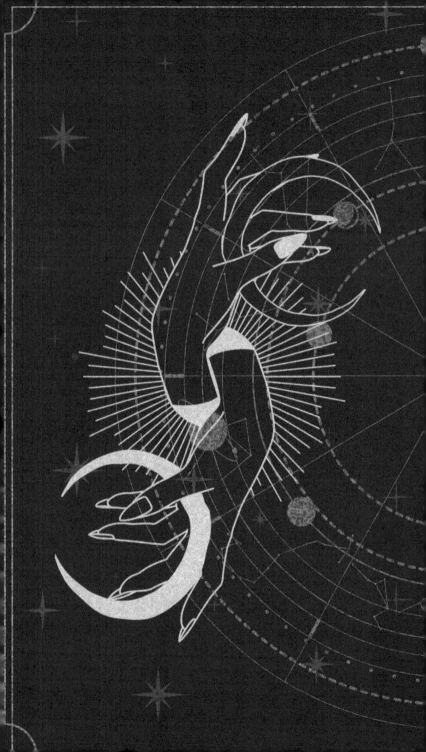

6

A MINT-GREEN MUG sat next to the beat-up Keurig Rus had brought with her to Moondale. It had a little white butterfly on it, and it said "anti-social butterfly" in a beautiful cursive font across the side that clearly indicated it was for someone left-handed. And it was bothering Rus.

It wasn't that the house had sat a mug next to the coffee maker; it did that every morning. It was that the mug existed in Rus's house at all. Because she knew she'd never seen it before. It hadn't come with her packed in a box. She hadn't bought it. And it hadn't been in the cabinet with the other basic-bitch-gray mugs the house had decided she liked. To top it off, or to make matters worse or whatever, sitting next to it *was* one of said basic-bitch-gray mugs. Like the house had just decided there should be a whole other coffee drinker with Rus in the mornings before she went to roll the girls out of bed and kick Fernando awake. A whole other person that liked pastels and bitchy mugs. Weird.

For a moment she contemplated throwing it away. It didn't belong, and the cabinet was already full. They didn't have space for this weird, out-of-place mug. But the poor kid in her cringed at the idea of throwing away something that wasn't broken. So instead, she just stood there, contemplating it as she sipped her almost too-hot black coffee.

"What're you looking at?"

Rus jolted at the sound of Fernando's voice, nearly spilling her coffee all down the front of her well-worn sweatshirt. When she turned to glare at Fernando, he shrugged innocently as if he didn't know he'd just snuck up on her before she was fully awake and thus should be ashamed of himself. Brat.

"Well?" Fernando prompted, tilting his head. "What is it?"

"That mug." Rus pointed without letting go of her own mug. "It wasn't in the cabinet when we moved in, and it's not one of mine. Is it one of yours?"

"You know I didn't bring anything like that with me." Fernando frowned.

"Right. No housewares, just clothes," Rus mumbled to herself, scrubbing at her still-crusty eyes. "You didn't pick it up in town yesterday or something, did you?"

"No."

"Of course not, that would have been too much to hope for." Rus forced her grip to tighten on the mug in her hand, hoping to hide how her hands had started to shake a little. "Then where the fuck did it come from?"

"Where does anything in this house come from?" Fernando shrugged, unbothered. "The house decided we needed it. I'll just put it away."

"There isn't room in the cupboard. It's full of—" Her mouth fell open as she blinked at the space where the pastel mug would fit quite nicely alongside the gray one she'd put back once she'd washed it, like she did every single morning. "Well, that's just—What the fuck is that about?"

"Who knows. Didn't Nesta tell you this house had a sassy streak?" Fernando said, unbothered by the house being weird as he grabbed a glass and poured himself some orange juice. "You better go get the girls up, or A-Ling is going to be late for school."

"Shit." Rus yelped, dumping what was left of her coffee in the sink and scurrying up the back steps to go get the girls ready for the day, not missing the soft laugh from Fernando as she went. The little shit.

WITH MEILING AT SCHOOL AND AIHUAN SAFELY SEATED in the booth they'd labeled as hers with a stuffed crow that looked vaguely like Darcy tucked in beside her, all her art supplies sprawled across the table, Rus pushed the mug from her mind. They'd never get the paint and crayon marks off the damn table, but Rus was all right with that. It would be a good marker that Aihuan had been there. That there had been happiness stored away in one little corner of the coffee shop.

It was peaceful, happy, relaxing. All of the things Rus hadn't allowed herself to feel in the last few months before they'd come to Moondale. Too busy trying to make sure they were all safe and hidden. If she looked out across the street, she could almost pretend she could see Az working at the register in Elwood & Co. It was nice to know that she was so close for all that she felt so out of Rus's reach. Literally just a short walk —

Rus's eyes landed on a white car parked off to one side of the occult shop, and something prickled at the back of her neck. Something like fear. It was normal for cars to park along Main Street. Normal for them to take up residence outside of shops. But it was a Tuesday in the middle of the autumn season. They got tourists around this time of year, sure, but not nearly as many as they'd get during the summer months when kids were out of school, and usually not in the middle of the week. The coffee shop itself had been relatively slow that morning, only serving townsfolk.

"Something's bothering you," Fernando said, sliding a cup with a tag for chai in front of her. It was Az's usual order. A gentle prompting from Fernando to do . . . what? Go see Az? Try to talk to her again? Because *that* had gone so well last time. Well, it hadn't gone badly, but that wasn't the point! The point was she was sure that Az didn't want Rus all up in her space. And Elwood's was definitely her space.

"That car across the way—how long has it been sitting there?" Maybe she was being paranoid. They were in Moondale, after all. They'd flown halfway across the world to escape their pursuers. Surely, they wouldn't have followed them here. "The white four-door."

Fernando turned so he could narrow his eyes on the car, his brow creasing. "I'm only just noticing it now."

"So you didn't see it pull up?"

"No. Why? What's going on?"

"Maybe nothing." But that wasn't quite true. Because there was something about the car that didn't seem right. Something about it that felt slippery, like her eyes could slide right off it and let it slip from her mind. "Keep an eye on Huaner. I'll take Az her drink and get a closer look."

Fernando shifted his weight on his feet, nervous, but he nodded.

"And remind me when I get back to call A-Ling's school. I don't want her walking home today. We'll pick her up."

"All right."

Rus wrapped her hand around Az's tea, took a deep breath, and pulled on the kind of fake smile that would make a beauty queen jealous. She watched the car from the corner of her eye as she approached, making a show of walking down the street a little to cross at the crosswalk properly, instead of jaywalking like the menace she was.

From the vantage point of the stripe-painted path on the pavement, she'd hoped to be able to see into the car, but she couldn't. The windows were tinted dark enough that there wasn't even the inclination of a shape inside. And that in itself should have set anyone within a mile radius off in Moondale.

That was if anyone else had noticed the damn thing. Which, considering the greasy smell of deflection magic clinging to the air around it, she'd be surprised if anyone else had. In fact, it had probably been sitting there all morning without *her* noticing it.

Whistling, she made her way past the car on the sidewalk, making sure her toe caught in that one root peeking out above the cement. She stumbled, hand flying out to catch herself on the tailgate. Something like burning fryer oil stung her palm, and she had to bite her tongue to keep from jerking back with a yelp that would no doubt draw attention from whoever was in the car.

"Sorry. Sorry." She laughed it off, making a show of checking to make sure the cup in her hand hadn't spilled any, and then continuing on her way to the front door of Elwood's. The bell over the door chimed softly, drawing Az's attention from whatever she'd been doing on the computer behind the desk. "Do you know how long that white car has been sitting out there?"

Az lifted her brows, looking a little put out by the lack of a proper hello, but her dark eyes flicked to the vehicle

Rus had indicated. A frown ticked at the corner of her lips, as if she was just noticing the thing herself. And that . . . *that* was worrisome. Because Rus was paranoid, but she'd also always been a big picture kind of girl. It was Az who noticed the details, and if she'd missed that one it meant whatever spell was on that car was strong.

"No. Why?"

"Uh . . . no reason." Rus laughed it off with a shrug. She knew it could have been her imagination. She knew it could have been her paranoia. There were hundreds of reasons why a witch might ward their car. She'd done it herself, so who was she to judge? But she couldn't escape the feeling of someone watching her. It prickled at the back of her neck. And she'd long since learned to trust that feeling. It had saved her life more times than she could count.

"Is everything all right?" Az asked, sounding genuinely concerned. And wasn't that just the sweetest thing that Rus had ever heard?

"Yeah, everything's fine." Rus pulled on that beauty-pageant smile again. The one that made her jaw ache and her eyes water a little. "I just wanted to bring over your tea and noticed it on the curb."

Az looked back out the window to eye the car, her lips pursed. "It has a deflection spell on it."

"It does." Rus nodded. "But there could be loads of reasons for that. It's probably nothing." She wasn't sure who she was trying to convince more: herself or Az.

"Hm. I will talk to the sheriff about it."

"No!"

Az's gaze jerked to Rus, her dark brows raised high above the reading glasses perched on her nose.

"Ah. Haha. No sense in bothering him, is there?"

"He's coming this way now." Az nodded toward the big front window, and when Rus looked out, Sheriff Greer was making his way across the street. Not at the crosswalk. Because cops could do whatever they wanted. *Fuck*.

"Oh. I should umm . . . I should go. You don't happen to have a back door I can sneak out through, do you?"

Az fixed her with a flat look, pinning Rus to her spot.

"Right. Of course not."

And then the bell chimed over the door, and the faint sulfur smell of electricity that always clung to Evander Greer invaded Rus's happy little bubble. "Well, well, well. Look what the cat dragged in." Greer jeered, his thin lips twisted into a sneer. "If it isn't the only witch to ever be kicked out of Moondale's coven system."

"I wasn't kicked out," Rus bit out, her hands tightening into fists at her sides. "I *left* before I was supposed to choose a coven. There's a difference."

There really wasn't. They all knew that. If she hadn't left, she probably *would* have been kicked out. Because that's what happens when the Board of Magic finds out you've been dabbling in necromancy. They could put up with her experiments with technology, but when she'd brought Darcy back after he'd been gunned down by some idiot human, that had been too much for them. Add that to the match between Az and Greer, and it had been the perfect storm. There really wasn't any reason for Rus to stick around.

"Sure, you did." Greer gave her a dismissive nod, then turned to Az.

Rus rolled her eyes. "I'll see you later, Az. I've got to get back to the shop."

She didn't wait for Az to respond before she bolted out the door, back down to the crosswalk—because Greer wouldn't hesitate to give her a citation for jaywalking, the utter bastard—and back to the relative safety of

Necromancer's. She'd just have to deal with whoever was in the car herself.

THE FEELING OF BEING WATCHED STUCK WITH HER FOR A couple more hours before Rus couldn't stand it anymore. There weren't enough customers to keep her adequately distracted, and that sensation sat like an itch under her skin that she couldn't scratch. So she told Fernando he was in charge and went to pick Meiling up from school early. Because anything had to be better than sitting around waiting for something to *happen*.

Except . . .

She realized perhaps a little too late that coming home with just herself and her girls, juggling Aihuan's bag of activities and listening to Meiling talk about her history class, was worse. Because the moment she stepped onto the path that led up to their house, she knew something was wrong. The very earth beneath her boots buzzed with it.

Darcy cawed from somewhere in the distance before he came to settle on Meiling's shoulder with a disgruntled noise.

"A-Ling," Rus said very quietly, drawing both girls' attention to her. They both went still; even as young as they were, they knew what that tone meant. They knew the danger it held in it.

"Yeah?"

"I want you to take Huaner and Darcy, and go down the street to the Elwoods'. It's the blue house on the corner, you know the one?"

Meiling nodded.

"Leave your things here. I'll take care of them." Already

Rus's fingers were twitching, putrid green swirls of magic gathering like thunder clouds around the tips. "Ring the doorbell as many times as it takes for someone to answer. And when they open the door, no matter who it is, tell them Icarus sent you and she'll be down to pick you up in a few minutes. They can call my cell if there's a problem."

Meiling, Goddess bless her, didn't ask any questions. She dropped her book bag without a second thought, ignoring the sound of her tablet hitting the ground probably harder than it should, took Aihuan's hand, and turned around to stride meaningfully back down the sidewalk. Rus turned to watch them to make sure they reached the Elwoods' door safely. She waited until the door shut behind them, and then she turned back to the house.

There was no open door, no broken window, not even any footprints to tell her that someone had entered without permission. But beneath her feet, the ground buzzed, unsettled. The roots of the grass and the cherry blossom tree out front told her that someone had been on her property without her permission.

Whispers, soft and hoarse, from the cemetery next door responded to the call of her magic. The dead turning over in their graves in anticipation. Eager to answer the woman who had tended to their final resting place, who had laid their souls to rest. Willing to fight for her if she should need it.

"Not yet. But stand ready," Rus said, and then she made her way up the path to the front door. It opened silently, the telltale creak that was normally there muted by the house itself as if it understood that Rus needed to be quiet, to be careful. She thought for a moment to toe off her boots to keep from making any unnecessary noise, but the house would hide her if she needed it. So she made her way inside.

The first floor yielded no signs of life, not even a breath of someone else's magic on the air. Nor did Meiling's, Fernando's, or the reading rooms. But when Rus entered Aihuan's room she smelled it there, still lingering—the tang of foreign magic. The person had gone, but they had been there. They had been there and they had *taken* something.

"What did they take?" she asked the house. She didn't know how it would answer, but when a little white cat slunk across the wallpaper of Aihuan's room and settled into the space along the wall left empty by one of Aihuan's favorite stuffed animals, Rus understood. "Fucking damn it."

Rus's knees shook with the knowledge that they'd found them. The understanding of what someone could do with a beloved toy. Of the havoc they could wreak on a child, even one like Aihuan. She'd have to take immediate countermeasures. She'd have to reach out to the covens. Fuck. She was going to need to call an emergency meeting with the board.

Her phone rang, pulling her out of that particular downward spiral, and she answered without even looking at who it was. "What?"

"Is the coast clear for me to bring the kids back over?" a young man's voice asked. *Indigo.*

"Yeah. If you could pick up their stuff on the way up the walk, that'd be great."

"Sure." Indigo hung up without another word, and Rus was left with the quiet of her empty house again.

"Did they leave anything behind?" she asked it, hoping maybe they'd dropped a hair, or some speck of dust, something she could use. But the house provided her with nothing, and she knew that had been too much to hope for. These fuckers were careful. They'd been hunting Aihuan for years. They weren't going to mess up now. "All right then."

THE KETTLE WHISTLED LOUDLY, MAKING RUS'S HEART stutter. She had drifted off, thinking about everything that had to happen in the hours to come. She'd need to reach out to Carmine when she was off work. Maybe the Jade Waters Elder would be willing to call the board together for her. Carmine Elwood had never been Rus's biggest fan, but she couldn't say no to a child, surely.

"Are you sure you want to do this?" Indigo asked. He'd settled himself at the kitchen table, helping Meiling with her homework while Rus made them tea to settle their nerves before starting on dinner. He was a good kid. All grown up, and much taller than Rus had ever thought he'd get. But she supposed that's what happened when you left home for more than a decade — cute, gap-toothed eight-year-olds went and became giants on you.

"I don't see where I have much choice. I can't protect the girls on my own, and we can't keep moving around like we are. This is . . . this is the closest they've gotten." She let out a breath that shook on the exhale. "And I was so sure we'd be safe here."

"Fine. But don't blame me when Aunt Carmine yells at you. It might be better to call Aunt Maureen and have her do it. But —"

"But I should go to the source. Just put the number in my phone." Rus dropped the device into Indigo's waiting hand, and the kid had the nerve to blink wide-eyed down at it.

"Good Goddess! Why is your phone so heavy?"

"It's not the phone, it's the case." Rus turned back to the stove, pouring hot water from the kettle into their waiting cups, including a little sippy one for Aihuan. They could all use something to settle their rattled nerves, Rus just wished it was something a little stronger. But not with the girls in the house, that was the rule.

"The case?" Indigo turned the phone around in his hands, examining it with curiosity. His wide brown eyes somehow looked so much like Az's that it made Rus's gut twist.

"There are protective wards carved into the inside of the case. It's the magic that's making it heavy."

"So . . . not to sound like a complete dumba—" He stopped, eyes jerking down to Aihuan before he cleared his throat. "Not to sound like a dumb dumb. But why do you have protective wards on your phone?"

Rus slid a mug across to Indigo and sat in the free chair, her fingers drumming on the ceramic under her hands. "Are you telling me they aren't teaching you kids how to protect your tech in school?"

Meiling looked up from her textbook with a wrinkled nose.

"No?" Indigo asked more than answered. His gaze flicked from Rus to Meiling. Rus wasn't sure what she was doing with her face, but she was sure that the horror on Meiling's was reflected across her own expression.

"Idiots," Rus huffed, rolling her eyes. "Okay. So. Riddle me this, Batman."

Aihuan hummed the Batman song as she moved on to color in a fairy.

"How much time do you spend on your phone every day?" Rus had a teenager; she knew the answer.

"Uhhhh . . ." Indigo shifted uncomfortably.

"Lots," Rus continued without any real prompting. She

already felt the heat of her annoyance coating her voice. Honestly, the board should know better! "Hours upon hours! And what do you do during that time?"

More uncomfortable shifting, because it was clear Indigo had never really thought about the threat his own device posed to him magically. Sure, there was always the threat of someone stealing his social security number and taking out a couple hundred credit cards. But anyone with any magical sense should know that's not all a phone is good for.

"You fill it with pictures, connections, searches, hopes, dreams, and even your identity."

"Identity?"

Meiling scoffed, ducking her head back to her textbook. She'd heard this rant before, perhaps even twice this week. Rus was so fucking proud of her.

"Social media." Rus snapped her fingers irritably in Indigo's face. "Keep up. Now add all that up and this?" She grabbed Indigo's phone to wave it around, nearly dropping it in her mug of tea. "Is as powerful as hair, nail clippings, spit, and even, in some cases, blood. All you've got to do is get close enough to clone it and . . ." Rus let out a long, loud whistle to emphasize her point. "Honestly, you traditional witches, all you ever think about is the basics. You never think about the human attachment to things, or other people, or even our devices. This is why the board—" She stopped herself, pursing her lips. "I digress."

"You should like . . . teach a class on that," Indigo said. He was still blinking at Rus as if she'd just gone off on some kind of political tangent.

"Yeah," Rus snorted. "The board would love that."

"Why couldn't you?" Meiling asked, her brows raised high. "You taught me everything I know. You're a good teacher, Aunt Rus."

"Because, A-Ling, mediums make people nervous. Especially the ones who dabble in necromancy. And I did more than dabble." She winked at Meiling, and then turned back to Indigo. "So, do you think the board will help us?"

"I don't know." Indigo frowned. His fingernails were scratching at the back of Rus's case, following the path of the wards as if trying to memorize them. "But you're right, you have to try. We—I don't want you to go away again."

He fixed Rus with a stare that rooted her to the spot, so much like his big sister's, and she couldn't ask what that meant before he slid her phone back to her and turned back to helping Meiling with her homework.

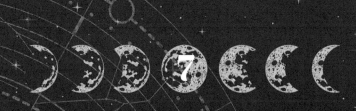

7

"I KNOW you're mad at me." Violet didn't even have the decency to look like it bothered her. Or that she felt bad about the fact that her younger sister hadn't spoken to her in days, and the only way she could get Azure *to* speak to her was by showing up at the store, unannounced, and demanding a tea break. And then proceeding to hound Azure until she turned the sign on the front door and led Violet back to the break room.

"No. What gave you that idea?" Azure asked in such a bland tone that she could tell her sister would miss the sarcasm laced through the words entirely before Violet's scowl had even started to form.

"Well. Firstly, you took my best baking sheet without asking, and you have yet to return—" Violet stopped, her frown deepening when she realized her sister was looking at her with a raised brow. "You're being sarcastic again, aren't you?"

Azure didn't bother nodding, she just continued to stare, unblinking, at her sister as she took a sip from her pale blue mug. It said, "Let's keep the tomfuckery to a minimum today" in gold letters on the one side, and Azure was both annoyed and amused to find her sister was not heeding its words. Because this whole *thing* was a bunch of tomfuckery.

"You know I hate it when you do that."

Azure did know. And frankly, my dear, she didn't give a damn. Violet had been saying she hated sarcasm for years, and Azure had decided long ago that that was a Violet problem. Indigo had promptly decided the same thing.

"I won't apologize for what I said about Icarus." Violet met Azure's gaze head on, no hint of shame or remorse in her expression. It made Azure's eyebrow twitch in irritation. "I do think you should let it go and move on. Maybe find someone more suit—"

"If you say *more suitable*, you'll never see your baking sheet again." Azure took another sip from her mug, waiting to see if Violet would try to call her bluff. It wasn't a bluff. It wouldn't be the first time Azure had abducted something of Violet's as punishment for her sister shooting her mouth off. Violet meant well, Azure knew that, but she also didn't know when to shut the fuck up.

Violet sighed, her shoulders sagging. "Look. It doesn't matter. She probably won't be here much longer anyway."

"Why not?" That was news to Azure. From what she'd seen of Rus since she'd arrived back in Moondale, it seemed to her that Rus was putting down roots. But that might have been wishful thinking.

"Didn't you hear?" Violet leaned forward a little as if she were going to tell Azure something juicy. "She called a meeting with the board. No doubt to petition for whatever she *really* came here for. They'll give it to her, to get her out of Moondale, and that'll be the end of that."

It took every ounce of self-control Azure had in her body to not roll her eyes at her sister. For someone who always saw the good in others, it was surprising how little she seemed to think of Rus. Well, maybe not surprising, considering how upset Azure had been when Rus had left. But still.

"When is the meeting scheduled for?" Because if Rus was going before the board, Azure was going to be there.

"It's not open to the—"

"When."

"Tonight. At midnight." Violet seemed to deflate a little in her chair. Azure wasn't sure what reaction her sister had expected from her, but this clearly hadn't been it. Too bad. "But I really don't think you ought to—"

"Evander will be there, I'm sure." Although the idea sat like something cold and dead in Azure's stomach. Slippery, and too heavy. It was like they thought Rus was dangerous. Like she might hurt them for telling her *no*. Oh how little they understood Icarus Ashthorne. Oh, how little they understood anything, really. They were all old goats who needed to give it up and retire, in Azure's opinion.

"Well, obviously, but—"

"Then I see no reason why I can't be there as well." Azure nodded to herself, the decision made.

Violet slumped forward, pressing her face into the wood of the table between them as she let out a long, loud groan. "Azure, you know that's just going to—"

"Piss everyone off? I'm aware." It was curious how Violet had yet to realize that Azure didn't care if she made the board angry at her. It had been years since they'd tried to force her to marry Evander. Years since that decision had cost her Rus. But she wasn't over it. And in the meantime, she'd done everything she could to make the board's job as difficult as possible. She didn't break the rules. She didn't put anyone in danger. But she had learned other ways to make a nuisance of herself. Like showing up to closed-door meetings and inserting herself into discussions the board deemed her too young or inexperienced to have a say on. Tough noogies, as Rus used to say when they were kids.

"Why do you do that? Why do you insist on antagonizing them?"

Azure wondered if that question was rhetorical or not. Violet knew the circumstances. She knew everything that had happened. She should not have been surprised that Azure took every chance she could to rebel. And yet still, she acted like every move Azure made was a direct attack on the board. Most of them were, but Violet didn't need to *know* that.

"Just . . . don't put your foot in your mouth. All right?" Violet asked hopefully, her brows drawn up high enough that they nearly caught in her bangs.

"I never put my foot in my mouth." Azure rolled her eyes. "Everything I say is thought over very carefully."

Violet huffed a laugh and lifted her mug to her lips to finish her tea.

THE BOARD WAS LOSING ITS COLLECTIVE SHIT. ALREADY. Rus hadn't even stepped foot on the grounds, and the elders from every clan and coven were buzzing with nervous energy. Azure couldn't make out what they were saying, but she could tell they were all in agreement about one thing: they were angry. How dare that ungrateful little guttersnipe think she could call an emergency board meeting. How dare she come into their town and kick up a fuss. How dare that little orphan—

Azure had to close her eyes to recenter herself, her hands reaching to adjust the traditional little pointed hat on top of her head. The damn thing itched, and it never really matched her outfits. But hats were a requirement of board meetings, and she was doing everything she could to not get escorted out of this one. Even if it was fun to watch Aunt Carmine's eye twitch whenever it happened. As if she couldn't believe an Elwood would be so spiteful. Which was funny considering the Elwoods had come to the town with all the others, running from the rule of bigger, more traditional covens. They'd been rebels once upon a time. Oh, how quickly people forgot.

"Are we going to talk about why you're here?" Evander asked, sliding into the fold-up chair next to her. He didn't sound angry at her, which was a surprise, because he had to know why she'd chosen to come. He had to know that it had nothing at all to do with him, and everything to do with Rus.

"No. We are not."

"Right." Evander scrubbed at his face, his rough fingertips making a soft scratchy noise as they rubbed over the five o'clock shadow on his sharp jaw. "Just don't get in the way if things go tits up, okay?"

"I can't make any promises." Azure's eyes flicked back to the entrance of the meeting room.

"Yeah. I thought you might say that. But I had to try."

He really didn't. Azure was an adult, and a capable witch. She could take care of herself if hexes started flying. But she didn't get the chance to say as much because a moment later the doors to the hall opened, and a chilly breeze followed Rus across the yellowed tile to the center of the semi-circle the board had set up with their peeling fold-up tables.

She was dressed in a long green velvet wrap dress that dragged across the floor in the back but had a slit at the front to reveal legs clad in black lace stockings that made Azure's throat feel like it had cotton in it. Scuffed black combat boots, untied, squeaked against the floor in the silence of the room. On top of her head sat a fedora-style black hat with a brim so wide it stretched out to her shoulders, which made the pointed felt hats of the elders look frumpy by comparison. And when Rus tilted her head back to meet the eyes of the elders, Azure could see crows embroidered on the bottom of the brim.

"Holy shit," someone muttered, and Azure only realized it was herself when she saw Evander whip his head around to shoot her a worried look. But she couldn't take her eyes off Rus, who had crossed her arms over her chest and was looking for all the world like every eye being on her made her feel validated instead of terrified. Still, there was something about her posture, something about the way the toes of her boots turned in just a little, that spoke to Azure of nervousness well hidden.

"Icarus Ashthorne," one of the elders said, the one from the Coven of the Silver Flame. Azure thought his name was Brant, but she wasn't sure.

"Rus, if you please," Rus offered, a smile peeling back her lips to show a mouth full of pearly teeth, the expression more threat than anything else.

"Icarus Ashthorne," Brant repeated, his wrinkled face pressing into a hard line as if he didn't find Rus or her antics amusing. Which was a crying shame if you asked Azure, because Rus's antics were . . . Well, maybe not amusing, but they were *something*. "You called an emergency meeting of the Board of Magic?"

"I did." Rus tipped her hat back a little more, revealing narrowed gray eyes.

"And what gives you the authority to do such a thing?"

Rus shrugged. "You're here, aren't you?"

Evander made a noise that sounded suspiciously like he had choked on his own spit. Aunt Carmine coughed into her fist to hide what might have been a laugh. And Azure didn't bother to cover the twitch of her lips as she leaned forward, drawn to the energy Rus was putting off. It wasn't just arrogance, there was competency there too. Rus had left Moondale, gone off to face the world without a coven at her back, and come back more powerful than anyone could have guessed, and there was something supremely sexy about that. Azure would have to unpack that later.

"Since we're already here," Cliantha, Evander's grandmother and the elder from the Coven of the Crimson Tide, said. She seemed to be trying to get the meeting back under control, but that was likely a lost cause. It had probably been a lost cause before Rus had even walked in. She had that effect on the elders. "Please, tell us what was so important."

At the question, Rus's shoulders grew tenser, her chin tilting back a little more. Azure felt the air around them shift with Rus's unease, but no one else seemed to notice. "I came to Moondale to seek sanctuary. My daughters and I are on the run from a group of witches who wish to use my youngest's power for their own gain."

The hall broke out in soft murmurs. Whispers of what kind of danger these witches posed to their own clans. Questions of if Moondale was safe. Fear. Nervousness. Cowardice. It all coated the group of old magic folk like a film and made Azure's stomach turn with bile. Rus had come to them, seeking help, and they were too concerned with their own skins to bother.

"These witches," Aunt Carmine started, breaking through the buzz of voices to silence her peers, "why are they after your daughter?"

Rus frowned, her hands gripping more tightly at the meat of her arms until it looked like her chipped black nails might tear holes in the sleeves of her dress. "Aihuan is a seer of the future."

The words were soft, but they carried with them the weight of expectation. The weight of knowledge. The weight of power. There was silence for what seemed like too long. And then the three witch elders looked at each other, gave a collective nod, and turned back to Rus.

"We can offer you and your children protection." Aunt Carmine's lips were pressed into a thin line, like she was going to say something that she didn't like. Something that turned her stomach. Azure had seen that expression many a time when Aunt Carmine was doing what she knew was expected of her, and what would ultimately be best for the Circle of Jade Waters Coven, but that she didn't necessarily agree with. She'd had that expression when she'd come to Azure with the announcement of Azure's match to Evander Greer.

"Thank you." Rus dipped her head, her shoulders relaxing a little.

"But," Cliantha picked up where Aunt Carmine had left off, her gaze near feral in its hunger. Azure gripped her short maroon skirt so hard she could feel the scratchy fabric of the crinoline underneath grit together. Her breath had lodged in her chest, and she was beginning to wonder if she'd ever breathe properly again. "You and your girls will have to pledge yourselves to one of the existing Moondale covens."

Rus stopped. Every muscle in her body went stiff, and Azure found she couldn't look anywhere else. She could only watch as neon green magic began to flutter around Rus's fingertips like smoke. As her eyes began to glow with the silent rage that boiled beneath. "Excuse me?"

"That is our offer," Brant said with a little shrug. "We

cannot provide protection to witches unassociated with one of our core covens."

"Cannot or will not?" Rus hissed, and Azure would swear she heard the whispering of spirits on the wind. The dead rising up to answer their mistress.

"I don't know what you're implying young lady, but—"

"I'm implying that they're *children*." Rus's tone was soft, measured, deadly. "I'm implying that if it were any other child—not mine, not a future seer—you'd have provided them protection regardless. I'm implying that the laws of the covenant of Moondale state very clearly that magical youth do not, under any circumstances, commit themselves to a coven or clan until they have completed their preliminary studies at the university. I'm *implying* that you're a greedy son of a bitch, Brant Ironwood, and you should be ashamed of yourself for trying to take advantage of a fucking *toddler*!"

"Regardless, that is our ruling." Brant's eyes hardened. "The board will not provide protection for the covenless. You have two days to choose a coven."

"And if I don't?"

"Then we can't help you."

Rus's jaw ticked. Her gaze narrowed on the elders for another moment. Then she turned on her heel and stormed from the room just as she'd come, the unsettled voices of the dead nipping at her ankles.

Azure didn't wait for the door to fully shut behind Rus. She didn't wait for the room to explode in discontent at the blatant display of disrespect shown to the Board of Magic. She stood from her chair, ignoring the skid of its rubber feet on the tiles, and followed Rus outside.

The air was crisp and cold under the waxing moon, and Rus's breath turned into puffs of steam as she muttered to herself, pacing on the cobblestone walk in front of the board building. It was a squat little thing, sitting in the shadow of the town hall, and most humans that lived in Moondale walked right past it, assuming that it was some kind of records archive. Which suited the Board of Magic just fine.

"Rus," Azure said, hoping to keep from startling her, but when Rus whirled around with wide eyes and her hands raised, ready for a fight, Azure knew she had failed.

"Oh. It's just you." Rus settled, her shoulders relaxing, but magic still flittered around her fingertips like smoke. Swirling up around her hands and wrists as if begging for its mistress to let it loose, to tell it to do something. And there were still those dull whispers, muted now that Rus had calmed, but they weren't far off. They were waiting. "I suppose you saw what happened in there."

"I did." Azure nodded, her own hands twitching at her sides. She wanted nothing more than to reach out to Rus. To pull her in close to her chest and tell her that everything would be all right.

"Fucking fuckers." Rus bit out the words so hard that Azure worried they'd bloody her tongue. "Moondale is supposed to be a safe space. A sanctuary for all magical folk who need it. That's why it was fucking *built*!"

"I can talk to my aunt. Maybe we can—"

"You heard them. They won't offer us any protection unless we pledge ourselves to one of the covens."

"Would it be so bad?" Azure asked, before she even had time to think about the words, and then she immediately wanted to kick herself. Maybe Violet was right—maybe she did put her foot in her mouth far more than she realized.

Rus laughed humorlessly, the sound like glass being run through a cheese grater. "You really haven't changed at all, have you? You know *this* is why we didn't work out."

Azure took a long breath through her nose that was *not*

a sigh, and refused to let the words festering on her tongue loose. Words that would remind Rus that they hadn't worked out because *she* had fucked off somewhere to chase a band, or find herself, or whatever the fuck else a twenty-one-year-old Rus thought she needed at the time. Instead, Azure pursed her lips and watched Rus pace for a long moment.

"I won't sign my girls up for that. They won't be tied to the covens, and their rules, and their narrow-minded *fucking* —No. Just no. I'll find some other way." Rus pushed the sleeves of her dress up, and Azure could see where the magic had begun to stick to her skin along her forearms too, settling into scars like it belonged there. "You should get back in there. Get back to your . . . Greer. I'm sure he's looking for you."

He wouldn't be, but Rus didn't wait for Azure to tell her that. She paced one last time in front of the building, then strode off down the street without a backward glance. Azure wanted to follow, but she felt rooted to the spot, her boots stuck to the cobblestones.

"That girl," a voice said behind her, and Azure turned to see Aunt Carmine shaking her head, "she's a whole lot of trouble."

Azure frowned, her gaze flicking back to where Rus was still walking down the street, her figure visible below the streetlights. Her dress billowing out behind her like a cloak.

"You should go by and charge her wards while she's out."

"What?" Azure turned again, her eyes wide as she drank in the expression on Aunt Carmine's face. There was something like understanding there. Aunt Carmine's dark eyes focused on Rus's retreating back instead of on Azure.

"Jade Waters can't officially provide her and her

daughters protection, but that doesn't mean the Elwood family can't do what they can to look after one of their neighbors. I'll have Maureen and Indigo do the same. It's the *neighborly* thing to do, after all."

"Right. Neighborly." Azure's fingers tapped against her thigh, her own magic climbing to the surface of her skin to dance like waves on the shore around her fingers.

"We can't do much. But we can at least make sure their home is safe."

"Won't the board be upset?"

"Do you really care?"

"No. Not really."

"You let me handle the board, Azure. You worry about keeping those children safe." Aunt Carmine patted Azure's shoulder lightly, stopping to give it a firm squeeze before she pulled her hand away. "You should go get that seen to before she gets home. We wouldn't want her to think that she owes us."

"No. We wouldn't." Azure looked back over Aunt Carmine's shoulder to the closed door of the board building and then nodded to herself before turning to head to her car.

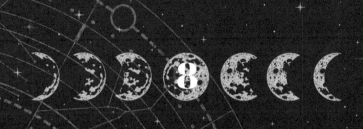

8

EVERYTHING WAS BLURRY AND INDISTINCT.
Hazy around the edges. A fuzzy feeling muting her senses enough that even weaving a simple light spell would send her reeling. It had been so long since Rus had been well and truly drunk that she'd almost forgotten what it felt like.

It wasn't the best idea to wander down to that pub on the corner. She should have gone to the house to get drunk instead. And not just because this meant she'd somehow have to find her way back while not being able to see straight, but also because the Drafty Draught held too many fucking memories. It seemed like every corner of the dark old bar had something for Rus to remember. The dart board where Rus and Cagney had gone head-to-head over who would be settling the bar tab every other week. The dark booth in the back corner where Rus and Az had had their first sloppy make-out session. Even the stupid barstool that Az had carved their initials onto the first time she'd gotten completely sloshed. It was all there, in technicolor, reminding Rus of everything she'd left behind all those years ago. And, fuck, she couldn't seem to drink it away.

Just like she couldn't drink away the sight of Az at that meeting, her long hair pulled back into a loose half ponytail, tucked beneath a classic black pointed hat. Evander Greer at her side, looking like he belonged there, looking like he was always meant to be there. Rus supposed that's what it meant to be set up by the board matchmakers; it made a couple look like a matching set, and they did. They looked *good* together. That alone had almost been enough to distract Rus from why she was there. Almost.

Rus took another burning sip from the glass in front of her. It was something dark and hard, and Ezra hadn't bothered to tell her what was in it before sliding the glass her way. Not that it would have mattered—Rus wasn't looking for something that would go down smooth. No. That would make this whole thing too easy. Would make this feel less like the self-flagellation that it was. She needed to feel every aching sip as it burned away her stomach lining and left her vision hazy and too bright around the edges. She needed to know that her head would hurt in the morning. That she'd be paying for the expression on Az's face when Rus'd told her she hadn't changed, for the cutting tone, and for the decision she had already made, in more ways than one.

Good thing Fernando is at home with the kids, she thought, taking another drink to either burn away the image of Az's wide dark eyes shining with hurt in the moonlight, or to brand that image into her memory. She wasn't sure. Who was she kidding? It was to sear that image into her mind so she wouldn't be stupid enough to do that again. Hurting Az was unforgivable.

"I'm calling someone for you," Ezra said, tone leaving no room for argument. Stupid fucker had always known exactly when to cut Rus off. Right before oblivion hit.

Goddess, she hated this fucking town. "Who do you want picking you up?"

The answer was simple, and it sprang to her tongue too readily. *Az.* She wanted Az to pick her up. Rus wanted to flop herself across Az's slightly shorter frame and listen to Az's bright K-pop music the whole way back to her house. She wanted to lean out the window of Az's hand-me-down Volkswagen Bug when Az wound it down to give her some fresh air to clear her head. She wanted—

"Cagney. She'll come get me."

Ezra's pale brows rose, like they knew that that hadn't been the first name on Rus's lips. They probably did. Every time Rus had gotten like this in the past, it had been Az to come get her, to lug her home and bundle her up in too many blankets so that they could crack the windows to let in the fresh air. "You sure?"

"Yeah. I'm sure." She wasn't and Ezra seemed to know it, but they shrugged and went to the phone to dial. Rus groaned, leaning forward to rest her forehead against the bar. The surface was slightly sticky, but not as much as it would have been on a weekend when the university kids would pile in to drink away their stress. Small mercies.

Either Rus was drunker than she realized or Cagney was already on her way, because it felt like no sooner had Ezra stopped rumbling softly into their phone than Cagney was sitting down beside Rus at the bar.

"Fuck. You're a mess," Cagney said without any real bite behind the words and flagged Ezra down. "Get her some water, I'm not having her puke in my car."

"Awww, Cags, you came," Rus slurred, leaning in to press her shoulder to Cagney's and nearly toppling them both off their bar stools with the effort. "You really do love me!" Rus launched herself at Cagney, throwing her arms around the other woman's shoulders and clinging to her like a damn leech, because that's what she was good at. Leeching off of others. Leeching and hoarding, those were Rus's specialties.

"Who loves you? Get the fuck off me." Cagney growled, her hands moving to try to brush Rus off. Rus held on tighter, her fingers tugging hard enough at Cagney's woolen jacket to make the seams groan. "Make that water to go. I need to get this dumbass home."

Ezra gave her a little salute and filled up a plastic cup before sliding it in front of Rus. "Was nice seeing you again, Rus."

Rus flipped them the bird and let Cagney drag her off her stool and out into the cold night air. It wasn't enough to sober her up completely, but the crispness of fall cleared her head a little. Too much, in her own opinion. For it brought it all back into sharp focus. The entire evening. The hunger in the elders' eyes. The way Evander sat too close to Az. The look of hurt that had flashed across Az's face when Rus had snapped at her. Each moment vivid and sharp enough that Rus found it hard to focus on anything else the whole way back to 157 Mourning Moore.

"This isn't my house," Rus said when they pulled up to a house on the outskirts of town. It was smaller than her own, or at least what she could see of it between the unchecked tangle of wildflowers that the front yard was, anyway. In the pale moonlight she could see bright pink shutters in sharp contrast against worn wooden siding.

"You're right. It's not." Cagney climbed out of the driver's seat without giving any kind of explanation and walked around the front of the car to manhandle Rus out of it.

"Why are we at your place?"

"Do you think I'm taking you home so my nieces can see what a fucking mess their guardian is?" Cagney's tone was sharp, but her hands were gentle as she looped Rus's arm across her shoulders and led her up the brick path.

"No. I guess not." The words came out wet as something that tasted like joy but felt like longing lodged in Rus's throat. Cagney was right—they were her nieces. They were her family just as much as Rus was. Cagney was also right that they really shouldn't see Rus like this. All sloppy drunk, and barely able to stand.

"I'm going to make you a snack. Something starchy. You remember where the guest room is?"

Rus nodded, scrubbing at her watery eyes with the heels of her hands. She didn't wait for Cagney to yell at her to stop crying like a little bitch; she just turned to the steps and crawled her way up to the second floor. The guest room was off to the right, but the bathroom beside it with its clawfoot tub and white tiles looked far more inviting. Rus leveraged herself up to a stand and headed into the bathroom instead.

The smell of alcohol clung to her like a second skin, seeped into her pores and the dress she'd worn to the board meeting. It only seemed logical that she run herself a bath and then proceed to climb in, still dressed in everything but her scuffed boots and hat.

Cagney joined her a moment later, a peanut butter sandwich in one hand, a big bottle of water in the other. "What the fuck are you doing?"

"I smell like bar." Rus sank down deeper into the water, letting the heat of it turn her skin pink everywhere it touched, and forced the air out from where her dress had puffed up.

Cagney let out a long breath, like a balloon deflating,

and made her way over to sit on the toilet, holding the sandwich out to Rus. "I assume it didn't go well."

"Decidedly not." Rus took a bite, ignoring the way her pruney fingers made the bread mushy.

"Do you want to talk about it?"

"Not particularly."

"Well, we're going to anyways."

Rus sighed heavily, taking another big bite from the sandwich, the peanut butter making it stick to the roof of her mouth so her next words came out garbled. "If 'e mus'."

"We must." Cagney sipped from the bottle of water before passing it over for Rus to take a deep gulp to clear away the food in her mouth. "What happened?"

"They said they won't help unless I pledge myself and the girls to one of the existing covens." Rus took another mouthful of water and held the bottle back out to Cagney for her to hold as she finished her sandwich. Already, she could feel the combination of the two sobering her up significantly. Which was just fucking *peachy*.

"Greedy bastards."

"That's what I said!" Rus sat up a bit, sloshing some water over the edge of the tub and onto the floor. Cagney's green eyes flicked down to it, but she didn't seem at all bothered by it. She lifted her gaze back to Rus, who was stuffing the last quarter of her sandwich into her mouth. "Dey ga' ma 'wo das."

"Chew and swallow before you talk." Cagney rolled her eyes. "Two days to what?"

She made a loud gulping sound as she swallowed the half-chewed mouthful, it ached the whole way down but Rus ignored it. "Pick a coven."

"And if you don't?"

"If I don't, then we're on our own." Rus slipped back down into the tub, closing her eyes as she submerged herself entirely. It was quiet beneath the water. The sounds of the world muted to dull thuds that could have been nothing more than a heartbeat in her ears. It gave her the space to think, if just for a moment. When she emerged again, Cagney's jaw had tightened so much that Rus could practically hear her teeth squeaking against each other. "I'm not going to do it."

"You're fucking right you're not." Cagney nodded firmly.

"We'll figure something else out."

"We will." Cagney shoved the bottle of water into her hands again and stared at Rus until she had drunk half of it. "But that's not what had you drinking yourself into oblivion, is it?"

Rus shrugged, brushing wet hair back from her face. Cagney wasn't going to let her off that easily, she knew that, but she also wasn't going to ask again. So they sat in silence for what felt like forever, while Rus took slow deliberate sips from the water bottle and the bath water cooled. When it finally got to be too much for Rus, she said, "She was there with him."

"Him who? Greer?"

Rus nodded.

"Are you sure she was there *with* him, and not just that they were both there?" Cagney frowned down at Rus, her green eyes searching, and that was impossibly worse than the sinking feeling in Rus's stomach. The one that made all her bones feel heavy.

"They looked good together."

Cagney snorted, rolling her eyes. "Like that means anything. Azure is so pretty, she'd look good with a potato."

Rus barked a laugh, the tightness in her chest easing. "She really would!"

Cagney's lips ticked up into a little smile.

"Do you think I should hex him? I think I should hex him. I just need his Twitter handle. He has a Twitter, doesn't he? He seems like a Twitter troll to me." Rus brightened, pushing herself to sit up straight in the tub as she brushed her wet hair back to plaster against her head.

"No."

"But he's going to steal my . . . my . . ." Rus floundered to think of a word, her lips pursed for a moment before she gave up. "Whatever she is, my Az."

"You're drunk. No, he's not."

"Yes, he is!" The water overflowed from the tub again, soaking the floor as Rus leaned forward to press her face in as close to Cagney's as she could reach. Which was damn near nose to nose. "He's a handsome son of a bitch, Cagney."

"His mother is actually quite nice." Cagney put her hand over Rus's face and shoved until Rus fell back into the tub with a squawk. It took her a moment to right herself, but once she did, she glared at her friend.

"Point stands. Have you seen his jaw?" Rus crossed her arms, pouting sullenly as her socked foot skidded against the side of the tub. "Cags, *his jaw*. It could cut fucking glass."

"I have noted his jaw. Yes." Cagney's tone had gone disinterested, her body leaning over the edge of the tub so she could reach down between Rus's feet and pull the plug. It made a loud gurgling noise as Cagney turned to grab a towel from under the sink.

"He's going to steal her," Rus insisted, poking her lower lip out further. "Maybe just a wittle hex?" She held up her pointer finger and thumb to show Cagney how small she meant, but Cagney rolled her eyes again with a huff.

"Rus. You're a fucking mom now. You can't be doing this shit."

Rus stopped, her hand slapping down against her wet dress as she blinked at Cagney. A mom. She was a *mom*. Legally, the term was *guardian*, but in every way that really mattered, she was Meiling and Aihuan's mom. They called her *Auntie*, but she was . . . she was all they fucking *had*.

"Oh fuck. You're right." Rus looked back up at Cagney, her eyes wide. "Well then . . . you hex him."

"What?! No." Cagney smacked Rus in the face with a fluffy towel. "I'm not going to hex Evander Greer just because he sat next to your girlfriend at a board meeting."

"Why not?"

"Because we're fucking adults. Now get up. Let's get you out of those wet clothes and into bed or you aren't going to be able to wake up in time to see A-Ling off to school."

Rus huffed but didn't fight any further. She leaned forward to shuck off her soaked socks before working herself out of the rest of her clothes quietly. After that, it was easy with Cagney's help to change into dry pajamas and curl up in the guest bedroom, the heavy quilt weighing her down into the bed.

"I'm not going to do it," Rus said into the quiet.

"Do what? Hex Greer?" Cagney leaned on the doorframe, her arms crossed.

"Join one of the covens."

"I didn't think you would."

"I might have." Rus chewed on the inside of her cheek, her nails digging into the quilt as she pulled it up tighter around her neck. "If they'd just wanted me, I might have. For my girls."

"I know that." Cagney's voice was soft with none of the teasing bite it usually held. "You're a good mom, Rus."

Rus ignored that last part, because it made something sticky cling to the insides of her throat, making each swallow thick as molasses. "But they wouldn't settle for just that. Not after I told them that Huaner can see into the future."

"Of course no—"

"And I can't have them looking at her too closely, Cags. I can't." Rus swallowed roughly, forcing down the words she knew she'd need to say. She hadn't told Cagney about Aihuan yet, but she'd have to soon. If Cagney was going to help her protect the girls, she'd need to know everything.

Cagney stilled, her breath seeming to be caught in her throat, then she let it out by force, her eyes narrowing as she went through the motions of turning off the light as a robot or a corpse might. Stiff and almost uncoordinated, or maybe too coordinated. "Get some rest, Rus. We'll deal with all of that in the morning."

"You're not going to ask me why?"

"I don't need to know why. All I need to know is that Huaner is family, and I'm not going to let anything happen to her. Now go to sleep."

"You're the best, Cags." Rus mumbled, feeling the heft of the quilt press her down into sleep.

"Tell me something I don't know." Cagney snorted and shut the door behind her, leaving it cracked so a sliver of light from the hall cut across the old floorboards. Rus drifted off a moment later.

ACROSS TOWN, HER TOES CURLING INTO HER BOOTS where she stood on the edge of the Ashthorne property, Azure looked up at the house, watching the lights in the windows. She had already layered her magic into the wards, reinforcing them with the magic of the Elwoods, the magic that had seeped into every inch of Moondale since its creation. It would be far stronger than anything Rus could do herself, not because Rus wasn't a strong witch, but because the Elwood magic saturated every inch of the land of Moondale. It was buried so deep into the soil of the place that Azure wondered if it hadn't seeped all the way down to the earth's core.

"We should go home," Indigo said, his arms curling tighter around himself in his oversized coat. It wasn't even that cold out, but Azure understood the dramatics behind grabbing the parka to wear over his pajamas and slippers. He was making a point that she'd put him out, even if he would have likely followed her without her asking. Azure knew he was as worried about Rus and her children as the rest of them were. "Aunt Maureen has already headed back."

"You can go. You have class in the morning."

"You can't stand guard out here all night, Az. You've got to get some sleep too."

"Rus isn't back yet." But she knew Indigo was right. She had work in the morning, after all.

"Cagney texted. She said Rus went on a bit of a bender." Azure wasn't sure what her face was doing, but whatever it was made Indigo's lips twitch into a knowing smile. "She's fine. Cagney set her up in her guest room. She'll be back in the morning."

"But the girls—"

"Have their uncle. And we're right down the street. We'll know if anything happens." Indigo slipped his arm through hers, tugging it a little. "Come on. Let's go home."

"You go. I'll wait until Rus is home."

Indigo let out a breath that rustled the limp hair in his

face. "All right. But I don't want to hear you bitching when you have to run the store on little to no sleep."

Azure cut him a look. Indigo laughed and spun on his heel to head back up the street toward their house. Once he was out of sight, Azure returned her gaze to 157 Mourning Moore.

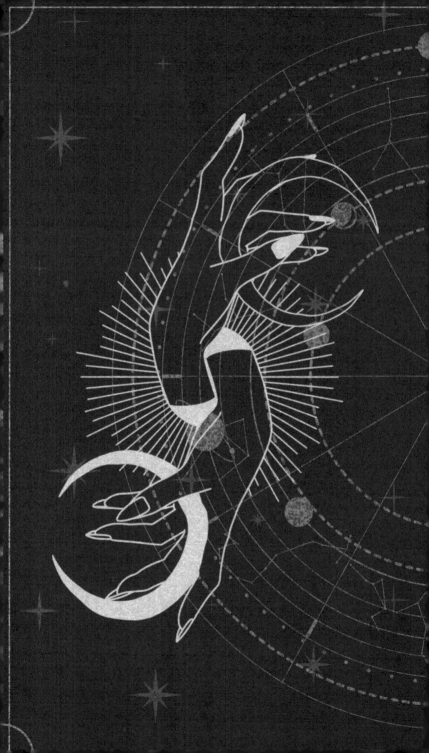

9

"FUCK!" Rus yelped, jerking away from the tiny cauldron before it could singe her eyebrows off. Again. "Fucking piece of shit. I know this should work. I've done this potion a million fucking—"

"Hey! If I'm not allowed to cuss in front of the baby, you can't either!" Meiling pointed her pencil at Rus, eyes narrowed in accusation, and had Rus not almost given herself an involuntary chemical peel, she may have felt guilt about the reprimanding tone. But as things stood, she didn't. *Fuck, I'm really bad at this whole parenting thing, aren't I?*

"What baby?" Aihuan asked, perking up from where she'd been sitting on the floor smashing four different colors of Play-Doh into one brown blob that she'd then want separated again. Rus thanked the Goddess that she'd decided to buy that shit in bulk; she didn't need a crying Aihuan on her hands along with everything else.

"Sorry. Sorry." Rus sighed, pinching the bridge of her nose where a headache had started to form. Two days of little to no sleep. Of constant research. Of running her magic ragged. It was all starting to catch up to her. But she didn't have time to sleep. Not when her girls were in danger.

"What baby?" Aihuan's head whipped around in search of the "baby" Meiling had mentioned.

"Uh huh." Meiling clicked her tongue, looking completely unconvinced by Rus's apology. Fucking teenagers.

"Where's the baby, jiejie?" Aihuan's lower lip poked out in a pout.

"You, Huaner. You're the baby," Meiling all but growled.

Aihuan let out a loud whimper, the prelude to a full-on temper tantrum. Rus wasn't sure if it was being called a baby, or the tone, but it didn't really matter. Not when Aihuan looked up at her with that wobbling lower lip.

"Oh, Huaner." Rus dropped to the floor beside the little girl, pulling Aihuan into her lap, bright green tulle skirt and all. "She didn't mean it, sweet girl. A-Ling is just stressed, and grouchy. We all are. She didn't mean it."

"Not a baby!" Aihuan wailed into Rus's shoulder.

"I know, little monster, I know. You're a big girl. And you're being so brave, with everything that's going on. So brave. We know that, right, A-Ling?" Rus raised a brow at the other girl. Meiling shifted uncomfortably in her seat, her eyes darting between Rus's expectant gaze and the back of Aihuan's curly head of hair. "Right, A-Ling?"

"Right." Meiling let out a long, loud breath, her shoulders slumping. "I'm sorry, Huaner, I know you're not a baby."

"There? See? Now, let's see that smile?"

Aihuan sniffled loudly before pulling back to bare her teeth at Rus.

"Terrifying." Rus grinned back at her, bumping her head against Aihuan's. "That's my little monster."

"Can I go paint a picture now?" Aihuan scrubbed at her face with the long sleeves of her black T-shirt.

"I think that's an excellent idea. Do you know where your art supplies are?"

"Mm-hmm." Aihuan stood on wobbly legs, her hands reaching out to grip Rus's shoulders to balance herself. Then she turned and went into the playroom to grab her art supplies.

"Can you watch her for a minute?" Rus asked, standing up and listening to her knees crack loudly from the movement. "I need to dump this shit."

Meiling shrugged but turned her head to watch Aihuan dig about in her art caddie. "What're you trying to make anyway?"

"I'm *making* an anti-tracking potion." Rus grabbed two potholders to pick up the little cauldron carefully.

"*Trying* to make," Meiling corrected. Rus could hear the smile in her voice. Brat.

"Your a-niang taught me. But I think I got the wrong amount of mugwort. I need to check the recipe in the grimoire."

"What's it do?"

"A couple drops sprinkled over your congee in the mornings and you both should be resistant to scrying magic. They'll have to get more creative to find you." Rus kicked the back door open, her boots thunking on the porch as she leaned on the door to keep it from shutting behind her. "I probably should have been making it all along. But . . . well, I thought your baba's talismans would be enough."

"Can I help?" Meiling's fingers twitched on the table in front of her. The homework they were giving her in school wasn't nearly challenging enough to keep the anxiety of their situation at bay; it had been clear with how little sleep she'd gotten over the last couple of days.

"Yeah. Just let me go dump this, okay?"

"Okay."

The door banged shut behind her, and Rus made her way across the yard to the edge of the graveyard. It wasn't the best place to be dumping fucked-up potions, but there weren't a lot of options. If she put it down the sink, who knew what the fuck that'd do to the house. And taking it out to the official board disposal site on the edge of town would mean a record of what she'd been doing. None of them needed that shit.

There was a caw from above, and Rus looked up to see Darcy nestled quite happily in the bare limbs of the big tree out back. He tilted his head, eyes seeming to narrow a little as he watched her.

"You're judging me. I can feel you judging me." She dropped the cauldron onto the ground, nudging it with her foot until it dumped next to the tree.

Darcy cawed, his head tilted the other direction as if that proved his innocence.

"Bullshit you're not."

He made a garbled noise that sounded suspiciously like he was about to hork up something half-digested.

"Look." Rus sighed, running her hand through her unwashed hair. Goddess, she needed a shower. "I know that it'd be easier if I got help from the covens and clans. But they don't want to help a covenless witch, so here we are."

Another head tilt, which was becoming increasingly annoying as Rus knew exactly what kind of criticism it was associated with, and Darcy made a chattering noise.

"Yeah, well, like I said, I haven't been given much choice. If I have to run myself ragged to keep the girls safe, then so be it." Rus shrugged. That choice had been made years ago, when she'd first met Meiling—all grubby hands and chubby cheeks, not much older than Aihuan was now. Rus had known immediately that she'd love that little girl for the rest of her life, and she'd give anything to see her happy. And then Aihuan had been born and everything had . . . happened, and Rus's resolve had been tested. Rus had done exactly what she'd vowed she would, and that was anything to protect those two girls.

Darcy grunted a low rumbling sound in his tiny bird throat.

"Fuck you. I *can* keep this up forever if I have to." She couldn't. She *knew* she couldn't. Darcy was right. But Rus would do it anyway. "I *will* keep this up forever, if I have to."

Darcy's eyes narrowed further, and he opened his mouth like he was going to make another dismissive sound, but he was cut off by the bang of the door on the back porch.

"Auntie Rus, that bitchy lady with the long hair is here again!" Meiling shouted through the screen door, the pale red sparks of her magic jumping from her hands to answer the call of the witch. She was likely already reviewing protection spells in her head. Good girl.

"You're not allowed to say *bitchy*." Rus huffed, picking up the overturned cauldron. "Which one?"

"The one with all the baked stuff."

"Oh, that's just Az." Rus's shoulders slumped a little in relief as she thudded up the steps to the back porch, and then across to the door. "Go let her in and bring her back to the kitchen. We can finish up the potion later. It's snack time anyway."

Meiling grunted her agreement, and Rus turned to grab the Cheerios from the pantry to pour some out for Aihuan before going to grab fruit and cut some for both girls. The soft sound of socked feet on hardwood let her know that the others had joined her.

"Kettle's on, what kind of—" Rus stopped, her eyes narrowing at Carmine Elwood, standing in the middle of her kitchen like she belonged there. Like she wasn't precisely the last person on the earth Rus wanted in her kitchen, near her girls. "You're not Az."

"Very astute observation." Carmine raised one dark brow, her expression impassive.

"Why are you here?" Rus's eyes narrowed and she gripped the knife in her hand harder than was likely necessary.

"The board hasn't heard from you. We expected you to come to us with your decision. But it's been three days."

"I thought that would have made my decision perfectly obvious." Rus forced herself to set down the knife. Forced herself to ignore the whispers of the dead in the cemetery next door, their souls unsettled with her fury. Forced herself to breathe in through her nose, out through her mouth.

"It did, for some of us. Others were . . . unconvinced. They sent me by to check in."

"They sent you by to *spy*," Rus hissed.

Carmine's dark eyes flicked away from Rus's narrowed gaze, and she looked almost ashamed at the accusation. Her shoulders slumped a little as she let out a long breath. "I am sorry for the decision they made."

"Are you? Because it sounded like you were on board to me."

"What's good for the gander isn't always good for the goose."

Rus opened her mouth to ask Carmine what the fuck *that* meant, but she was cut off by the sounds of little shuffling feet.

"Auntie Rus, who is this?" Aihuan asked from the

doorway to the playroom. She'd clearly walked off to put away her art supplies when she realized they needed the table.

Carmine's eyes darted to Aihuan too quickly for Rus to do anything to hide the little girl. They narrowed for a moment, assessing, and then widened. It didn't take a genius to know exactly what Carmine saw when she looked at Aihuan. Carmine had a knack for seeing auras—many of the elders did—which is why Rus had kept Aihuan away from them as much as she could. "Is this the child?"

"Huaner, go wash your hands in the bathroom upstairs. I'll have your snack ready in a minute." Rus moved, putting herself bodily between Carmine and the toddler too little too late. She could see by the wrinkle of Carmine's brow that the old witch had seen everything.

Meiling blinked at her, her own hands twisting with magic, posture defensive where she stood behind Aihuan.

"Go help your sister."

"But—"

"A-Ling. Do as I say."

Meiling huffed, but she whirled to follow after Aihuan, and Rus waited until she heard the upstairs bathroom door shut before she turned her fury on Carmine Elwood.

"You will tell no one what you've seen, Carmine, or so help me Goddess, I'll go scorched earth on this fucking town until there isn't a Jade Waters witch left. That includes Az." Rus ignored the way the words shook on the exhale. It didn't matter. None of it mattered, not if the board got it into their heads to take Aihuan away.

"This is blasphemy, Icarus!" Carmine's tone was all self-righteous indignation, her posture posed to do what, Rus wasn't sure, but she was sure it wouldn't be good. "You know that as well as I do. How could you experiment on a—"

"I didn't do it as an *experiment*," Rus said coldly, but she could feel her own anger waning. The long days dragging her down with exhaustion. "Or like . . . to prove how powerful I was, or whatever the board thinks of me. I did it because she was two, and she deserved a chance to live. She didn't deserve to die. Not like that. Not because someone wanted her power. And I'd do it again, for either of them. No matter *what* it cost me."

Carmine must have seen something in Rus's expression that she understood, because she relaxed and nodded. Maybe it was the understanding of another woman who had given up her life to raise someone else's children when they'd needed her. Rus had never really thought of how having that in common with *Carmine Elwood* would change things, but she sure as fuck was thinking about it now.

"Sit. Tell me what happened." Carmine turned to grab the screaming kettle from the stove and pour them both mugs of hot water before adding tea bags.

Rus let herself slump into the chair, hoping Meiling would understand the hint and keep Aihuan away long enough for this story to be told. She hadn't planned to tell Aihuan about this until she was a bit older. A bit more likely to understand. "When Aihuan was two, her power manifested. I mean . . . her mother had had visions when she was in the womb, that's how we'd known what it would be before she was born. But it didn't really manifest until she was two. And it was . . . it was so *loud*, Carmine. You know how powers can be when they first manifest. They're like the north fucking star, and anyone even remotely curious can follow them right to the kid."

Carmine nodded, but she didn't say anything as she adjusted the tea bag in her mug, letting it steep more.

"And especially a seer. People are always looking for one of those. So we were in . . . Ireland? I think it was?

Fuck, I don't even remember. We traveled all over in those days: me, and their parents, and the girls. But anyway, the next thing I know we're being tailed by witch hunters. They've got Huaner's scent, and they've decided they need that power for themselves. I don't even know how they got her away from us. We were being so careful, maybe too careful, I don't know. One minute Huaner's giggling, her chubby hand in A-Ling's, and the next she's just fucking *gone*. They probably got some of her hair or something and used a summoning circle, fucking assholes. We hadn't even thought that would be a problem.

"A-Ling was inconsolable, she thought it was her fault. So I go after them. I tell Xueming and Eamon to let me handle it. That I'll bring their baby girl back safe, because I'm her moonmother and that's my job." Rus took a sip of her tea, letting it scald her tongue and her throat to try to burn away the pain of what came next. The memory of what she'd found.

"By the time I found her they'd left her in this . . . this *shed*, exposed to the elements. Apparently getting visions of the future from a two-year-old is harder than they'd bargained for, so they'd just . . . they'd *left* her." Rus choked on the words. She could feel her eyes burning, but she knew she couldn't stop. Not now. Not until Carmine fully understood what had happened, and what it had cost her. "She'd already gone blue by the time I got there, Carmine. No amount of warming magic was going to help. I couldn't —there wasn't even a brink to bring her back *from*. So I did the only thing I could think to do, the only thing that made *sense* to me.

"I didn't have any small animals to sacrifice, and the fuckers who'd left her there were gone already. So I . . ." Rus shrugged, swallowing thickly, her hand twitching around her mug, wanting to reach for her stomach. She wouldn't. She didn't want Carmine's pity for *that*. Not when she'd given it up willingly. "I offered up some of myself."

When Rus looked up, Carmine was watching her with an unreadable expression. Rus frowned, her fingers tightening around the mug in her hands. "What would you have done? If it were Az? Stolen away by someone who just wanted her power. Abandoned and left to freeze because she didn't do exactly what they wanted. Two years old and just . . . just *gone*." She choked on the last word. It scraped raw at her throat, but she managed to breathe past it, somehow. "What would you have done? Don't tell me you wouldn't have done everything you could to bring her back. Sacrificed any part of yourself you had to to give her a *chance*. Don't lie to me like that, Carmine."

Carmine shook her head. Rus wanted to ask what that meant, but a moment later Aihuan came into the room, squealing and launching herself at Rus's legs.

"Auntie Rus! I'm all ready for snack time! Can I have strawberry?" Aihuan peered up at her through a mess of curled black hair, her brown eyes sparkling.

"Of course you can, little monster. Have A-Ling help you into your chair, and I'll grab your plate." Rus stood, giving Carmine a long, assessing look, but Carmine was watching Aihuan with that same unreadable expression. "Say hello to Mrs. Elwood. She's Miss Az's aunt."

"Hi!" Aihuan waved eagerly as Meiling all but wrestled her into the booster seat. "I'm Huaner and this is my sister, A-Ling. What's your name?"

"I think you can call me Miss Carmine," Carmine offered, a softness to her tone that Rus hadn't heard since she'd been a child herself.

"Okay!" Aihuan grinned, and then was promptly distracted by the plate of strawberries Rus sat down in front of her. Meiling settled in the seat between Carmine and Aihuan, watching Carmine mistrustfully.

"A-Ling, manners." Rus tutted softly.

"I'm Meiling," Meiling offered but didn't say anymore before she stuck her earbuds into her ears again and turned her eyes back to the homework she was working on.

"Teenagers. What're you gonna do?" Rus laughed, sitting on the other side of Aihuan, sliding a cup of juice her way.

"She's very . . . energetic." Carmine's brows raised in interest.

Rus shrugged. "Necromancy, *real* necromancy, is about more than raising a few corpses to fight your battles for you."

Carmine wrinkled her nose in distaste but didn't fight Rus on the subject. Which was good because of the two of them, Rus was the expert. No one in Moondale had fiddled with necromancy before her, and she doubted anyone had after. Too afraid of the judgment of the board. "How many times have you done it?"

"Only twice that really mattered." Rus's eyes flicked to where she could see Darcy out the window, napping in the tree out back, and then back to Aihuan, who was counting her Cheerios out with a soft whisper into groups of five before eating them.

Carmine nodded, seeming to take that answer for what it was. Then she finished off her tea and pulled her hands away from the mug. "I will tell the board of your decision not to join a coven."

"What about—?" Rus jerked her head to Aihuan.

"I do not think it would be in their best interest if they received a full report on Huaner's . . . circumstances. They are already in a frenzy over the fact that this is the first time we've had a future seer in Moondale in centuries. No need to rile them up further."

Rus slouched in her chair, relief washing over her. "Thank you."

"No need to thank me. I'm just doing what's in the best interest of my coven." And my family, Carmine didn't say, but Rus heard it all the same. She shook her head, and stood. "I'll see myself out. But if you should need anything from myself or my family, you know where to find us."

"Yes. I do. Thank you, Carmine."

Carmine turned to head out of the kitchen, and stopped in the doorway, taking a breath. "You're not planning to run again, are you?"

"No." Rus let the word out on a breath. She hoped Carmine wouldn't hear the hopelessness in it. The insinuation that they didn't have anywhere else *to* run. That this had been her last resort and now she hadn't any other options.

Carmine nodded. She exited stage left, leaving Rus running the conversation over and over until her head spun with it.

10

IT HAD BEEN A WEEK. A week of secretly charging the wards on 157 Mourning Moore when Rus was busy elsewhere. A week of watching Rus through the window of Elwood & Co., her appearance slowly becoming more and more haggard. A week of wanting to reach out and not knowing how, or if she even had a right to anymore. A week of running that conversation after the meeting with the board over and over in her head.

It was that more than anything that stopped Azure from reaching out. Because Rus had made it quite clear that night that she didn't *need* Jade Waters' help. And that she didn't *want* Azure's help. Still, Azure couldn't completely extricate herself from the matter. She'd been sending Indigo and Aunt Maureen over regularly with little things, as well as stopping by herself—though she never stayed long past the dropping off part. Scones for the girls. A draught to help with Rus's energy when she flagged. Little signs that Azure was still out there, somewhere, caring. It would come to naught, Azure was sure of that. But it was all she could do, really. She couldn't force Rus to accept her help, but she could do this, at least.

Azure was so distracted with thoughts of another talisman she might be able to make up to act as a portable ward for the girls that she didn't even hear the bell above the door. In fact, she didn't notice Cagney's presence until the druid was right in front of her, green eyes blazing, breath coming in short, seething pants.

"I know you sent her." Cagney pointed at Azure, her hand shaking with her fury, and Azure could feel every plant in the room stand up to attention. Even some of the newer books seemed to be answering the call of the druid.

Azure didn't bother to dignify the accusation by asking who Cagney meant. She knew. And now Cagney knew as well, she supposed. Not that it would change anything. Azure wasn't about to—

"Is that how you *help* them?" Cagney asked with a disgusted scoff. "Send your aunt by and dig up all those— all that *hurt*?"

Azure stilled, her face freezing in what must have been a look of impassivity because Cagney's gaze only burned more angrily. "What?"

"Carmine was by the other day. As if you didn't *know*." Cagney rolled her eyes. "Asking all sorts of questions about Huaner. She dragged up the whole bloody business. Rus was so—" Cagney stopped, blinking at Azure for a moment. "You didn't send Carmine."

"No. I have asked Indigo and Aunt Maureen to check in with Rus periodically, but I did not send Aunt Carmine. I thought she would be . . . indelicate about the situation." Azure frowned. "What bloody business?"

Cagney pressed her lips together, biting down on them as she let out a loud breath through her nose like a kettle that'd started to boil.

"Cagney," Azure said patiently, her tone soft. "What bloody business?"

"I shouldn't tell you. It's not my place."

But she was going to. Azure could see it before Cagney had even given in. Because Cagney would do anything to protect Rus, even if that meant she had to divulge her secrets. She was a good friend, and she'd always do what was best for Rus, even if it wasn't what Rus wanted.

"I can't help protect them if I don't know what's going on," Azure pressed gently. Rus would be mad at both of them for this conversation, she was sure of that. Fuck it. Rus could go on and be angry, so long as she was safe.

"Huaner died, a couple of years ago. Some witches— different than the ones after her now, we think—took her. And when she couldn't give them answers, they left her to die. Rus brought her back." It looked like there was more Cagney wanted to say. Like there were words pressing at the back of her teeth, but she swallowed them down, and Azure wasn't going to force any more from her. Because already Azure felt . . .

She needed to sit down. Yeah. She definitely needed to sit down. What the *fuck*? Azure stumbled back into the chair behind the counter. The one that had been there since some other Elwood had run the store even though Azure never used it. Maybe Aunt Maureen had pulled it from the back to give herself a way to get off her feet for a few minutes at a time. It didn't matter. All that mattered was it was there now, and even the sturdiness of it didn't keep Azure from feeling like the ground might reach up at any moment and swallow her whole.

Aihuan had died. Rus had used necromancy to bring her back. Rus had . . . Rus had paid a price for that, Azure was sure of it. She didn't know what the price had been, but she could guess. Her mind flicked back to the scars that littered Rus's arms. The ones that looked newer and deeper than the ones from when she was young and just learning how to use her own blood to call the dead. She didn't seem to need to spill it as often these days, now that she'd gotten —No. It wasn't that she had gotten more powerful. It was that she was closer to the dead than before. One foot in the grave would make it easy to call forth those who had already passed to help her when she needed them.

Cagney gave her a few brief seconds of respite before she pulled her face into a scowl again. "You see why you can't keep doing this, right?"

Azure looked up from where her gaze had drifted to her own hands. She didn't remember looking down at them. When had she begun to compare the unblemished brown skin of her own hands to Rus's scarred and calloused ones? Azure shook her head, not understanding what Cagney was trying to say.

"This loving and protecting them from a distance bullshit," Cagney clarified. "It's not what Rus or those girls need. It's not what they deserve. You're either all in, or you're out."

But it wasn't that simple, was it? It couldn't be. Not with Rus. Not with all the history that was behind them, and all the years that had spanned between them. They had been tangled up in each other for years. Since she was five years old and moving to Moondale to live with Auntie, far away from the life she'd known in Boston with her parents and her sister. Since a little girl with bright gray eyes, missing her two front teeth, with a smear of freckles across her nose had offered her hand to Azure. Azure's life had been tangled up in Rus's for so long, she didn't think she would ever be able to cut out the parts of it that belonged to Rus. It would be like amputating a limb. No. It had been that, exactly. Even with Rus gone, Azure had still felt her there in everything she did. So much of herself was made up of parts of Rus.

Cagney snorted, as if Azure's silence was confirmation enough of the choice she'd made. Maybe it was. Maybe her inability to stand up right away and say she'd protect Rus no matter what was answer enough. "If you're out, you need to get your shitty laundry-scented magic out of her wards. It's just going to muddle things up."

Azure frowned, her brow wrinkling as she ground her teeth together to keep from making some biting remark about how Cagney's smelled like damp earth and fungus.

"All you're doing is confusing the land." Cagney narrowed her eyes on Azure, as if expecting a challenge to the statement. There would be none. Because Azure was still processing the fact that Aihuan had died. That Rus had brought her back. Cagney snorted when she got no answer. "That's what I thought."

Then she turned and left just the way she'd come, with Azure hardly noticing. The bell chimed again a moment later, and Violet walked in, her hair neatly wound up in a bun, a pair of glasses perched on her nose.

"What was that about?" Violet asked, her head turned so she could watch Cagney storm across the street to Necromancer's and disappear inside.

"I have no idea," Azure lied. She couldn't tell Violet the truth. As much as she loved her older sister, she didn't think Violet would understand the choice Rus had made. Violet, who had given up her own dreams of a family because her wife didn't want children. Who had married Taryn without a second thought in spite of the fact that Azure knew she was in love with someone else. Who always followed the rules and did what the board told her to. No. Violet wouldn't understand the sacrifices that Rus had made and continued to make for her girls. She also wouldn't understand the bone-deep feeling of need that lingered in Azure, had lingered in her since the day Rus left.

"It sounded like a jealous tantrum."

"Did it?" Azure resisted the urge to roll her eyes. For an empath, Violet could be surprisingly dense when it came to other people's emotions. She could feel the shape of them. She could recognize upset, and anger, and even love, but she always seemed to struggle to connect those feelings to their root cause. Of course she would mistake the protectiveness Cagney was feeling toward her best friend for jealousy.

"Yes! Taryn told me they've been spending all sorts of time together lately."

Taryn Elwood was a little shit-disturber who liked licking the boots of the board and would do anything in her power to gain esteem in their eyes. Azure knew this about her sister-in-law. But it didn't make this whole conversation any less annoying. "They're friends."

"Are they?" Violet tilted her head, one piece of hair that she'd artfully pulled from her bun to frame her face falling across her shoulders. "Taryn said Cagney visited Rus while she was away."

"Taryn says a lot of things." But the truth of those words didn't take away the sting of what Violet had said. Azure hadn't been lying when she'd told Cagney weeks ago that she was the only one Rus hadn't seen fit to keep in touch with. Rus had spoken to Cagney and Nesta, her two best friends from before she'd left, regularly. And even Phyre Ironwood, a girl who had lived at the orphanage for a few years with Rus before being adopted by the Ironwood clan, had received an email at least once a month updating her on how Rus was doing. But for the Elwoods, there had been nothing. Not an email. Not a text. Not even a poke on social media. And that had left something aching in Azure that she had yet to identify.

Violet was still yammering on about something that Taryn had said, but Azure had wisely decided to tune her out. It was better not to engage with Taryn's underhanded attempts to climb the Moondale social ladder. Especially as all it usually did was piss Azure off.

STILL, AZURE REALIZED THE FOLLOWING DAY WHEN SHE was back home on her lunch break, her fingers tight around a book of protection arrays she'd pulled off the top of her shelves at home to send over to Rus, that perhaps everyone had a point. Violet. Cagney. Maybe they were right. Rus had made it very clear she didn't want Azure to interfere in her business, and Azure didn't want to push her away, not again. So maybe it would be better if she extracted herself and her magic from the situation entirely. At least until the threat had passed.

She nodded to herself. That decision made, she went in search of someone to deliver the book. With Indigo out at a friend's, and Aunt Maureen at the greenhouse, that left only Aunt Carmine. Who was sitting in her reading nook looking quite cozy in a thick shawl Indigo had crocheted for her, her reading glasses perched on her nose.

"Can I help you with something, Azure?" Aunt Carmine asked, not even looking up from her book.

"I would like you to deliver this book to Rus. It has some arrays in it that I think could jog some ideas for her. She may not be able to use —"

"Why don't you just deliver it yourself?"

Azure bit back a curse, letting out a long, annoyed sigh.

"I have decided to take a more hands-off approach to the safety of the Ashthorne family."

Aunt Carmine huffed, placing a finger in her book to mark her spot, closing it, and lowering it to her lap so that she could look up at Azure with those narrowed brown eyes that Azure was told were so much like her own. She'd been told on more than one occasion that she looked just like her Aunt Carmine when she was younger, but Azure never really noticed the family resemblance unless Aunt Carmine was looking at her like this. Disappointed.

"What?" Azure shifted on her feet, unsure under that penetrating stare.

"May I ask why you've come to that decision?"

"The board has made it very clear that—"

"And since when do you give a flying fuck what the board wants? Pardon my language." Aunt Carmine's lips tipped up in a smile.

"Sticking my nose into Rus's business will only draw more attention to—"

"Nope. Try again."

Azure huffed out an annoyed breath, but Aunt Carmine just sat there, waiting and watching, patiently. Like she had all the time in the world for Azure to get over herself and say what she needed to say. It was frustrating how this old trick, the one Aunt Carmine had been using on her since she was five years old and unable to explain why she didn't want to go to her parents' funeral, still worked so many years later.

"What is it really?" Aunt Carmine pressed gently.

"I don't think she wants my help."

"And when has that ever stopped you before?"

Azure frowned, looking down at her socked feet as she flexed her toes against the hardwood. Aunt Carmine was right; she'd never let Rus's resistance to help stop her before. She'd never let Cagney's opinion of her change her mind either. Nor had she ever let Taryn's words sway her. So why now? Why this time?

"It's the child, isn't it?" Aunt Carmine asked, putting a bookmark in her book and setting it aside. "Something about Aihuan's nature has you bothered."

"It's not . . . *not* Huaner." Azure puffed her cheeks petulantly. If she were honest with herself, it was a little bit Aihuan. But it was also a little bit Meiling. And it was less about them as people and more about—"I'm not sure if I fit in Rus's life anymore. Now that she has . . ." Azure wrinkled her nose, chewing on the words.

"Now that she has a family." Aunt Carmine nodded in understanding.

"It's not that I don't want her to be happy." Although Azure wasn't sure why she felt like she needed to say that. Aunt Carmine knew that. She had to. Because Azure had done everything in her power for years to make Rus smile. Even when it had gone against what Aunt Carmine wanted, or the board rules.

"Of course not."

"I just—"

"You don't need to explain it to me, Azure. I understand."

Azure let out a breath, her shoulders relaxing. She was glad someone did, because she hadn't understood it herself until just now when she'd said it out loud. "What should I do?"

"You should take her that book. Maybe sit down with her and go over some of your ideas for protection arrays." Aunt Carmine shifted in the chair, pulling one leg up to cross under the other as she got comfortable to go back to reading.

"But the board—"

"You let me worry about the board."

Azure frowned, chewing on the inside of her cheek. "I don't want to push her away again."

"Then don't do any pushing. Just go and offer your help. If you're meant to be there, a place will open up for you. Icarus Ashthorne, for all her . . . Icarusness, has never been the type to keep the people she loves at arm's length. She'll make space for you. Just—" Aunt Carmine broke off, seeming to consider her words carefully. Then she nodded. "Just remember that you're essentially starting from scratch. You have history, yes, but it's been over a decade, Azure. Be her friend first. If anything more is meant to come from it, it will."

"Right." Azure bowed her head, her hands clutching at the book cover hard enough that she could feel the spine bending. "Thank you, Aunt Carmine."

Aunt Carmine grunted. "Go on. Get out of here. And don't tell anyone I gave you love or life advice. I don't need Indigo coming in here asking me about his newest crush. Or, Goddess forbid, Maureen starting to think I've gone soft." Aunt Carmine shuddered.

"Of course not." Azure bit back a little laugh. Aunt Maureen already knew Aunt Carmine had gone soft. There really was no hiding it from her. But they let Aunt Carmine think she was the strict disciplinarian.

"Well? What are you still standing here for? Go on. Get." Aunt Carmine threw a pillow at her, and Azure choked on a giggle as she fled the room, her hurried steps leading her down to the front hall to slip into her coat and boots. Once she was buttoned up, she headed out into the chill autumn evening air, retracing the path she'd walked at least a dozen times in the past week to 157 Mourning Moore.

SOMEONE NEEDED to look after the graves of the forgotten. Rus knew this better than most witches. Being a medium put her in direct contact with the spirits of the nameless, faceless dead. The ones who sometimes didn't even have grave markers. No one wanted to be forgotten, even the dead, and when their graves were left to sprout weeds, or go untended, that's when the spirits got the most unsettled. Even those who had had loving families sometimes got lost on their way to wherever they were headed if the families moved away, or just didn't take the time to go through the rights.

It was no one's fault. These things just happened. Life was for the living, and it was in the nature of the living to want to distance themselves as much as they could from the dead. Out of fear, maybe. Or lack of understanding, perhaps. Even witches seemed to feel the same way.

Which was why when a child was born a medium, it was seen as unlucky in this corner of the world. A curse. A blight. Against the family, and sure to bring ruin to the parents. Maybe that's why Rus's parents had died—because she was a medium. Or maybe people were just making connections where there were none to be made. Either way, Rus understood the dead probably better than most witches could. She knew what it was to be left behind and forgotten.

Which, in her opinion, is what had made her such good money over the years. Everyone wanted easy solutions to hauntings, and Rus was the easiest they came. Not the cheapest, perhaps, but definitely the least involved. It was also why when she'd moved into 157 Mourning Moore, she'd taken one look at the overgrown cemetery next door, and the lingering shades of people long since passed, and known that they were going to become a problem if she didn't do something about it.

Plus, there was something . . . meditative about cleaning the graves. Something that left her mind at peace about pulling the weeds and wiping down the headstones. Like laying them to rest, finally, brought her a sense of wholeness that she couldn't exactly explain. And she needed that right now with how unmoored she felt: jittery and panicked ninety percent of the time, and almost too tired to function the other 10.

She murmured a soft prayer for the woman whose name had long since faded. It was something with an *m*. The woman had been a midwife and a mother, and she had probably lived a good life, all things considered. But she also had probably outlived anyone who had ever cared for her.

The shade of the woman lingered over Rus's shoulder, a coldness at her back that Rus had to resist the urge to shiver from. Her focus so wholly on the task that she hardly noticed it when another pair of knees sank down into the grass beside her, and a voice joined her own. The prayer ended, and the cold pressure at her back drifted away on the soft autumn breeze, the woman's spirit finally finding the rest she needed.

"You didn't have to do that, you know," Rus said, lifting her head from where she'd had it bowed to look at Az beside her.

"No. But I wanted to." Az shrugged, like it was that easy. Like her kneeling beside Rus at some grave marker without a name, and sending the soul off to rest, wasn't something they'd done a hundred times before. Like Rus hadn't been missing Az's calm and warm presence at her side all these years when she did this. "You always use the same prayer."

"Yeah, well, it's the thought that counts really. The dead don't care about religion or language. They just want someone to acknowledge them and care about them. That's all they need. You know that."

Az nodded her agreement. She did know that. Because Rus had told her on more than one occasion. Because they'd spent a lot of time in their teens in graveyards, sending the spirits to rest when the negative emotions of the shades grew too desperate and threatened the safety of Moondale. There had been a lot of that when Rus had been a child—malevolent spirits upsetting the balance of the magic of Moondale, and her people. There wasn't as much now. She wondered why.

"Was it bad when you moved in?" Az asked, breaking off that train of thought.

"Not terrible." Rus stood, brushing off the knees of her jeans. "Not like when you and I first started back when we were fourteen."

Az hummed in some kind of smug satisfaction that Rus didn't understand and would have questioned her about had they been on better terms.

"It was more that I just didn't want the girls to see." She

offered Az a hand up, and Az took it, letting Rus pull her to her feet. "They weren't a threat, but they were looming, and those things still scare A-Ling."

"I see."

"I learned other prayers, when I was traveling." Rus led the way through the cemetery back toward her house. "Different languages, different sentiments. But this is Moondale. Most of the people here spoke English, so there hasn't been much call for it. I've found a couple of stones with Celtic knots on them; they get the Gaelic version. It's really beautiful."

"I'd like to hear it."

"Maybe next time." Rus laughed a little, ignoring the heat that pooled in her chest, making her hoodie uncomfortable in the glaring sunshine. "I hope I'm not—I hope I'm not stepping on anyone's toes doing this."

"You aren't."

"How do you know? The board gets very persnickety about people who trample into graveyards and mess with the dead." Rus would know that from experience. And she didn't honestly think that the board would be happy to know that the necromancer they'd chased out of town was making herself very well acquainted with the unsettled spirits of their town.

"Do you actually care what the board wants?" Az turned to her at the door, one dark brow lifted as if to ask if she was allowed in. Rus grabbed the door and held it for her, making the invitation apparent.

"Not really," Rus said, following her inside to the screened off porch, and then through to the kitchen at the back of the house. "And it's not like I could ignore the spirits even if I wanted to. I've never been able to ignore someone who needs me."

There was a twitch at the corner of Az's lips, the

beginnings of what Rus thought might have been a smile as Az said, "No. I suppose you haven't." Then she shook her head and it was gone. "The board focuses their attention on the newly dead, mostly. I'm sure they hadn't even noticed any lingering bad energy from this land, being it was so minimal."

"Right. Of course. If it's not an obvious problem, just let it fester until it becomes one." Rus grunted, heading over to the stove to start the kettle more out of habit than actual desire. "Why are you here anyway? Come to lecture me again on how much easier I could make my life if I just joined one of the covens?"

Rus kept her back to Az, not wanting to see how her words cut into Az. There was a tiny, tired voice in the back of her head that told her she didn't want this to turn into a fight. That she shouldn't be so outright combative toward Az. But there was a much louder, furious one that said that Az had no right to waltz into her home and demand she turn herself and her girls over to the board's clearly limited mercy.

When she did finally turn, Az was watching her with those unfathomable, dark eyes, squinting a little like she could see right down to Rus's very soul. And fuck. She probably could. She'd always been able to. Why would now be any different?

"You look tired," Az said, not answering the question.

"No fucking kidding." Rus grabbed her mug from that morning and took what was left of her coffee in a quick gulp. It was cold and tasted mostly like sludge now, but she needed something to do with her hands. And she needed the boost. Nothing was working these days. It felt like everything she did to try to keep herself going was failing her. And she was failing her girls. *Goddess*, she was failing her girls.

"Where are the girls?"

"A-Ling is at school, and Huaner is upstairs napping. She should be waking up any minute now." Rus turned to slam a fresh cup into the Keurig and make herself another cup of watered-down coffee. "I just wanted to get that shade dealt with before she woke up."

"You left her in the house, alone?" Az frowned, her nose wrinkling.

"So you've come to tell me how to parent now too then?" Rus bit the words out, and they ground against her teeth like rubble.

Az pursed her lips then sucked them in so she could chew on them, silencing herself. And that was worse, because Rus knew what that meant. It meant whatever Az had been about to say was deemed too bitchy, and she needed to think some more about what to say instead.

But Rus didn't get a chance to hear whatever it was that Az had decided to say instead, because a moment later Aihuan joined them in the kitchen, rubbing at her big brown eyes and poking out her bottom lip. "Auntie Rus, is it snack time yet?"

"Yeah, little monster, it is. What do you want for your snack?" Rus scooped the girl up, perching her on her hip as she shuffled to take the kettle off the stove and pour some tea for Az in the hideously pastel mug from the cabinet.

"Cheese and crackers." Aihuan leaned heavily on Rus's shoulder, burying her face in the thick hood around her neck.

"Cheese and crackers, huh?" Rus hummed thoughtfully, moving to the fridge with the girl still on her hip as Az's tea steeped. "You sure you don't want . . . peas and carrots?"

Aihuan let out a raucous giggle right in Rus's ear that left it crackling for how loud it had been. "Nooooo. Not peas and carrots. Cheese and crackers."

"Peas and carrots. Okay." Rus nodded, but she grabbed the block of cheese from the drawer and made her way back to the counter after bumping the fridge closed with her hip.

"Noooo! Auntie Rus, I don't like peas *or* carrots."

"Really? You don't like peas *or* carrots? Weren't carrots your favorite vegetable last month?" She pulled the pack of crackers down from the cupboard.

"Well, now peppers are."

"I see. My mistake. Next time you change your favorite vegetable, please write me a four-page essay on why. That way I'll remember."

"An essay?"

"Yeah, you know, like A-Ling does for school? Remember when we helped her write that paper on how she'd lived in other countries?"

"Okay. Five pages," Aihuan said, holding up five fingers, looking very proud of herself.

"Perfect." Rus leaned in to brush a kiss to the little girl's forehead and frowned at the temperature of her usually cool skin. "You feel a little warm, little monster. Are you feeling all right?"

Aihuan shrugged. "Cheese and crackers time?"

"Cheese and crackers time." Rus nodded, but she couldn't shake the feeling that something was off. She lowered Aihuan to her feet carefully. "Go get up into your chair."

"Oh! It's you!" Aihuan stopped, her mouth agape as she looked up at Az.

Az was watching them, an expression on her face that Rus couldn't place. In all the years Rus had known her, she didn't think she'd ever seen Az look at anyone like that before. She wished suddenly she had time to parse out what it meant, or the balls to ask, but Aihuan was tugging at the end of her hoodie.

"Auntie Rus, it's her. Miss Azerrre."

"It's me," Az said with a little smile. "You can just call me Miss Az. If that's easier."

"Mm!" Aihuan nodded happily and made her way over to the table. She stopped by Az and held her hands up to the woman expectantly. "Help me into my chair."

"Huaner!" Rus huffed out, exasperated.

"Please," Aihuan added.

"Of course." Az bent to lift her up and twisted to sit Aihuan in her booster seat just as Rus was setting the plate of crackers and cheese in front of her.

"Thank you!"

"You're welcome. You're very polite, Huaner." Az smiled gently at her, and Rus had to turn to busy herself with finishing up Az's tea and her own coffee lest she do something stupid like ask Az to move in. Because if anything would be putting the broomstick before the wand, that would be it.

"Mm-hmm! Auntie Rus taught me all the manners."

"All of them, huh?" Az teased gently, her tone warm in a way that Did Things to Rus and made her nearly choke on her own spit.

"Yup!"

"Well, that's wonderful."

"It is," Aihuan mumbled around what Rus could only assume was a mouthful of crackers. Rus turned to see her stuff another whole cracker into her mouth and then open it as if to say something else. "I—"

"Not with your mouth full, Huaner," Rus chided gently, and Aihuan grumbled but focused on chewing instead of saying whatever embarrassing thing she'd been about to say to Az. Rus slid the mug of tea to Az and sat down beside her, ignoring the wide-eyed look that Az gave her. "You never told me why you came to visit."

"Oh. I brought this book of protective arrays and talismans that I found on my shelves. I thought you might find it useful." Az ducked to pull the book from her purse and slid it across to Rus.

Rus's fingers brushed Az's when she took the book, the touch sending a shock like static up her arm, raising every hair in its wake. "Umm, thanks."

Az nodded, a soft look of happiness crinkling the corners of her eyes. "You're most welcome. And if I come across anything else I think might be of assistance, I'll bring it over."

Rus felt something catch in her throat. She cleared it, trying to force it away, but it remained lodged there. Some wet and sticky emotion that she didn't have time for. Not when there were literal witch hunters on her ass trying to take her daughters. "Thank you."

"Of course," Az bowed her head, then took a deep breath like she wanted to say something else. But she stopped herself. "I should get back. I was only supposed to be gone from the store for an hour . . ."

It took a moment for the words to filter through the happy hum in Rus's mind at the reminder that Az had taken time out of her day to come and offer help where it hadn't been asked of her. And then she jerked. "Right. I'll see you out."

"No need. I know the way." Az stood, taking her mug with her to sip it before pouring it out in the sink. "Thank you for having tea with me, Huaner."

"See you later, Miss Az!" Aihuan waved cheerfully, bits of cracker stuck to her fingers and splattering the table in crumbs.

"You be good for your auntie, all right?"

"Mm-hmm!"

Az turned to head out of the kitchen and stopped just in the doorway to the main hall, her shoulders tightened a little. She let out a breath, letting them relax again before she turned to look over her shoulder at Rus. "Get some rest, Rus. You're no good to anyone if you don't."

Rus opened her mouth to argue, her cheeks flaming at how well Az knew her. But Az didn't wait for a rebuttal. She turned and left without another word. Rus had half a mind to chase after her and tell her that she wasn't the boss of her. That she didn't get to come into Rus's home, into her life, after a decade and try to tell her what to do.

Then Aihuan looked at her and said in the most pitiful, reedy voice Rus had ever heard, "Auntie Rus, I don't feel so good."

"What's wrong, little monster?" Rus whipped around, her hands moving to comfort the little girl. But it was too late. Aihuan had already started retching, everything from her stomach landing in a wet pile. Including crackers, and cheese, and the bread from her sandwich at lunch and . . . and . . . a greasy-looking ball of curly black hair about the size of Aihuan's fist. Aihuan's hair, Rus didn't have to look very hard to realize.

Aihuan whimpered softly, and Rus scooped her up, pulling the girl into her chest and away from the table so neither of them had to look at that . . . that . . . that *thing*. Her phone already in her hand, Rus tucked Aihuan closer.

"Fuck," she hissed under her breath, going to the pantry to start pulling out ingredients like a mad woman. "Fuck."

"Auntie Rus," Aihuan slurred. "Whassat?"

"Nothing you need to worry about, sweetie. Auntie Rus, Uncle Nando, and Aunt Cags are going to take care of it. We're going to make it all better. You just hang onto me, and don't let go. Don't let go for any reason. Do you understand?"

"Why?"

"Because I—" Rus bit down on the inside of her cheek hard enough to draw blood, letting the pain ground her. "Because I'm very upset right now, and I need you to help me feel better. Is that okay?"

"Okay." Aihuan snuggled in closer, burying her little face in Rus's shoulder, smearing what crumbs and grime had been left on her mouth into the fabric of Rus's sweater, but it didn't matter. None of it mattered. Because that had been a poppet. Or the beginnings of a poppet. And if they were building a poppet, then they'd gotten their hands on some of Aihuan's hair, or blood, or nail clippings, and it wouldn't be long before they used it to hurt or control her.

Cagney picked up on the third ring, and Rus thanked the Goddess that it was the druid's off-season because she didn't think Cagney would hear her phone over the sounds of whatever gardening tools she used. And Rus needed her now.

"What is it?" Cagney asked, already on high alert.

"Huaner just—" Rus swallowed hard, her throat thick with bile. "They've built a poppet. Not a very good one, not yet at least. But they're experimenting with it. Refining it. It won't be long before—"

"I'll be there as soon as I can. Tell the house to lock all the doors and windows, and keep her close to you."

"Right."

Cagney was silent on the other end of the line, but she didn't hang up as Rus pushed her phone onto her shoulder so she could grab an empty box they hadn't thrown out yet from the floor of the pantry and start to stack in it everything she thought they might need.

"There won't be much we can do, will there?" Rus asked when the silence got to be too loud.

"Maybe. Maybe not. But we aren't going down without a fight."

"Right."

"I've got some ideas, but I need to call around for some ingredients and books. I want you to call Fernando and stay on the line with him until either he or I get there. All right?"

"Yes. Yes. All right." Rus swallowed thickly against the tightness in her throat. "Thank you, Cagney."

Cagney grunted and hung up. Then Rus was dialing Fernando and telling him everything as she hauled the box to the kitchen and put the little cauldron on the stove top, Aihuan still tucked close to her chest, a comforting weight.

"I'm going to close up and pick up Meiling early from school," Fernando said, his words soft but crisp. Rus hardly heard them over the pounding in her own ears.

"No, she's already missed too many days as it is. And we can't keep closing up the shop at random. Just . . . just stick it out till the end of the day. I'll be okay."

Fernando let out a long sigh, and Rus could picture his shoulders sagging a little. But he would trust her judgment in this. He always had. "I'm going to leave the call connected and put in my earbud. If anything happens, I want you to shout at me and I will be there as quickly as I can."

"Okay." Rus huffed affectionately, already feeling better now that they had a plan in place.

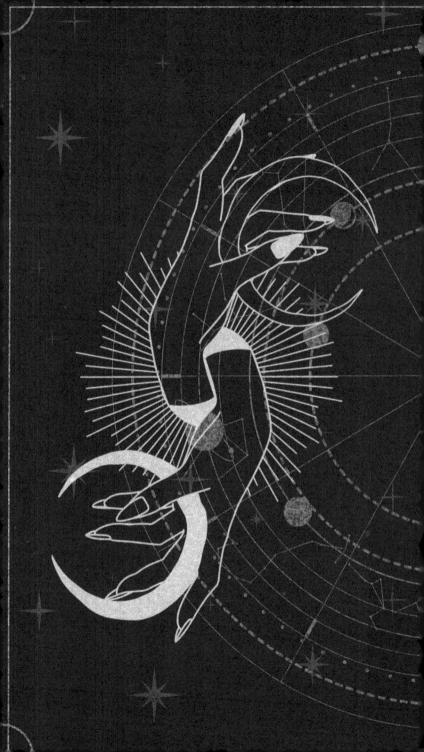

12

AZURE'S PHONE WAS RINGING. It had been ringing for three solid minutes so far, and she wasn't sure why the unknown number wouldn't give up. Didn't they know that Azure didn't answer numbers she didn't recognize? And even if they didn't, after the third call that should have been pretty obvious. Plus, she was *working*, for fuck's sake.

The shop was unusually busy for midday on a Thursday during the off-season, and she had yet to even be able to check the three voicemails the person had left. Probably a robocall considering that they hadn't given up. There were three people waiting in line for her to ring them out, and another five or so in the back of the shop browsing. Where they had all come from, she didn't know, but she sincerely wished they'd all fuck off. Especially as not a one of them had come in knowing what they were looking for. Not. A. One.

Who the fuck did that? Who just went into a shop and didn't know what they were looking for? Who wandered into a shop just to *browse*? The idea was completely foreign to Azure, who never went into a shop unless she knew they had exactly what she wanted. And she would know if they did because—abuse of power or not—she would use her sight to make sure before she so much as set foot in a place where a salesperson might hound her the entire time, making her feel guilty for not buying anything.

The bell over the door rang, the autumn wind carrying in the scent of rotted leaves and dirt, and Azure looked up to greet the person with her signature polite nod. But she stopped, mouth falling open just a little. Because there stood Cagney looking frazzled. Hair loose around her shoulders, curls sticking up everywhere, and a flush to her cheeks.

Azure's stomach dropped. Something had happened. Something with Rus and the girls. Something was wrong.

Cagney marched to the counter, ignoring the queue, and said, "I've been calling you for the last ten fucking minutes. Why don't you pick up your damn phone?"

"I don't answer numbers I don't recognize," Azure responded coolly, going back to ringing out the man who had a stack of about twenty books that looked like he'd just grabbed them at random off the shelves. No two authors the same. The genres all over the place. It was weird, but who was Azure to judge?

"Of course you don't." Cagney let out a loud breath, running her hand through her hair. It got stuck somewhere in the unkempt curls and she had to yank it out hard enough that it made her wince. "I'm calling in my favor. Now."

Azure stopped, a book on home gardening tight between her fingers, the magic of the debt she owed Cagney zinging under her skin like static. Favors were not taken lightly in the magic community. In fact, Azure made a habit of never owing them, but Cagney had offered a small insight into Rus's life when she'd been at a particularly low point a few years back, and Azure would be damned if she hadn't taken it.

"Okay," Azure said, her fingers speeding up the process of scanning the man's purchases and bagging them.

"You aren't going to ask what it is first?" Cagney cocked her head, her lips pursed as if she were trying to solve the riddle of some strange creature the likes of which she'd never seen before.

Azure resisted the urge to roll her eyes and tell Cagney that there wasn't anything she could do about it if she didn't like the favor. Cagney was calling it in, and maybe she could wriggle out of it, but she knew Cagney well enough to know that there was slim chance of that. So there really was no choice in the matter.

"It's to help Rus," she said instead. She'd felt that fear enough times to know it in Cagney's eyes.

"Yes." Cagney did roll her eyes, letting out a long puff of air.

"Then tell me what you want me to do, and I'll do it." Cagney probably didn't even need to call in her favor. But the idea of owing the druid for an indeterminate amount of time until Cagney decided to call it in didn't sit right with Azure. It had already been too long. She didn't know how it was for others who owed a debt, but hers had sat under her skin like an allergy for years. It would flair up every once in a while, when she remembered it was there, and make her break out in hives.

"I need you to go to the house and stay with her until I can get there. And I need the key to your back room."

"Right this minute?" Azure reached for the key under the counter and held it out to Cagney, who snatched it up without a second thought.

"Right this minute."

Azure nodded and turned to her customers. "All right, if you've already decided on your purchases, come here and grab a bag and get out. If you haven't, just leave. The shop is officially closed."

There was a chorus of disgruntled noises, voices, and questions, but Azure didn't hear them over her heart thumping in her ears as she shut down the computer, pulled out a bunch of bags, shoved them hastily into the people's hands who did have things they wanted, and pushed everyone out the door. It took her less than five minutes to shove everyone out, and then she was locking the door behind herself.

She sent a quick text to Cagney to tell her that the druid was free to take anything she needed from the shop, knowing full well it would make inventory hell the following month. Not that it mattered—that stunt she'd pulled with the customers would have fucked her inventory system up anyway. At least Cagney would remember what she'd taken.

Then she was off, her boots smacking a little too hard against the sidewalk as she made a run for 157 Mourning Moore. She didn't stop running until she'd made it to the little wrought iron gate in front of Rus's house. Her breath coming in hard pants, creating puffs of steam in the chill late-autumn air. Azure realized just then that she'd forgotten to grab her jacket from the back of the shop in her rush to get to Rus, but it didn't matter. None of it mattered.

Because the air in front of 157 Mourning Moore tasted of sulfur and was full of the unsettled murmurs of the dead. Azure saw movement out of the corner of her eye, but didn't dare to turn her head and meet the corpse's gaze lest it decide she was a threat.

One. Two. Three . . . Five. Five sentinels off to her right. And another six to her left, if the slowly moving shapes were any indication. There might have been more. Rus had already exceeded the amount that Azure knew she could control at once when they'd been twenty-one and stupid, just learning to push their limits. So who knew? Still, they didn't seem to be moving much. Just shifting from side to side. Likely keeping watch. Reporting back to their mistress if they noticed anything amiss.

Azure let out a low breath and said to the air in front of her, not taking her eyes off the house, "Tell your mistress Azure Elwood is here."

One of them let out a soft grunt, its tongue thick in its decaying head. And then she heard the whispers, the sound barely audible over the shuffle of those uncoordinated feet in the dry grass and leaves.

Azure tried not to hold her breath as she waited in the silence that followed, but it was hard. Rus could turn her away. Rus could decide she didn't want Azure's help. If she did, Azure *could* push her way onto the property if she wanted to. Eleven corpses was nothing, especially when it didn't seem like Rus was putting that much magic behind them. But that would mean going against Rus's wishes and—

"Az," Rus let out on a breath where she stood in the front door, Aihuan perched on her hip, a stain of some kind across her shoulder. Rus looked so tired. The dark circles that Azure had noticed from earlier in the day were more prominent, likely the drain of magic fueling the sentinels, and where her hoodie sleeve was rolled up, Azure could see dried blood from the magic needed to raise them. There had been eleven at the front of the property, but Azure wouldn't be surprised if there were some stationed all around. Especially as Rus was slumping against the door frame, almost relying on the house to hold her and Aihuan's weight.

"Can I come in?" The question so loaded, Azure could feel the heaviness of it as it left her tongue. Because it wasn't just her coming in for a cup of tea. No. Once she was inside, she'd be staying for as long as Rus would have her. She'd be there to weave her magic into the land and protect them all so long as she was allowed. Which, admittedly, might not be for very long, but Azure wouldn't leave until Rus told her she had to.

"Yeah . . ." Rus took a breath, the motion lifting her shoulders as she nodded. "Yeah, I think you'd better."

The gate opened with a screech loud enough to wake the dead, and Azure saw some of the corpses twitch out of the corner of her eye.

"Don't worry about them. They're just watching. For now." Rus turned to go back into the house, not even waiting for Azure to get up the path to the front door before she was heading back through the main hall to the kitchen.

"I'm assuming you have a veil over them." Azure kicked off her shoes at the door as it shut behind her without her touching it. The lock clicked into place loudly in the too-quiet foyer.

"The normies can't see them, if that's what you're worried about." *Don't need the board on my ass for anything else* went unsaid, but Azure heard it anyway. Not that the board should really fault Rus for protecting her home and her family when they had refused to help her, but Azure knew that wouldn't matter to them. What would matter to them was that Rus had raised eleven fucking corpses to keep watch on the property. Even if it was for protection, necromancy was still necromancy in their book.

"What happened?" Azure stepped into the kitchen, and her nose was immediately assaulted with the ozone smell of some potion or other brewing in the cauldron on the stove. No. Not one cauldron. Two, and Rus had also pulled out two soup pots to use as well, all four burners on the little gas stove full up.

"That," Rus said pointing to the table over her shoulder with the wooden spoon in her free hand, "happened."

Azure turned to look at the table and blanched at the wad of hair among the sick still there.

"Who's there with you?" a quiet, tinny voice asked from the phone on the counter.

"It's Az. I'm okay for a bit, Nando. You can go and focus on dealing with the little shits at A-Ling's school." Rus blew a piece of hair out of her face, her eyes focused on the bubbling concoctions.

"All right. I'll see you soon."

Rus grunted her response, not willing to take her attention from whatever she was making.

"Bye bye, Uncle Nando," Aihuan mumbled, her face smashed against Rus's shoulder.

"Bye bye, Huaner." And then the phone beeped, and the line went dead.

"Do you want me to clean it up?" Azure stepped closer to the table to get a better look. The hair was curly and dark brown in the way that Aihuan's was, and looked like it was coated in something other than stomach acid. Something greasy and dark like an oil slick. But not oil.

"No. I need to examine it once I'm done with these."

"What about the . . . rest?" Azure swallowed around the feeling of a gag forming in her throat as she looked at the half-digested crackers and cheese, and other things she didn't recognize.

"I don't know what's a part of the poppet, and what isn't. So we'll leave it for now." Rus shrugged, bouncing the little girl on her shoulder and making Aihuan grumble. "Sorry, little monster. I think I can put you down now, so long as you stay in the kitchen with me and Miss Az. What do you think?"

"Noooooo," Aihuan whined.

"No? Why not?"

Azure let the quiet bickering of mother and daughter become background noise as she dug around in the cabinets until she found something she could put the mess in that wasn't the table. It was a glass container, and she returned to tilt her head at the mess. "Do you have any gloves?"

"Under the sink." Rus turned to look at her, her nose wrinkled. "You really don't have to do that. I'll deal with it when I get done these potions."

"It's going to dry if we don't seal it away in something soon. Then none of the wet ingredients they used will be viable." Azure squatted in front of the cabinet under the sink and pulled out a pair of long yellow dish gloves. "Besides, I'll need the table to draw out some talismans."

Rus huffed but didn't say anything else, so Azure set to work cleaning up. Once the table was cleared and the container was sealed, she turned back to watch where Aihuan was still hanging off Rus's hip. Rus was starting to sag on that side, her weight resting heavily against the counter as she monitored the potions.

"Huaner," Azure said gently, calling the little girl's attention. "Why don't you show me where you keep your art supplies, and I'll teach you to make some warding talismans?"

Aihuan perked up, but she looked to Rus for her approval, brown eyes wide.

"Go on then. I've got another ten minutes on the stomach potion, and Miss Az is genius with talisman work. She'd be the best one to learn from." Rus brushed a kiss to the little girl's chubby cheek before letting her down to her feet.

"I wouldn't say *genius*." Azure rubbed her palms against her long skirt, hoping the embarrassment didn't show on her cheeks.

"Good thing I'm the one who said it."

"Talismans?" Aihuan held her hand out to Azure without hesitation now that she'd gotten her mother's approval, and Azure took it, letting the little girl lead her into the playroom on the back corner of the house. A quick glance out the window revealed that some kind of veil had been put over the windows as well, to keep the shambling corpses from view of the little girl.

"Yes, talismans. You can do a great many things with just a little bit of magic, paper, and some ink."

"Can we protect Auntie Rus with it?" Aihuan whispered in that way all children did, like she could keep the sound from echoing back into the kitchen, but it was still too loud and Rus probably heard her anyway.

"Huaner." Azure squatted in front of her, putting her hands on the little girl's narrow shoulders. "I'm here to help. You don't need to worry about your Auntie Rus because she has me and your Uncle Nando and your Aunt Cagney. We're not going to let anything happen to her, or you, or your sister. Do you understand me?"

"You promise?" Aihuan's lip wobbled a little, her eyes gone glassy with tears.

"I promise."

Aihuan looked at her for a moment longer, those big brown eyes searching Azure's face as if looking for the hint of a lie. And she probably would have found one if there was anything to find; children were extraordinarily perceptive that way. Especially the ones who had gone through as much as Aihuan had. Then she said, "Okay," with a little nod, and turned back to digging through the

messily organized cabinet where Rus had stored all her
craft supplies. "What do we need?"

"Paper," Azure said, and waited until Aihuan dropped a
thick stack of construction paper into her hands. She hadn't
used construction paper for talisman writing since she'd
been Aihuan's age and still practicing them herself. But it
wouldn't make much difference, not once Azure had put
her magic behind it. "Brushes. The nice raindrop-shaped
ones." Aihuan held up a couple of brushes, and Azure
smiled gently with a nod. "Yes, those. And whatever color
paint you want to use."

"Green?"

"Yes, I think green will work quite nicely." Azure took
the bottle of paint, along with a couple of palettes, and led
the little girl who was carrying the brushes back into the
kitchen.

An hour later found a table full of Aihuan's tries
at talismans, a napping four-year-old, and six bottled
potions. Aihuan was in Rus's arms again, snoring softly on
her shoulder as Rus followed Azure around, the little tape
dispenser in her free hand.

"You're good with her," Rus said from nothing, her
voice soft with awe.

"She's easy to be good with." Azure shrugged. It was
true. Aunt Carmine had told her to come to 157 Mourning
Moore and see if she could find a place for herself, and she
had. It wasn't the place she'd wanted when she heard Rus
was back in Moondale, but it was more than she could have
hoped for standing on the slick curb of the bus station
watching Rus ride away a decade ago.

Rus cleared her throat, her eyes looking away from Azure's pointed gaze. "You should head home. Cagney will be here soon. I think I've got it from here."

"Do you want me to go?"

Rus's head jerked back up, meeting Azure's dark eyes with a wide, surprised gray gaze. "What?"

"I said, do you want me to go? If you want me to leave, I will. But don't tell me to leave because you think that's what I want to hear." Azure shrugged and went back to hanging the red construction paper from the big bay window in the living room at the front. It hurt her eyes to look at for too long, what with the bright green paint Aihuan had chosen to make them. But that was all right.

Rus didn't say anything, and really, that was answer enough for Azure.

"You should go rest. I'll finish hanging the rest of these."

"Someone has to keep the corpses going." Rus shifted Aihuan so her weight rested on her other hip.

"I didn't tell you to sleep."

"Oh." Rus puffed out her cheeks and nodded. "Okay." Then she turned and went to the couch to stretch out across it with Aihuan still bundled against her chest. Azure felt her heart clench, watching the two of them in the reflection of the window.

No. There's work to be done. No time for that, she told herself, and she set back to plastering every window and door in one of the talismans.

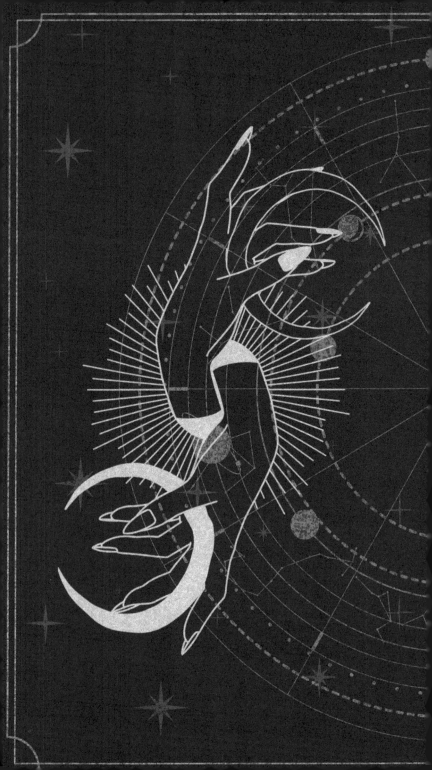

THE FOLLOWING morning dawned too bright, and too early, in Rus's book. She managed to doze at some point — not sleep, not really, but doze. Let her mind wander, and her body rest, while her magic did its thing and kept the corpses going.

She shuffled to the bathroom feeling not much different from the shambling dead outside the windows of her home. They weren't a permanent solution. She'd have to sleep eventually. No matter how many energy potions she managed to down. All the magic in the world couldn't make a mind immune to the need to shut down every once in a while. But that was future Rus's problem. For now, she could hear the house waking up beneath her feet.

The soft grumbles of Meiling as she went about getting dressed. The delighted chatter of Aihuan as she brushed her teeth. A quick glance in the mirror told Rus that there was nothing she could do for the bags under her eyes, so she just splashed some water on her face and headed down the back stairs to the kitchen to get started on breakfast.

Blessedly, the house had already set out a fresh mug for her coffee.

"Thank you," Rus mumbled, grabbing a Keurig cup and smacking it into the machine before moving to pull out the boxes of cereal. She should make a real breakfast, featuring protein, to give the girls a good start, but she didn't have the energy for it. She half wondered if she'd ever have the energy for it again. Probably not, with the way things were going.

Her coffee was just spluttering into the mug when Aihuan came screaming down the steps, her slippered feet skidding across the hardwood. "Auntie Rus! Auntie Rus! Auntie Rus!"

"What? What? What?" Rus asked, reaching down to grab her up and spin her around the kitchen for a moment, breathless with the joy on the little girl's face.

"Good morning." Aihuan giggled and then kissed Rus's nose before hugging her neck tightly.

"Good morning, little monster. Did you sleep well?" She settled Aihuan into her booster seat before setting a bowl, a spoon, and the box of cereal in front of her. She'd likely make a mess of the table, but that was fine. Messes could be cleaned up. And they all needed a little extra joy that morning.

"Mm-hmm. Noooooo nightmares."

"Well, I'm glad of that." Rus chuckled softly and spun to grab her mug, gulping down the too-hot coffee.

"Auntie Rus. I'm missing something," Aihuan grumbled, and when Rus turned back to her the little girl had crossed her arms over her chest, glaring down at the bowl in front of her where she'd poured a ridiculous amount of cereal. Too much. Rus would be throwing a good quarter of it into the bin.

Rus frowned in confusion for a moment, looking at the

bowl of cereal, the little cup of juice, the spoon, the . . . Oh. Right. She snorted, rolling her eyes, and went to grab another little bowl for Aihuan to separate the marshmallows out into. "Of course, little monster. How could I forget."

By the time Az woke up and came into the kitchen, running her fingers through her hair to try to untangle it from where it had gotten horribly mussed from sleeping on the couch, Fernando and Meiling had joined the ruckus, their soft chatter making the kitchen feel less lonely and fuller than Rus knew what to do with.

"Well, look who decided to join us," Rus teased, moving to press a cup of coffee into Az's sleep-warm fingers.

"Can I do anything to help?" Az asked, her eyes still a little blurry as they swept the kitchen. She'd been up after Rus had gone to bed the night before, which was unusual for her, being an early riser. Rus half expected to wake up and find her gone, already off for her morning run before work. It had made something warm, and a little confused, curl up in Rus's chest to see Az's dark purple head peeking out over the side of the couch when she shuffled past the living room.

"Sure." Rus smiled, the expression feeling real for the first time in what felt like weeks. "Do you have a spell to pull all of the marshmallows out of Huaner's cereal and put them in a separate bowl?"

Az blinked at her for a long moment, her wide brown eyes looking somehow even bigger with the soft morning light glinting off them. Goddess, she was beautiful. "No, I don't . . . I don't believe that I do."

The laugh crawled up Rus's throat completely unbidden, leaving her mouth first as a snort more akin to pig than woman, and then as a full belly chuckle. Fuck. She really was tired. And maybe losing her mind a little bit. That really wasn't good. When her laugh finally abated, Az was staring at her, her full lips parted to let out a startled breath, the crinkling around her eyes telling Rus that maybe she'd been about to laugh too.

"No. It's fine. Come have breakfast," Rus said, hoping to cover the embarrassment compacting her spine. From the knowing look Fernando shot her, she didn't quite manage it. He raised one dark brow and she narrowed her eyes on him, daring him to say anything.

With a shrug, he rose from the table, taking his glass to the sink and pouring it out. "I'm going to head to the shop. Do you want me to take Meiling to school?"

Not really, was the answer. Rus didn't want either of her girls where she couldn't see them after what had happened the day before. She wanted them within arm's reach so she could spirit them away when things started to look well and truly bad. The whispering started at the back of her mind, soft and incessant, begging, pleading with her to let them free. To bring them back to the world of the living and let them slake their blood lust on the people who threatened her and hers.

"Rus," Az said, her voice too close and too loud, and Rus had to take a step back when she realized that Az was suddenly right in front of her, her brown hands tight on Rus's wrists, the sickly green magic wrapping around both of them in something more akin to a threat than a greeting.

Rus shook herself. "Yeah, take her in to school." Meiling would be safer there. She pulled her wrists from Az's warm, dry grip, and poured herself another cup of coffee. She was slipping. Goddess above and below. She was slipping.

There was silence behind her, and in the reflection on the kitchen window she thought she saw Fernando and Az share worried glances, but that might have been a trick of the light.

"You should head out too, Az. I know you need to get

the shop ready for the day." She'd already wasted enough of Az's time with this mess. She wouldn't waste anymore.

"Indie doesn't have classes today, so he's agreed to open the store." Az settled into the chair Fernando had just vacated, making herself quite at home there. It left something aching in Rus that she didn't have time to think about. She shook herself again.

A long-fingered, slightly damp hand pressed into where Rus hadn't realized she was clutching at the counter. She looked down to see Fernando's darker fingers wrapped around her own. "Cagney will be here soon. She's finally gotten everything she needs."

"How long?"

"A couple of hours."

Right. So if there was ever a time to do something intolerably stupid, it's now. Rus nodded and watched as Fernando and Meiling gathered their things before leaving with soft goodbyes, and even softer hugs. All the while, Aihuan continued separating her cereal, every once in a while stuffing a handful of marshmallows into her mouth, and Az watched her over the rim of that frankly ridiculous pastel mug.

The door creaked shut behind them, and Rus turned to Az with a raised brow. "Can you watch Huaner for a hot minute? I'm going to go up to my room and grab some things."

Az's eyes narrowed, a look of suspicion pursing her lips, but instead of calling Rus on the obvious bullshit, she just said, "All right."

Rus took what was left of her lukewarm coffee and headed up the back steps, not waiting for Az to realize what a mistake it might be to leave her alone at that particular moment. Once she was in her bedroom, she shut the attic behind her and settled the mug on the desk in the window.

Then she set to work gathering everything she'd need for the ritual to fuel the corpses while she slept.

A metal talisman was pulled from a drawer, and sat on the floor, an athame, a jar of dirt, some herbs, and a small chalice joined it, Rus's fingers drummed hard against the wood as she glanced out the window at the cemetery again. There wasn't any time to waste. If Cagney caught her at this shit, she'd flip. So Rus nodded, knelt in the center of the rug, and got to work.

IT TOOK APPROXIMATELY TEN MINUTES FOR AZURE TO realize that the buzzing she was feeling under her skin was from magic and not from her own anxiety at being left alone with a three-year-old.

"Shit," she hissed to herself when the lights blinked.

"Miss Az, what's that?" Aihuan asked, her fingers tight around what was left of the marshmallows from her breakfast. "What's going on?"

"Nothing, Huaner. Nothing. Can you do me a favor?" Azure moved quickly, scooping the little girl up into her arms and already halfway up the stairs before she could even respond.

"Yeah? I'm sooooo good at favors."

"Of course you are. You're the best." Azure smiled softly, pressing her face into Aihuan's curly hair and taking a steadying breath. "I'm going to put you in your room, and I need you to stay there for me."

"Why?"

"I need to go up and check on your auntie for a moment. It shouldn't take more than a few minutes. Do you think you can do that for me?" Her hands were shaking, and she didn't know when that had started. Likely before she'd even realized what the subtle ringing in her ears meant. Fuck. Fuck. Fuck. She might be too late already.

"Mm-hmm. Can do!"

Azure sat her on her feet and Aihuan disappeared into the nursery, her little slippers scuffing against the floor. A silent prayer to the Goddess slipped through Azure's mind, and then she was climbing the steps up to the attic and turning the knob to press inside.

Rus was on her knees on the floor, fingers fiddling with the sharpened end of her athame, blood coating the floor in front of her. But it wasn't that that disturbed Azure—that she'd seen a thousand times growing up with the medium. No. It was the black-and-green fog that was so thick that Azure couldn't see the floor for it. It was the voices that weren't whispering anymore, but near screaming. It was the way that something dark and twisted looked like it had latched onto Rus and wasn't going to let go.

Azure lost track of things after that. One moment she was standing at the door, staring at her worst nightmare, and the next she had Rus in her arms and was using every ounce of magic in her body to dispel whatever dark thing Rus had called upon to protect them.

"Stop, Rus. Just stop. This isn't the way," she gasped against Rus's neck when the darkness lingered, threatening to sink its teeth into her too, sharp enough to draw blood. "Stop! Just stop!"

Rus shrugged her off, getting enough space between them somehow to give her a shove that sent Azure reeling, her shoulder hitting the floorboards hard enough to jolt her back. But she was up again, on her knees, pressing forward as she clutched at her hopelessly wrinkled skirt. "Let me help you."

"No," Rus growled, the thing in the room with them

looming and whispering in a language Azure was almost glad she didn't understand.

"Why won't you let me help you?" Words choked in her throat, threatening to turn into a sob. She wouldn't cry. She couldn't, not right now. Not when Rus needed her more than ever.

"Because I don't need your help!" The anger was raw and real, but it sounded like Rus was losing the thread of it, her voice going high and breathy like she was beginning to hyperventilate, to panic. "I don't . . . I don't need anyone's help!"

"You could die," Azure said, quietly furious. Like the calm before a storm. The quiet before the thunder. "You can't keep doing reckless magic like this. Spreading yourself so thin you're near transparent. You can't. You can't!"

"Why not?" Rus met her watery gaze with a razor-sharp smile, lips pulled back from her teeth like a knife wound. "I'm only hurting myself."

For a moment, Azure thought to say something horribly, dangerously, undeniably true. Something that would expose all her own ragged edges and the places where Rus had left her aching all those years ago. But she forced it back, swallowing it down like glass, and said, "What about your girls? What happens to them without you?"

Rus's eyes widened, her mouth falling open to draw in a short, wet gasp, and then she let the magic go. Released the thing that she was trying to tie to herself and this place to protect them. And crumpled to the floor in a heap of beautifully unconscious, foolish woman.

Azure had lifted her to the bed and was tucking her in when Cagney knocked lightly on the door.

"Come in," Azure said, her voice a soft hush.

Cagney had Aihuan on her hip and was leaning against the door frame. "I see I missed all the drama."

Azure shrugged, not really wanting to talk about it, and gathered up the things Rus had been using for her spell. A quick thought caught the herbs on fire, hoping that at least that would deter Rus from trying again in a hurry. Then she was crossing to the door and brushing past Cagney and Aihuan.

"Thank you," Cagney said, catching her elbow to stop her in the doorway. "Thank you for stopping her when I wasn't here to do it myself."

Azure nodded, Cagney released her, and they both made their way back down to the kitchen.

"Show me what you've been working on to protect the house," Azure ordered. Without Rus's magic to fuel the corpses, all they had was the wards, and those hunting Rus and the girls had already proven they could get past them. They needed something else. Something stronger.

"You're going to love this." Cagney grinned, setting Aihuan on her feet and moving to grab a cloth grocery bag from the front door that was bursting at the seams before dumping it on the kitchen table. "We're going to turn the whole damn place into a maze array."

"What?" Azure blinked down at the contents from the bag. Most of it looked like it had been taken from Elwood & Co.'s storeroom, but there were other things—flint, a mason jar of water, another of mud, a collection of maple and sycamore seeds—that must have come from Cagney's personal stores. "Don't we need four elementals for that?"

"No. Just four people wielding the elements. You and I have earth and water covered. That just leaves fire and wind."

"Rus isn't up to this kind of magic. Not right now. And even if she were, we still need one more person whose magic is tied to the land. It won't work without Moondale magic to ground it." Azure shook her head. It was a solid idea, but they didn't have the power they needed to do it.

"Good thing I called Phyre and Nesta then, isn't it?" Cagney's grin widened to something near feral, and Azure had to hold back a groan. Just what she wanted: a cupid and a forge witch up in her space while she tried to keep Rus from doing something moronic.

"How long before they get here?"

"Couple hours. Plenty of time for you to have some tea, or meditate, or go for a run, or whatever it is you need to do to stay calm."

"Delightful." Tea. She was going to need a fuck-ton of tea.

14

HER FEET WERE COLD. There was a pounding headache forming behind her eyes from Nesta's voice. And Azure hated everything about the last thirty minutes of her life.

"It won't keep something from entering," she'd tried to argue about ten minutes before Nesta and Phyre showed up.

"Maybe not, but it'll damn sure keep them from leaving with our girl," Cagney had said with a wink, downing the last of a bottle of seltzer water she'd found in the back of Rus's fridge.

And that had been the end of that, so to speak. Discussion closed. Or at least, Cagney considered the discussion closed; Azure still had her reservations. Either way, she found herself standing in the middle of Rus's backyard ten minutes later, barefoot and holding a jar of murky water that Cagney had fished out of the bay presumably sometime in the last decade. Aihuan was sitting on the bottom porch step, Darcy perched two stairs above so he could be near her head. He was chattering softly to her, and Azure couldn't quite make out what he was saying, but whatever it was it seemed to settle Aihuan's nerves. Good. A crying toddler would only make this whole thing harder.

"All right, everyone ready?" Cagney asked, although it sounded rhetorical, like she was going to start the ritual whether they were or not. Everyone nodded anyway, and Aihuan gave an encouraging little cheer from where she sat that drew smiles to all their faces. It was nice, Azure thought, to remember what they were doing this for. To remember who was being affected by all of this.

Cagney's chanting started as a low, constant hum, her hands cupping the open jar full of mud tight enough that her tan knuckles turned white with it. When she struck the right chord with her voice, the mud lifted from the jar, swirling and slapping against itself in the open air between them like a child throwing mud pies on a bank. Next was Phyre, the flames of a forge licking over her outspread fingers as her voice joined Cagney's, then they too rose into the air, swirling over the mud but not drying it out, not baking it as it normally might.

Nesta met Azure's eyes from across the circle, their head dipping into a little nod to signal it was time to start, and they both began chanting at the same time. The low hum of words grew and swelled as the murky water and seeds joined the slowly rotating ball of elements in the middle of their circle.

There was a moment when Azure thought that the power of the grave dirt that surrounded the property on two sides would be too much for the elements they were trying to wield. When she thought that their distance from the docks and the lack of warmth would smother the spell. But then the fog came, rising from the ground as if the land itself had breathed it out.

They continued chanting until the fog had settled at waist height, and then their voices grew quieter and quieter until there was only silence, the fog, and the swirling mass of elements hovering in the middle of their circle.

"Do you think it'll be enough?" Phyre asked, her voice all soft hope.

"I don't know what else to do, honestly," Cagney replied, her shoulders hunching in something that looked like defeat. Azure wanted to go to her, to wrap her arms around her and tell her that they'd done the best they could. But she and Cagney had never been friends like that, and they weren't about to start now. "You two will have to stick around. If you leave the property, it'll all fall apart."

"Yes! Sleepover!" Nesta cheered, lifting their fist into the air in triumph.

Azure groaned. "I'll go and ask the house for some blow-up mattresses. There's only the one couch." When she made her way back to the stairs, Aihuan was looking at them with wide eyes, her mouth slightly agape. "What's wrong, Huaner?"

"That was big magic," she whispered in wonder, and Azure felt a smile twitch at her lips. Maybe she could put up with Phyre and Nesta sticking around for a couple of days if it meant that Aihuan kept that amazed look on her face.

"Sure was. Come on, let's head in and check on your auntie."

"Mm." Aihuan nodded, holding her hands up so Azure could bend down and scoop her up into her arms.

Rus was groggy when she woke up. A hazy mess of thoughts and feelings and a pounding ache in her ears and temples. Her tongue stuck to the roof of her dry mouth, and it tasted like she'd eaten nothing but yesterday's garbage. Honestly, she'd had hangovers that didn't feel this fucking bad. She groaned, rolled over to grab her phone off the nightstand, and checked the time.

5:43 p.m.

Well, that would explain all the noise downstairs. But what it didn't explain was what had happened between ten that morning and now. Scrubbing at her crusty eyes, Rus rolled out of the bed and headed for the bathroom. She'd feel better once she washed her face, she was sure of that much at least. It might not fill in the gap, but—

Oh. Oh fuck.

The gray eyes of her reflection widened in the mirror as it all came rushing back. The spell. The tying of a bit of herself to the land itself. Arguably not her best choice, it would mean she'd be locked into Moondale for the foreseeable future, and the board could very well arrest her for doing it without their approval, but if that protected her girls then Rus didn't care that she'd be stuck in this place. And then, lastly, but most terrifying, Az's face, all broken and scared and pale. Fuck. No wonder she felt hungover.

Rus groaned, leaning heavily against the little sink she'd claimed as her own until the ceramic dug into her waist and her forehead left a greasy, fogged up spot on the mirror. The question now was, had it worked? Had the land of 157 Mourning Moore accepted her sacrifice in exchange for protection?

Sucking in a breath—in, in, in—Rus spread her fingers wide across the side of the sink and let her magic roll from her fingertips out into the air around them. The land didn't resist, but it likewise didn't draw her in like it should have, chaining her to it.

Damn it. Az must have interrupted too early. Well. No matter. I'll just have to try again when —

Something clattered to the floor downstairs, jerking Rus's attention from the feeling of the land beneath them. When in Hecate's name had her house gotten so fucking noisy? The girls were never that loud, especially not when they thought she was resting. Rus huffed, grabbing a clean hoodie from the basket of laundry she still hadn't managed to put away and tugged it over her head.

"You know you could help by putting that away," she muttered to the house, her slippers making loud clomping noises on the way down the back steps into the kitchen.

The house didn't say anything. It sat silent and smug at forcing her to do menial chores like laundry when there were about fifty other things to worry about at any given moment. *Sassy streak* her ass—the house on 157 Mourning Moore was a complete and total asshole.

"What in the name of the Goddess are you little miscreants doing down—" She stopped, her feet landing at the bottom of the steps, eyes wide as she took in the chaos that was her kitchen.

"Good morning, sunshine!" Nesta piped up from where they were at the table, rolling dumplings with Meiling.

Phyre was at the stove, her hair streaked with gray and pulled up into a high ponytail, smile lines pinching at the corners of her eyes and a careless grin thrown over her shoulder, just like old times. "Sorry for making a mess of your kitchen, but we have quite the horde to make dinner for."

"What?" Rus squeaked.

"Auntie Rus! We're having a sleep over!" Aihuan squealed, barreling into her legs and nearly knocking her back into the steps. "Nesta and Phyre and Miss Az and Aunt Cagney and Uncle Nando and A-Ling and Huaner and you! All of us!"

"All of us, huh?" Rus asked, her voice an octave too high. She cleared her throat.

"Mm-hmm. All of us." Aihuan nodded firmly, the motion almost rocking her out of Rus's arms, and then she was squeezing Rus's neck too tight, and pressing her face in against her jaw. "And they did big magic," she whispered like it was a secret.

"Big magic?"

"Come help me set the table, and I'll explain." Rus looked up to find Cagney standing at the back door. Phyre handed Cagney a thick stack of plates and forced silverware into Rus's hands after she'd set Aihuan back on her feet.

The back door creaked closed behind them, hushing the voices that were loud inside the kitchen, and providing some release for Rus's throbbing head. Cagney moved around the table, setting the plates in their places, and Rus followed behind with chopsticks and spoons.

"We did a maze array," Cagney said at length. "That's why everyone's here. It was the only way I could think to keep anyone from leaving with Aihuan without us knowing."

Rus's shoulders sunk a little. "How long do you think that will last?"

"Hopefully long enough for us to find a more permanent solution. I also contacted Greer. I thought—"

"You what?!"

Cagney turned from where she'd just put the last plate down, her hands on her hips and an incredulous look on her face. "I get that you two aren't friends, Rus. Believe me, I do. But he is the sheriff, and he needs to know if a child goes missing. Don't look at me like that. I thought it'd be better to give him a heads up."

Rus slumped into one of the chairs, her neck stretching over the back so she could stare up at the unmoving ceiling fan. "What did he say?"

"He was surprisingly understanding." Cagney shrugged. "Said if we had any other trouble, I should call him and let him know. I don't think—" She stopped, pressing her lips together and taking a breath. "I don't think he gives one flying fuck what the elders on the board are saying. It's his job to look after Moondale's citizens, and he will. He's not a bad guy, Rus."

Dragging a hand down her face, she let out a loud breath. "Fine. Fine."

"He said he'd send some patrol cars by tonight, just to keep an eye on the place."

"Fucking brilliant." Goddess above, she needed a drink. Preferably a hard one, but she'd settle for a glass of wine. "And Az?"

"What about Az?" Cagney tapped her fingers impatiently against one of the speckled ceramic plates, her nail making a soft clicking sound. When Rus didn't do more than flap her wrist in Cagney's direction, she huffed an annoyed tsk. "I told you before, Greer and Az don't have anything to do with each other. They're not even really friends. So please, for the love of the Goddess, get your head out of your ass." She didn't wait for any further reply, and a moment later the sounds in the kitchen were louder than ever, then the door shut and she was in silence again.

"Right. Good talk," Rus mumbled, scrubbing at her face again. The porch light turned on, burning at her sensitive eyes, and Rus hissed, covering them with her hand. "Oh, don't you start on me too," she grunted to the house and rolled herself to her feet before heading inside again.

WHEN ALL WAS SAID AND DONE, IT WAS ACTUALLY NICE having Phyre and Nesta in the house. The extra voices filled in the spaces and the cracks that Rus hadn't even known were there.

And hours later, after everyone else had gone to sort out their sleeping arrangements and the girls were put to bed, Rus settled on the back porch with a glass of wine warming her belly and the sounds of crickets chirping in the distance. Her eyes only just barely focused on the overgrown graves and drying grass as her mind wandered.

The door into the kitchen behind her opened, letting a strip of bright light out into the night, and then closed again as someone stepped out.

"If you're coming to tell me to go to bed, Nando, it's not fucking happening. I had a nap today, and I'm wired." She took another sip from her wine glass. The nap wasn't what was making her wired and jittery, for all that she would pretend it was—it was the shift in the air. The electricity of a coming storm. It wouldn't be long now before whoever it was made their move.

"It's not Fernando," Az said, stepping around her to pull out the chair on her left. "I want to talk about that spell you were performing earlier."

"What about it?" Rus tipped her head back, finishing off what was left in her glass before turning her eyes back onto the yard. She didn't think she wanted to be looking at Az when they had this conversation. Not after how horrified Az had looked when she'd found her.

"Whatever you were—" Az drew in a breath, the sound too loud in the quiet of the night, and then let it out again. "You cannot call on malignant spirits to help with this. I know it's something you did in the past, but you can't take those kinds of chances now. You know what they'll do if you let them in. You know what kind of control they could have over a medium once they're invited. Especially a medium with your threshold for—"

"Hold on a minute." Rus sat forward, bracing herself on her knees so she could peer up at Az through the darkness. "You think I was making deals with dark spirits?"

"I saw—"

"Not that it's any of your business, but that is one hundred percent not what you saw. What you saw was me —" The swirling ball of elements out on the lawn flared to life with a light brighter than the sun, near blinding them both. "What the fuck?"

Rus's hand flew up to shield her eyes, and then she heard the screaming and she was out of her chair so fast she sent it toppling to the floor. Her boots thumped hard against the back stairs, Az hot on her trail. She shoved open Aihuan's door, stumbling through just in time to see the long-eared little creature trying to drag Aihuan through the window, which was stubbornly remaining closed.

"Let her go!" Rus roared, lunging forward to scoop up the child and kick the creature in the face so hard it stumbled backward, smacking its head against the window frame with a crack before crumpling to the floor. Aihuan was still wailing into Rus's neck from where they'd both sunk to the floor when the others appeared in the doorway.

"What's going—" Phyre stopped, her pale eyes narrowing on the creature lying unconscious in the middle of the nursery. "Nesta, help me get it up. We'll go tie it to a chair downstairs. Maybe we can get it to answer some questions. Fernando, you and Meiling can come down to the living room to sleep while we work."

Nesta nodded, and they and Phyre both moved over to

the goblin, scooping it up between them and dragging it out into the hall. Rus could hear Meiling's and Fernando's slippers shuffling against the floor as they made their way downstairs.

"Are you all right?" Az asked, kneeling beside Rus and Aihuan, her hands half raised like she wanted to reach out but didn't know if she'd be welcome.

"Fucking *goblins*, Az?" Rus spat, holding Aihuan closer as her cries slowly petered off. "Who sends fucking *goblins* after a toddler?!"

"I don't know," Az admitted, sounding a little lost.

"Well, we're damn sure going to find out," Cagney said, rolling up the sleeves of her ridiculously comfy-looking dressing gown and marching toward the stairs. She called, "Come down once you've gotten Huaner settled," over her shoulder and then Rus was alone with Az and a sobbing Aihuan.

"It's all right, Huaner." Rus rocked them both a little, side to side, humming a soft lullaby that the girls' a-niang used to sing to them. Az picked up the tune after a couple of bars, and together they wove a soft, calming spell into the air until Aihuan had relaxed entirely against Rus's chest.

"Should we put her back to bed?" Az's voice was quiet, her hands still twitching a little where they clung to the sweatpants she'd borrowed from Rus to sleep in.

"No. I don't . . . I don't want her too far. We can put her on the couch while we deal with the goblin. I'm sure Phyre would be happy to sit with her."

Az nodded, pushing to her feet, then helped Rus to stand by way of a gentle grip on her elbows. She strode to the window while Rus waited by the door, checking that it was shut tight and latched before they followed the others downstairs.

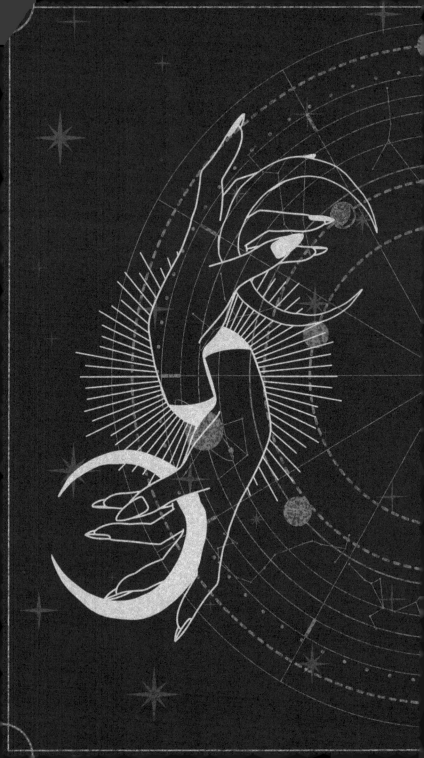

15

"I CALLED GREER. He said he'd be here in the next ten minutes," was what Cagney said by way of greeting when Rus and Az joined her in the kitchen to glare down at the struggling goblin after putting Aihuan in the living room with the others.

"Fucking brilliant," Rus muttered, bracing her hands on her hips and meeting the goblin's yellow eyes. She wondered, idly, how much fear of the Goddess she could put into the little creature before Greer showed up and demanded they treat them humanely in accordance with the magic statutes of the Americas 1637, or whatever bullshit law he'd cite as a means to get in her way. "Well, until then, you're going to tell me what I want to hear."

"Or what?" the goblin spat back in their high, reedy voice.

Rus knelt before the goblin, a slow, eerie smile pulling up her lips. "Or I will call on every poor, sad soul you've ever had a hand in taking their life. And I will lock you in my pantry with them until you're screaming so loudly, you'll wake our neighbors."

"You don't have any neighbors." They snorted, rolling their eyes in a way that Rus supposed was meant to make them look confident, but really just made them look foolish. "You're next to a cemetery."

"I know." Rus's smile spread wider, curling up her face like a living thing.

"You wouldn't. You *couldn't*." But their eyes were wild, jumping from Rus to Cagney and Az over her shoulder. Whatever they saw there must have been enough to make them realize that neither of her companions were going to stop her. And since the rest of their little group had moved into the living room to watch movies with Meiling and Aihuan to keep them distracted . . . Well, it wasn't like Nesta, Phyre, or Fernando would have stopped her either.

"I assure you, I could." With the silent rage at the hunters sending a goblin into her home to steal her daughter still crawling under Rus's skin, it was easy to call the dead to her. The whispering started up before the goblin could even take a breath for their next foolish refusal, putrid green magic crawling against their gray skin, wrapping, and undulating, and forcing its way into them. All the while the whispering grew faster, more insistent, as Rus searched for the spirits that had attached themselves to them.

It would be a simple task. Pluck the loudest voices and set them loose. She'd done it enough times over the years to have developed quite the knack for it. But just as she was about to pull the wailing cry of a pixie from the lot, the wards screeched loud in her ears, letting her know another magic user was on her property. Humanoid this time. Not some smaller, lighter magical being that could slip through the wards like the goblin had.

What is it? she asked the spirits she'd managed to pull back from their eternal resting place after dinner.

Coven of the Crimson Tide, they answered, voices a hiss in her ear. *Crimson Tide. Crimson Tide.*

"Fuck." Rus stood up, stretching out her back and letting the magic she'd been about to use to torture the goblin dissipate. "Greer's here," she answered Az and Cagney's questioning looks. "No doubt he'll want to do this by the book." She kicked the leg of the chair the goblin was tied to, making them grunt.

"I'll get the door," Cagney volunteered.

"Please do. And don't let him be too loud in the hall. I don't particularly want him waking the girls if the others have managed to get them to sleep."

Cagney grunted her agreement.

"And make him take off his fucking boots at the door. You know the rules."

"Yeah, yeah, yeah."

"Well?" Rus asked Az when she didn't move to follow behind Cagney, instead stepping forward so close that Rus could almost feel the heat of her against her side.

"Well what?" Rus saw Az tilt her head out of the corner of her eye. They were both looking at the goblin, but Rus got the strange feeling that Az's sole focus was on her, and little else. It sent a shiver of something warm and liquid down her spine, something like delight and arousal tied into one. But she ignored it in favor of the more pressing matters at hand.

"Aren't you going to go and greet your fiancé?"

"Evander isn't my fiancé," Az said, and she sounded undoubtedly grumpy about the insinuation. So much so that Rus couldn't help but turn to look at the frown that wrinkled her nose and scrunched up her lovely brown eyes.

"Boyfriend then," Rus pressed, feeling vicious and almost raw with something that might have been hope.

Az huffed. "He's not my—"

"I hope you haven't done anything to them yet," Greer cut in from where he had stomped right into the kitchen without so much as an invitation from its owner. Honestly, it was amazing she hadn't heard him coming with how loud he was. But then wrapping herself up in Az, and focusing on little else, had always been shamefully easy for Rus.

"Just scared them a little." Rus shrugged, turning away from Az to meet Greer's hard look with a wide smile. "We were swapping ghost stories. Weren't we, friend?"

"Right. Of course." Greer stomped to stand in front of the goblin, hardly even waiting for Rus and Az to move out of his way so he could loom over them. "I want you to know, I didn't come here in my squad car," he said in a tone that sounded hard and gravelly.

"Wha-what?" the goblin squeaked.

"I need you to know that. I also need you to note that I'm not in uniform, nor am I carrying any sort of Moondale sheriff equipment."

"Okay?"

Rus's eyes flicked to Cagney behind Greer's back, but Cagney was too busy watching him with wide green eyes, and a little bit of a blush staining her freckled cheeks. Rus jerked her gaze back to Greer, tilting her head in interest. She wasn't sure what he was doing, but she thought she just might approve.

"I need you to make a note of this," Greer continued, completely oblivious to the women around him, who were all watching him with varying degrees of intrigue, "because it means I didn't come here on official Moondale sheriff department business. It means my actions don't speak for the department. It means I came here as a free agent, and as a friend."

Rus mouthed the word "friend" in disbelief. Half of her

wanted to argue the term, and the other half wanted to thank Greer for what he was doing. He didn't have to, she recognized that. He could lose his job, his status among the board, his place in his family. And if he wasn't with Az, as Az had just said, she had to wonder *why* he was doing all of this. She'd have to ask him later. After they'd gotten what they wanted out of the goblin.

"Nod if you understand what this means," Greer pressed.

The goblin nodded, although they looked rather like they had swallowed their own tongue, their big yellow eyes practically bulging from their head, their gray face suddenly ashen.

"Good. Then I'm going to stand back and let Rus do her thing." He patted the goblin's knees and straightened up.

"You aren't going to—"

"Maybe I would have." Greer grinned down at them, his eyes dark with promise. "But fear is a much better motivator than pain. And no one does fear quite like a necromancer."

The goblin gulped audibly.

Greer took a step back, a dark little grin twisting up one corner of his mouth. "Right. They're all yours, Rus."

Rus laughed softly, the sound far less bright and kind than it normally was, and squatted in front of the goblin again, her magic already hissing against her skin. "As I was saying. I think I found a pixie who'd like to take a bite out of you. Her name was—"

"I'll tell you anything you want to know," the goblin blurted. "Just—just don't leave me alone with her, please. Please." They were begging Rus, but their eyes lingered on a shape that had begun to form in the roiling green smoke of Rus's magic on her forearm. The pixie's unsettled spirit.

It was a shame the goblin was ready to blab now—the pixie really needed to be put to rest. If not, she'd linger, stirring up trouble. And while the goblin may have deserved whatever befell them, the pixie didn't deserve to be stuck in limbo because of their actions. "Please. Please. I'll—I'll tell you everything about them."

A firm hand gripped Rus's shoulder, and she looked up to see Az standing beside her, grounding her back to the earth. Pulling Rus back from whatever edge she'd been teetering over. Because that was the thing about a medium: sometimes they lost themselves to the wants and needs of the spirits. Sometimes they could forget about the living altogether. Sometimes they needed grounding. Az had always been extremely good at that—bringing Rus back to herself, her own body, when it felt like the spirits might rip her away from it entirely.

"Please," the goblin was still begging, uncaring of the silent moment shared between Rus and Az. "I'll—I'll—I'll —" Their voice cut off with a choked sound, garbled and wet. Their yellow eyes going wide with fear.

"Shit," Rus hissed, flinging herself forward to try to get a good grip on the goblin's arms, their shoulders, their jaw so that she could see what was happening, but they had already started convulsing.

"Get their mouth open," Az commanded, her hands beside Rus's, trying to keep their shaking from knocking the chair over.

"I'm trying! I'm trying!"

Cagney and Greer were beside them a second later. A soft murmured chant coming from Cagney, something old and in Gaelic that Rus didn't understand. Greer had grabbed a wooden spoon from the counter, and as Rus and Az pried the goblin's mouth open, he tried slipping it between their teeth. But it was too late, Rus realized before the others did, much too late. Whatever was strangling them had already done the work long before they had even realized what was going on. For when the goblin stopped convulsing, although they still breathed, their eyes were vacant and empty.

"Fuck," Rus rasped, awed and horrified at what she'd just seen. "Fuck!" She kicked the leg of the chair, nearly sending it and the comatose goblin to the floor.

"Rus," Az said, her tone a warning.

"No, Az! No! That was our only lead and they just . . . they just put it into a fucking coma. From a distance! Through our fucking wards! I can't . . . I just . . . I can't right now." Rus tried to breathe deeply, but there was panic building in her ribs, threatening to choke the air from her lungs. The goblin must have had something on them that Phyre and Nesta had missed when tying them up. A talisman, or a cursed object. A fail safe.

"Can't you just . . ." Greer wiggled his fingers in the air and made a "woo woo" sound that she supposed he must mean to be an imitation of a ghost.

"Sure, if they'd actually fucking *killed* them, I could call upon their restless spirit and get some answers. But not like this." Rus raked her hands through her hair and scuffed her slippers on the way to the sink to clutch at the countertop, hoping it would help her keep her balance in a world that was tilting like a ship at sea.

"Maybe we can track the source of the spell that did this," Cagney said, her voice forced into hopefulness when there was none. They all knew there was none. The witch hunters would have covered their tracks. Maybe even made someone else cast the spell that had sent the goblin into their coma. The trail could lead them halfway across the fucking country for all Rus knew. No. It would do no good.

"We could solve that," Az suggested, and Rus jerked to

narrow her eyes on where Az was still looming over the creature, her fingers twitching a little at her sides.

"What?"

"Well, if they're dead, you can interrogate their spirit, right?"

"Theoretically. If the hunters haven't sucked it away somewhere and put it in a bottle." Rus turned to lean heavily against the counter, letting it hold her up.

"Someone could do that?" Cagney asked, her face twisting in disgust.

"Sure." Rus shrugged, scuffing her slipper against the hardwood floor. "You'd be amazed what a medium can do with a wayward spirit. You just need—"

"It doesn't matter what you need, we aren't killing them," Greer growled. "I draw the line at that."

"You draw the line at killing someone but not at torture?" Rus raised a brow, an incredulous snort leaving her lips.

"They can't defend themselves!"

"What's it matter now? They're a fucking vegetable! And they'll stay that way. Whatever the hunters did to them is permanent. The best thing we can do for them is to set their spirit—"

"I won't be an accessory to murder!" Greer shook a finger at her, stepping into her space.

"I thought you weren't here on official Moondale sheriff business? That's some official police jargon you're throwing around there, *Sheriff* Greer!" Rus sneered.

"Look here, you pompous, two-bit, no account—"

"Aunt Rus?" Meiling's voice cut through the shouts like a knife. It was wobbling, on the verge of tears. Everyone stopped what they'd been doing and turned to her. Meiling was in the doorway, her face gone pale, tears streaming down her cheeks. "Aunt Rus. She's gone."

"What?" Rus asked, her long gait eating up the floor between the counter and the door into the hall. "Who's gone?"

"Huaner. Huaner's gone." Meiling choked on the words, her breath hitching.

"What?" the other three adults said, but Rus didn't pay them any mind. Her heart was pounding against her chest so hard she felt like it might leap up her throat and out of her mouth. Her hands were shaking as they reached forward to grip Meiling's shoulders perhaps a little too hard.

"What happened? You need to tell me exactly what happened."

"I don't—" Meiling hiccuped, her hands jerking at her sides. "I don't know."

"What about the adults? Where are Nesta, Phyre, and Nando?"

"They umm . . . They ummm . . ." Meiling shook her head, her shoulders beginning to shake even more under Rus's hands.

"I'll go see what's going on," Az volunteered, bless her, and nodded to Greer, who followed, going the long way round through the playroom and office into the living room.

"It's my fault again, isn't it?" Meiling asked, her voice a whisper.

"No, sweet girl. No. It's not your fault. And don't you worry. I'm going to get Huaner back, just like I did last time. I promise." Rus pulled Meiling into her chest, hugging her tightly, and made a motion to Cagney to move the goblin into the pantry. They'd have to deal with them later; there were more important things going on now.

The chair scraped loudly across the kitchen, but Rus couldn't give less of a fuck about the damage Cagney was probably doing to her floors. All that mattered was keeping

Meiling safe and getting Aihuan back before the witch hunters did something to her that not even necromancy would solve.

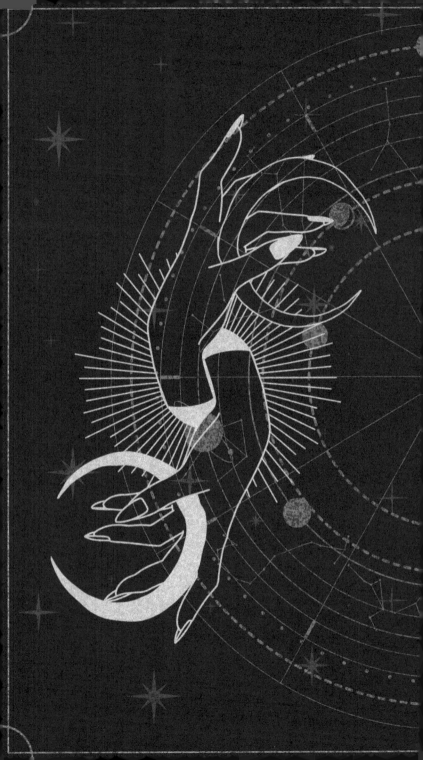

16

IF THERE WAS one thing Azure didn't want in that moment, it was to step away from Meiling and Rus, to leave them in the kitchen holding each other like their lives were falling apart around them—which they fucking were—but someone had to. And Azure Elwood trusted herself above all others to keep them and Aihuan safe. So she pulled herself away from them and went in search of Aihuan, forcing herself to breathe calmly. But what she found in the living room wasn't what she'd been expecting at all.

She stopped in the doorway, blinking at the red poppy petals that carpeted every inch of the place. Covering the slumbering adults, the furniture, and everything in between. All except a vaguely Aihuan-sized patch that must have been where the toddler had been sleeping.

Drawing in another deep, calming breath proved dangerous as Azure felt her own eyelids grow heavy with fatigue and her muscles begin to relax. She frowned, pulling the neck of Rus's black T-shirt up over her nose to block the smell of the flowers.

"Shit. They've got a druid," Greer hissed beside her, the

words muffled through where he'd lifted his hand to cover his nose and mouth.

"We need to let Cagney deal with this." Azure reached down to brush her fingertips over one of the silken petals. Poppies were well out of season for Moondale. But if Rus was right, if they were performing some magic via proxy from points unknown, it'd be easy enough to get their hands on poppy petals. The question was, how had they convinced a druid to help them given that druids were known for being a peaceable people? Cagney notwithstanding.

"Come on, I'll set up a perimeter to keep the smell in there." Greer stepped over the threshold of the room, back into the office on the other side, and squatted down to press his palms into the floor under the wide doorframe. Azure nodded and stepped out after him. The magic went up like a window between the two spaces, transparent and a little distorted but impenetrable. "Hopefully they won't send any more."

"They'd need a power source to get them past the wards. That's likely what happened to the goblin." Even as she said it, her stomach twisted with nausea. It was common to use blood in magic—Azure was used to that and hardly noticed it anymore. But to get past the kind of magic Rus had used to protect herself and her home, they'd need more power. They'd need a dramatic boost. More than blood, or even just draining the power off another magical creature. They'd need a life force.

"Shit. Man, that's dark," Greer shook his head. His hands were shaking at his sides. "Rus really got herself in deep, didn't she?"

"This wasn't her fault," Azure grumbled, turning to scowl at Greer. "This had nothing to do with her ability to make enemies."

"I know, but—"

"Let's go tell the others what happened." Azure turned on her heel and headed back through the house without a second glance at him. She wasn't in the mood to argue about whether Rus had brought this on herself, especially when it was clear she had not. Besides, fighting with Greer would take more time they didn't have. They needed to find Aihuan as soon as possible. If Greer was going to get in the way of that then he could go the fuck home, and Rus would probably tell him as much, saving Azure from having to be the bitchy one, as per usual.

The goblin was gone by the time they returned, likely tucked away in the pantry to keep Meiling from seeing what had become of it. Rus, Meiling, and Cagney had settled at the table, and someone had prepared steaming mugs of what smelled like chamomile for each of them, but no one appeared to be drinking any.

They all looked up when Azure and Greer returned, and Azure set a couple of petals on the table in front of them before taking Rus's mug and gulping down half of it in an attempt to settle her stomach.

"Poppies?" Cagney asked with a wrinkled nose.

"Looks like." Greer shrugged, settling into the chair beside her, leaving nowhere for Azure to sit. Not that she planned on it anyway. She needed to feel like she was doing something, and she wouldn't if she sat. "The question is, why didn't they knock Meiling out like everyone else?"

"Because she's a medium." Rus shrugged, taking her tea back from Azure to finish it off. "Stuff like that affects mediums differently because of their connection to the land of the dead."

"That is both very useful and slightly terrifying. So if I were to give you a sleeping potion right now, it wouldn't do anything?" Greer leaned forward on his elbows, a look of interest on his features that Azure would very much like to smack off. Not because she was jealous, certainly not. But because Rus was not some kind of science experiment to be poked and prodded and used for research for whatever the board might want. That was the root of this whole mess, after all.

"Potions are a different matter since they alter the . . . You know what? No. We don't have time for me to give you a lesson on basic magical biology." Rus pushed to her feet, and it was only then that Azure saw the way her legs shook under her weight. Like she might collapse at any given moment and take all of them with her.

"Rus." Azure reached for Rus's elbow, hoping to stop her before she could crumple to the floor. But Rus brushed her off so she could lean heavily on the table, looming over Greer threateningly.

"Go read a fucking book if you want to know why different magic users are affected differently by plants and herbs."

Greer rolled his eyes as if he were annoyed, but held up his hands in surrender.

"Great." Rus straightened up, tugging uselessly at her hoodie, likely trying to make herself look either more imposing or more put together, Azure couldn't really figure out which. Either way, when she spoke next it was with a tone of such authority and competence that Azure swore she felt her own knees buckle. "Cagney, I need you to deal with the mess in the living room. The others likely won't wake up tonight, but we should get rid of the poppies before the smell sinks into the fabric in there."

"Right." Cagney rose to her feet and disappeared into the hall without another word.

"Greer, I know you said you aren't here on official business but . . ." Rus shifted from foot to foot.

"I'm already on my way." Greer pushed his chair back with a scraping sound. "I can get an Amber Alert out within the next hour. It might not really do much; they've probably cloaked themselves from the normies, but the more people keeping an eye out, the better. Do you have a recent photo?"

Rus nodded, pulling her phone from the big pocket on the front of her hoodie, and with a couple of taps she slid it over to Greer, who forwarded the photo on to himself. "Thank you for this," Rus said, her tone more serious than Azure thought she'd ever heard it before. "I really owe —"

"You don't." Greer shook his head and offered Rus a smile that was a little sad. "You don't owe me anything. Aihuan is a kid, and if I can't protect a kid in my town, what kind of sheriff am I?"

"A shitty one." Rus grinned back.

"A shitty one," Greer repeated. "I've added my number to your contacts. Call me if you need anything else, all right?"

"All right." Rus gathered up the mugs of now-cold tea as Greer headed for the door. When he was gone, that left Rus, Azure, and a dozing Meiling in the kitchen. "A-Ling, you should go back to bed. If you don't want to go up to your room, you can sleep on the couch in the office. I'm sure the house will provide you with some blankets."

"Okay," Meiling mumbled, shuffling out, and then it was just Rus and Azure. Azure looked across the kitchen at where Rus was bracing her hips against the sink, letting the counter hold up her weight because it looked like her legs were too weak to. How was she even still standing?

"This happened before," Rus said into the quiet, her voice near unrecognizable for how broken it was. "That's why she's —" She shrugged one shoulder, the mugs clanking loudly in the sink.

"Reanimated," Azure finished for her, the word tasting strange on her tongue, but not a bad sort of strange—not like she would have thought it might two months ago. She'd known Rus all her life. Seen Rus call upon the dead to do things the likes of which no one else would even imagine. But until Cagney had told her about Aihuan, she'd found the reanimation of Darcy grotesque in its way. She'd thought of necromancy as something dark and forbidden, just as the board had always taught them. But now, seeing Aihuan and the way her family loved her? Azure couldn't help but think that Rus had made the right choice.

"Someone told you." Rus laughed, the sound dry and humorless. "Of course they did. Was it Carmine?"

"Cagney."

"Fucking bitch. Can't even trust your best friend to— It doesn't matter." Rus let out a breath, her shoulders hunching forward. "None of it matters. It was all for fucking nothing. Wasn't it?"

"I don't believe that." Azure took a step toward her, her palms itching to reach out. To stroke away the worst of whatever Rus was feeling.

"It will be if they—" Rus spun, her eyes wide and wild, and then she was wilting into Azure's arms. Sobbing against her shoulder. Clutching at the back of her borrowed T-shirt. Hiccuping. Choking. Whimpering. Breaking apart and trusting Azure to hold all the pieces lest any be lost. "I can't . . . I can't bring her back a second time. It wouldn't work."

"We'll find her before that becomes an issue," Azure promised, her arms tightening around Rus, guiding her to one of the chairs at the table. Azure held her close, stroking her hair until Rus had settled for the most part.

"This isn't a solution," Rus said after what felt like hours of silence between them.

"What?" Azure sat beside her, dragging her chair closer.

"Getting Huaner back is just a temporary fix to a permanent problem." Rus huffed, running her fingers through her hair as she let out a breath. When Azure continued to stare at her like she didn't understand, Rus let out a long sigh, her hands moving to fiddle with the strings of her hoodie. "So long as Huaner has the ability to see into the future, and it's shining like a fucking beacon, people are going to come for her. We might be able to stop this group, but what about the next ones? Or the ones after that?"

"So, what do you want to do? Bind her powers?" Azure's stomach twisted sickeningly at the thought. Binding a young witch's powers wasn't entirely uncommon back in the old days, but these days it was well known that such a thing could stunt the witch's growth, making it harder for them to grow fully into and control their abilities later in life.

"Bind her . . . Oh Goddess, no," Rus spat, her face turning pale at the mere thought. "No. Definitely not."

"Then what? There's really no other way to hide a witch's power signature until they learn control. Unless, of course . . . their hometown . . . does it for them . . ." Azure felt her heart kick at that very thought. If Moondale was Aihuan's home, her *real* home, then Moondale's magic would rise up to protect her from outside threats. That was one of the many benefits of the covens and their less nomadic lifestyle.

"Exactly." Rus smiled at her but it looked a little pained, even for how the single word made Azure's stomach flip flop in a whole different way.

"So you're going to . . ." Azure couldn't say the words. She couldn't breathe life and hope and love into them, but she wanted to desperately.

Rus set her jaw, all grim determination, and said, "Start my own Moondale coven."

Which was not what Azure had been hoping to hear. She'd being hoping that Rus would say she'd join Jade Waters. But she could work with this. If Rus was going to start her own coven in Moondale, then that meant she was going to put down roots. It meant she planned to stay. And anything else . . . well, fuck anything else.

"Do you think Carmine could get me the necessary paperwork?"

"Yes. Yes, of course." It wasn't what Azure had dreamed of or wished for, but it was enough. Oh Goddess, it was enough.

"Can you ask her to get that together first thing in the morning? The sooner I get the paperwork filed, the sooner Moondale will start working its magic."

Azure nodded, the motion too fast and too jerky, but she didn't think Rus noticed as she was already rising from her chair and heading for the study. "I need to consult my grimoire on some stuff. You should try to get some more sleep. You're welcome to take my bed if you want. I'll probably stay in the study with A-Ling."

"Good night, Rus," Azure murmured, although she knew that there would be no sleeping. Not for her. Not tonight. Maybe not for the next few nights. Excitement and happiness buzzed in her veins like fizzy water. She reminded herself that it was unfair to be happy about this, not with Aihuan missing. But that didn't seem to change anything.

"Night, Az." And then Rus disappeared into the dark recesses of the house, and Azure was left to try to swallow down a nervous, excited giggle. It worked, but only just barely.

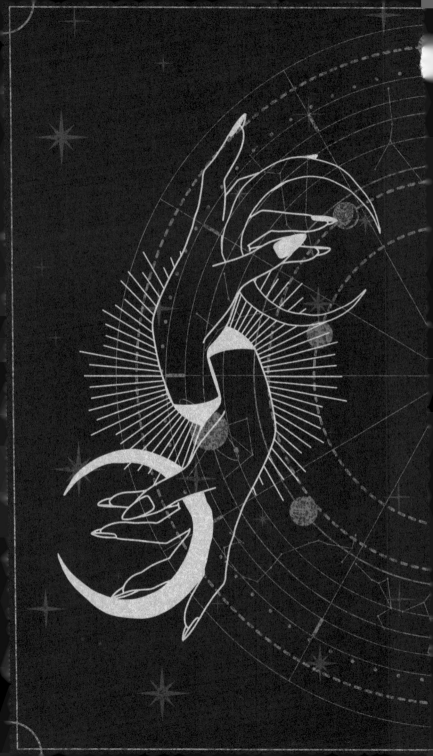

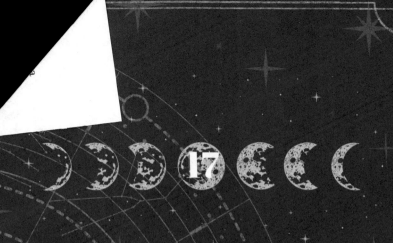

17

AZURE WAS PRACTICALLY TRIPPING over herself in her hurry to get to Aunt Carmine and get her hands on the paperwork Rus would need to start her own coven. She couldn't remember the last time she'd been so jittery. Maybe not since she'd been twenty-one and buying an engagement ring for a woman who she thought she'd spend the rest of her life with. Of course, that had all come to nothing, but now she was getting a second chance!

A second chance! It sounded ridiculous even to herself. She was thirty-two. Who got a second chance at thirty-two? Certainly not grumpy bookstore managers. Especially not ornery, pessimistic ones. Funny how her pessimism didn't seem to apply to all things Rus. No. With Rus, there was always hope. Always had been. Even when things had looked like they were at their worst. Really, it was that that had made Azure fall in love with Rus in the first place.

Silly little thing, hope. It always hurt more than anything else when it was dashed.

Azure shook her head; she wouldn't think about that

now. Not now that she had a second chance at things, second chance to convince Rus to stay.

Aunt Carmine looked up from her computer at the rapid knock on her door, her dark brows raised high to wrinkle her forehead. "Something I can help you with, Azure?"

"I need the paperwork to start a formal coven in Moondale." The words left her in a rush so fast, Azure half expected Aunt Carmine not to understand them. And if the tilt of her head was anything to go by, maybe she hadn't.

"What?"

"The paperwork," Azure said, sucking in a breath and forcing herself to slow down, "for starting a coven in Moondale, an official one, with a board seat and a say in the governing body, and all the trappings." Rus deserved all the trappings. She deserved to see her coven grow and become something that was beautiful, and whole, and as much a part of Moondale as Jade Waters was. As Rus was.

"May I ask what for?" Aunt Carmine asked, but Azure could already hear the printer in the corner warming up for printing. Azure was struck, not for the first time, with how wonderful her aunts were. How they understood her. How they'd been good mothers to her, even if they weren't her birth parents. Violet may still have memories of their mother and father, but Azure had this—two women who loved her so wholly they'd do anything for her, almost no questions asked.

"For Rus." As if that weren't perfectly obvious. Aunt Carmine knew that almost anything Azure did that seemed out of character was for Rus. Azure had never really tried to hide how weak she was for Icarus Ashthorne. "And for the girls. If she starts her own coven—"

"Then Moondale will extend its protection to them without the need for the board to extend their reach." Aunt Carmine nodded with a thoughtful hum as the printer began spitting out pages, each landing orderly in the tray. "It also means she won't be able to leave Moondale for an extended period of time as she has in the past. She'll be tying her magic to the land," she continued, her back to Azure where she stood waiting for the printer to finish its work, her fingers brushing the edges of the crisp white papers. "Are you sure that's what she wants?"

"It was her idea."

Aunt Carmine let out a loud breath, her shoulders hunching forward a little. "Make sure she thinks this through, Azure. I know you want Rus to stay, and I know she'll do anything to protect her girls, but this is a big commitment, a big decision. Tying yourself to a plot of land by blood . . . it's not something to take lightly. Make sure she knows that?"

"I will." Azure took the papers in her sweating hands, ignoring the way they trembled with her excitement. It wasn't right to be excited about this, not with Aihuan missing, she reminded herself. But she also knew that they would find Aihuan; there was never a question of that. And this was just . . . this was wonderful. It was . . .

"I've got everyone in Jade Waters looking for her."

Azure looked up from where she was clutching the papers hard enough to bend the edges and blinked. "You have?"

"Of course I have. I let them know as soon as Greer sent out the alert." Aunt Carmine clicked her tongue with annoyance. "No matter what the board says, Rus is right— we cannot abandon a witchling in need. We'll find her, Azure. Make sure Rus knows that. Make sure she doesn't do anything foolish until we do. Those girls . . ." She pursed her lips, taking another long breath. "They need her."

"I'll make sure she's safe." She would. Because what

was the alternative? There was none. "Thank you for this, Aunt Carmine."

"Of course. I'll let you know if we find anything." Aunt Carmine settled back into her chair, her nails tapping loudly against the keyboard—a dismissal. Azure wasn't sure what she was doing, but she had little doubt that it was something to help find Aihuan.

For all Rus thought the people of Moondale didn't care about her, they were already coming together to bring her daughter home. The thought warmed Azure from the inside out, and that warmth followed her all the way back to Rus's front door.

The house had been quiet when she'd left a little under an hour ago, trusting 157 Mourning Moore to do its thing and lock the door behind her. It was still quiet when she returned, the door creaking open loudly as it did every time, as if none of the residents had woken yet.

Azure moved on socked feet to the living room to check on where Cagney and Fernando had wound up a few hours ago after Nesta and Phyre had left to report Aihuan's disappearance to their respective families with the hopes that they'd help find the child. There was no guarantee that the Ironwoods or the Holyores would go against what their elders had decided, but they had to try.

Next it was to the office where she'd left Meiling still sleeping fitfully on the couch and Rus with her face pressed against the desk, snoring lightly. How Rus had fallen asleep there, Azure would never know, but it was good to see her finally—

Azure stopped in the threshold, her hands fisting around the paper she was holding. The chair Rus had propped herself up in for her impromptu nap was empty. That was all right, Azure told herself, maybe she'd just gone into the kitchen to—

That was empty too. No sign of anyone having been there recently. Azure sat the papers on the table before her damp palms could cause permanent damage to them. They were too important for that. Much too important. And then she was tearing off up the back steps, and checking every room for any sign of Rus. There was nothing.

Her socked feet slipped on the edges of the stairs on her way back down, almost dumping her onto her ass in her rush to get back to someone, anyone who could explain what the fuck had happened.

Cagney grunted, smacking Azure's hand away as she shook her shoulder hard enough to nearly smother her with the back of the couch. "Cagney, Rus is gone."

"What?" Cagney muttered, still half asleep, her speech so slurred Azure was beginning to wonder if Rus hadn't used some sleeping magic to keep them all under while she did whatever she'd done.

"Rus is fucking *gone*!"

Cagney jerked awake, sitting up so quickly Azure toppled onto her ass on the rug. "What do you mean *gone*?"

"I mean I left to get the paperwork from my aunt, and came back, and she's not fucking *here*."

"How long?" Cagney was on her feet, already headed for the office on the other side of the living room.

"I wasn't even gone an hour."

"Is her car still out front?"

"Yes."

"She couldn't have gotten far." Cagney retraced Azure's trek through the house to look for Rus with Azure hot on her heels. "Can you use your sight to find her?"

"No. I—I uh . . ." Azure shifted on her feet, her eyes drifting down to where her bright white socks stood out in glaring contrast against the black floorboards. "I cast a spell when Rus and I were still together that blocks her from my sight. I thought it was only fair seeing as how I—" Azure shrugged.

"Well that was really romantic, but also stupid as fuck." Cagney finished her search upstairs, and they made their way back down to the kitchen. "Remind me to go back in time and shake the absolute shit out of baby Az."

Azure snorted a chuckle, and then swallowed it down. "How do we find her?"

"I've got some blood samples from Rus back at my house. They're like a decade old, but they should still be viable. I'll go grab them; you wake up the others." Cagney stuffed her feet down into her boots, not even bothering with the zippers on the sides.

"You have Rus's blood just . . . lying around?" That didn't seem terribly safe. She couldn't imagine Rus allowing someone to keep samples from her on hand like that.

"They're in a safe." Cagney shrugged. "Don't remind her I have them, though, or she'll demand I destroy them and the next time she does something stupid as fuck, we'll all be screwed." She pointed her finger at Azure, then she was out the door, down to her bicycle on the sidewalk, and gone.

Leaving Azure alone with the quiet of the house, and the weight of the realization that maybe Rus had been lying to her. Maybe she'd gotten her hopes up for nothing. Again.

IT WASN'T A LIE, NECESSARILY, RUS REASONED. SHE DID mean to petition for the right to start a coven. It was just . . . well, she knew how bureaucracy worked in Moondale, and she knew how slow the board could be about things. Filing the right paperwork and doing the right rituals would be easy enough. But getting that shit passed by the closed-minded fuckers on the Board of Magic? That was another story entirely. There was no way in fuck they'd let the process go as quickly or as smoothly as she needed. And she didn't have time for that. She needed to get Aihuan back right now! Before something horrible happened to her again.

So when Az had slipped out early that morning to visit with Carmine, Rus had cast a sleeping spell to make sure everyone who was left over would stay safely tucked into their makeshift beds. Then she'd grabbed a reusable grocery bag from the pantry—checking on the still-comatose goblin—filled it with everything she could think she'd need, including a bit of Aihuan's hair that she kept tucked away behind the allspice, which she never used, and left the house as quietly as possible. The house, for its part, hid her footsteps and kept the doors from creaking on their hinges as if it knew what she was doing and approved.

The graveyard was silent around her in the chill early morning, and she pulled her hood up over her head, hoping that and the shielding charm sewn haphazardly into the lining would keep anyone from seeing the figure clad all in black looming in the middle of an abandoned cemetery. She was no stitch witch, but she'd made a decent practice of needlepoint over the years. Well. Decent enough to manage the most basic charms.

Whispering started up the moment she let her awareness slip below the murky surface of the veil that separated the living from limbo. She had one spirit in particular she needed, and she had its name. No others would do.

She hadn't lied either when she said she couldn't use the goblin to track Aihuan's pursuers, but she had been stretching the truth a little because the goblin had been used by that same group of witch hunters multiple times. And the goblin, along with the witch hunters, had caused plenty of creatures to lose their lives over the years. Some of which were not resting peacefully in the afterworld.

Something dark and looming skittered out of the corner of Rus's eyes, but she knew better than to look at anything she hadn't called upon directly by name when she stepped through the veil. It was too easy for something to latch on and stay there, uninvited. The gray-on-gray world of limbo spread out before her like a black-and-white movie. All the same details as the world she knew—the graveyard, her house, her yard—but the color washed completely away.

"Jin," Rus said the name, loud and clear, using it to call upon the creature whose spirit still clung to the goblin. She couldn't have gone far. And in moments, the little pixie fluttered up to her, stopping midair in front of Rus's face.

"And what do you have to give in trade for the information you seek?" Jin asked, her nearly transparent head tilting to the side as she skipped all the usual pleasantries. Well, Rus liked a spirit who got right down to business.

"Vengeance on the ones who killed you." It was an easy enough proposition, one Rus had given to plenty of spirits when she needed them to help her with something. Usually, that vengeance didn't require her to spill any blood. Spirits were as complicated as the living could be, and very often they didn't wish death on others, even for all they had died themselves.

"Whatever form that vengeance takes?" Jin raised one brow that may have been blonde when she was alive. "Even if I want them dead?"

"If that's what you want, yes. They took my daughter; I'm not above ending them in any way you see fit."

"And I will be able to come along?" Jin pressed

forward in the air, her fingers reaching for Rus's face, sending a chill down Rus's spine. She didn't like inviting spirits into her body. Sometimes they wanted to stick around, and with her threshold as low as it was, it was hard to force one out once they'd been invited in. But she didn't exactly have a whole lot of time for negotiations. The longer this took, the more likely it was she'd be too late for Aihuan.

"If you can lead me to where they're keeping my daughter, I will let you ride along. But if you don't know where she is, or you lead me somewhere else, it is within my rights to force you out." She had to be careful and specific when dealing with spirits. She had to let them know that there were rules. Especially with immortal magical creatures who'd died. They tended to be really pissed about the whole dying thing. "And when this is done, you will depart, and move on to the afterworld. That's the bargain I'm offering."

Jin huffed, crossing her arms over her chest, washed out gray eyes narrowing in consideration. "And if I don't want to go?"

"That's not an option. If I let you ride along, you leave when this is finished, and you move on. Those are my terms."

"Oh, very well." Jin flapped her little hand through the air flippantly. "Honestly, you witches are always so uptight." She smiled at Rus, all sharply pointed teeth and promise. "So do we have an accord, Icarus Ashthorne?"

"We do." Rus held out her hand, palm up, and waited as the little creature swooped down and pressed her face against the skin. Then those teeth sunk into the meat of Rus's palm, and for all they were not on the physical plane, they sure as shit felt like they were. Rus hissed a breath, her eyes narrowing at the bright flash of light as Jin disappeared, and a moment later the pixie's presence settled into Rus's mind like a softly glowing weight.

"Well? What are you waiting for, witch? This place gives me the willies. Let's go!"

Rus rolled her eyes, took a step forward, and slipped back through the veil onto the physical plane, the world washing itself in colors once again.

18

RUS HAD FORGOTTEN how notoriously bad spirits were with directions. It had been nearly a year since she'd let one ride along with her after contacting it, and minor irritations like a spirit not knowing its left from its right were easily pushed aside and swept under the rug in the interim. She had also forgotten how little they seemed to understand distance.

"How much farther?" Rus asked, standing in the middle of an intersection of Moondale proper, her feet aching in her boots, and her head starting to pound from the incessant nattering of Jin the pixie. That was another thing she had forgotten in the three-plus years since she'd had a pixie ride along—they were fucking annoying. Going on and on for what felt like hours about this time they had tripped Jennifer Lawrence, or that time they had ridden in a flower on the Queen's hat for the entirety of a royal parade—as if anyone who didn't have the sight could even see them. Seriously, the attraction to celebrity that pixies experienced was damn near legendary. Which might have been funny if Rus weren't currently sharing a head with one.

"And then I said to Sting—" Jin stopped, only just noticing that Rus had asked a question. "What was that?"

"I said, how much farther? We've been walking for forty-five minutes. I should have brought my fucking car." She scuffed her boot against the ground, looking one direction and then the other before crossing the street.

"Can't do. Too much iron," Jin said, her tone distant like she was only half paying attention to the conversation. "Anyway, where was I?"

"You were going to tell me how much farther we were from where the witch hunters have taken my daughter." Rus gritted her teeth, inhaling deeply through her nostrils to keep from screaming.

"You know, if you're just going to give me attitude, then you can find them yourself." Jin huffed, and Rus could imagine her crossing her arms over her little chest and turning up her nose.

Rus pinched the bridge of her own nose and forced her tone into something that might be considered more polite in some circles, but would have an edge of annoyance to anyone who knew her. "Apologies, Jin. Please, if you could tell me how much farther, I'd greatly appreciate it."

Pixies, thankfully, did not understand sarcasm. "Oh. It's around here somewhere."

"Somewhere, where?" Rus spun to look up and down the street she was standing on. It was one street over from Main Street, and while it wasn't as obviously commercial as the street where Elwood & Co. and Necromancer's was, it was lined with old homes that had been converted into little shops with apartments above them when the town had become a tourist attraction. A few shoppers were meandering down the broken sidewalk, and Rus couldn't imagine that the witch hunters would bring Aihuan here; it would draw too much attention.

"I'll know it when I see it," Jin said in a tone that might have been a shrug, and Rus nearly lost the battle to not scream.

"Of course, you will." Running a hand through her unbrushed hair, Rus exhaled loudly, flipping the bird to the human couple who walked past her, cutting her strange looks for talking to herself before continuing in the direction Jin was steering her. "Lead on, Macduff."

"My name isn't Macduff, it's Jin, remember? You called it when you summoned me in limbo."

Rus shook her head. "I know that. It's just a . . . It's a stupid thing humans say to be funny sometimes."

"I don't see how being called by the wrong name would be funny. Names have power, you know. I had this very same discussion with David Bowie once when . . ." Rus tuned her out after that, because while it was impressive that Jin knew so many musicians by name, her high and nasally voice really had begun to grate on Rus's ears, even for all the fact that it was in her head.

They walked a couple more streets over, leaving behind the commercial properties of Moondale to head deeper into the residential neighborhoods. Az and the others would have realized she was gone by now, the sleeping spell having evaporated into the aether so their internal clocks could wake them. Cagney would be up first. Then Fernando. And then Meiling. That was if Az hadn't raised the alarm and dragged them all from their beds.

Rus had expected Az to take some time convincing Carmine to hand over the proper paperwork, if she even managed to at all, so she should have at least an hour-and-a-half to a two-hour head start on the others by her own estimate.

"What does this place look like?" Rus asked, cutting off another long-winded explanation about how it had really been *Jin* who wrote "A Whiter Shade Of Pale" that sounded not only patently false, but like Jin had never actually heard the song before.

Jin made a noise that was the verbal equivalent of a shrug and sounded vaguely like "I'unno."

"What do you mean *you don't know*?" Rus threw her head back to glare up at the sky and bite down on a cry to the Goddess asking why she had created pixies to begin with.

"I told you I'd know it when I saw it."

"I thought you'd been there!" Goddess above and below, her temples were throbbing. She didn't know how much longer she could keep up letting Jin steer them wherever they were going before she collapsed. It'd been too long since she'd had a spirit that wasn't human or witch in her head, and the hangover of having magic that didn't quite fit with her own, and was arguably more potent, was already starting.

"I have." Jin sounded affronted, like Rus had called her a liar, which they both knew she wouldn't because pixies couldn't lie—not directly, anyhow. "The warehouse is around here, somewhere in this direction."

"Warehouse?" Rus stopped where she'd been walking down a row of neat and orderly little brick townhouses. They were fairly new, by Moondale standards, but had probably been there for at least a hundred years or so. "There are no warehouses in Moondale."

"What? Of course there are."

"No. There aren't. They tried to bring an industrial park to Moondale back in the eighties, but the Board of Magic blocked it, said they didn't want any big businesses here. Everything like that is in the next town over, Ironport. Their clans and covens have less of a hold over the—"

"Right. Right. Right. I don't need a history lesson." Jin grumbled, flippant. "Fine. It's in Ironport then. How far's that?"

"We definitely need the car." Rus scrubbed at her face, letting out a long, irritated breath. She'd shout at Jin for wasting her fucking time, but it was hard to get up the energy past the ringing in her ears. She definitely should have thought about what a power-suck pixies were before she agreed to let Jin ride along.

"I can't ride in a car. Too much—"

"I know, too much iron." Rus took another deep breath. She wished the world would stop spinning for one fucking second so she could figure out what street she was on again. "But I can't walk ten-plus miles like this."

"Is that how far it is?"

"Yes, Jin! That is how far Ironport is!" Was the world starting to look blurry or was that just Rus? She stumbled back, leaning against someone's whitewashed fence to try to catch her breath.

"No need to shout," Jin grumbled.

"Sorry. Sorry." Rus held up her hands placatingly. "I just . . . I need to get some air, I think."

"Air? You're outside." She sounded annoyed, and Rus couldn't blame her. She was kind of annoyed with herself at the moment. She should have known her body's limitations. But she hadn't taken on a passenger that wasn't humanoid since before she'd brought Aihuan back. Fuck. This wasn't just about a magic overload, was it? No. This was a spiritual overload. That was . . . that was *dangerous*.

"You need to . . . You need to . . ." She was going to say Jin needed to get out, but she couldn't breathe through the spinning of the sidewalk under her feet.

Jin gasped, the sound startled and almost bewildered, like when someone misses a step on their way downstairs in the middle of the night. And then it was strangely silent in Rus's head, so silent, all she could hear was her ears ringing from the absence of sound.

"Jin?" Rus asked, almost afraid of what would answer in the place of the pixie. She hadn't invited anything else in when she'd been beyond the veil, but that didn't mean something hadn't hitched a ride. Her threshold may have gotten lower since the last time she'd stepped over six months ago. Or maybe it had been the exhaustion from all the days without sleep lowering it. Or maybe it was the moon, or her fucking menstrual cycle. There were so many factors, she couldn't account for all of them.

"Jin's not here right now," a deep growling voice said in her ear.

"Who the fuck are you?"

Whoever—or whatever—it was laughed, deep and throaty, and then Rus wobbled again on her feet, her vision narrowing to a point.

AZURE HISSED, HER BOOTS SCUFFING AGAINST THE sidewalk as she ran to catch Rus before she could hit the ground. It was a near thing. Had they been but a few steps behind, Rus would have fallen and cracked her head open on the pavement. They both wobbled a moment before Azure managed to get her balance, and then bent to scoop Rus's prone form up into her arms. Goddess, she was so light. Had she not been eating?

"What happened?" Meiling asked, her voice quivering in a way only the young who thought their parents invincible could.

"Magical overload would be my guess." Cagney

squinted at Rus's too-pale face, brushing her hair away from where it had begun to stick to her sweating temples.

"It looks like she took on a passenger." Azure nodded to the strange double glow of Rus's aura—she wasn't as good at reading them as Aunt Carmine, but she was intimately familiar with Rus's—and adjusted her hold on Rus to keep her from slipping out of her arms. "The goblin?"

"No. She said she couldn't contact them." Cagney strode to the curb to open the back door to her car, her hand reaching out to cushion Rus's head as Azure set her in the seat. "The pixie, would be my guess."

"Do you think the pixie told her where they were keeping Huaner?" Fernando looked up and down the street as if he could make out where Rus had been headed. There was no way to know really. By the time they had gotten eyes on her, Rus seemed to be focused on the voice inside her head and wherever she was walking. She hadn't even noticed when they started following her.

Azure shook her head, her shoulders slumping a little as she bent over Rus to buckle her safely into the seat. "Likely not. Rus always said spirits were horrible at giving directions. The best she could hope was to use it as a compass."

"She could have been walking for miles." Cagney slid into the driver's seat and slammed the door, the others loaded in around her—Fernando up front, Azure in the middle between Rus and Meiling—and then they were headed back to 157 Mourning Moore.

"Then why bother letting that thing inside her?" Meiling shifted nervously, which was understandable. Not all mediums were as open to letting a spirit ride along as Rus seemed to be. Although Azure wished she would be less open to it. It was dangerous, letting something else into your body without really understanding who or what it was. But Rus had never been the type to think these things through, not when it was only herself that might get hurt in the process, and others may benefit from it.

"She probably thought it was the only way to find your sister." Azure reached down to pat Meiling's knee gently.

"But it's not! We can use my blood. You even said so. Why would she—"

"Because your Auntie Rus is a self-sacrificing idiot," Cagney said, her hands gripping the steering wheel hard enough to make the leather creak under her grip. She met Azure's gaze in the rear-view mirror and nodded. "I'm sure she was worried about what bloodletting on soil that wasn't home turf would open you up to."

"Well, that's just . . . that's just *stupid*." Meiling huffed, curling her arms over her chest and turning to look out the window at the slowly passing street.

"It is. And we won't be letting her do it again." Azure gave Meiling's knee a little squeeze and felt her lips twitch when Meiling's shoulders relaxed.

"No. We won't." She was still glaring out the window, but Azure thought she saw Meiling's expression smooth out from the scowl it had been in for the last forty-five minutes while they searched for her wayward guardian.

19

IT WAS amazing that Rus was still sleeping, honestly, with how noisy 157 Mourning Moore was, everyone arguing over everyone else. Azure wouldn't have been able to sleep through all of it, but then Rus had been running herself particularly ragged, and carrying a passenger with her had always been the kind of thing to leave her so drained it'd be a miracle if a hurricane woke her. Azure knew this from experience because they had had a hurricane once after Rus had had a leprechaun in her head for a couple of days in an attempt to find his lost gold, and Rus had slept right through it like it was nothing.

"I still think we should wait," Phyre said, her voice steadier than Azure thought she'd ever heard it. She was wringing her hands though, a clear indication that the confrontation was making her nervous, which . . . same. Azure rubbed her own sweating palms on the sweatpants she'd borrowed from Rus and still hadn't had the heart to take off. There wasn't time anyway, she reasoned. Too much else to do.

"She's right. The board should be involved in this. We

can't just go storming into another magical territory without some kind of—"

"That's not what I meant," Phyre huffed, cutting Greer off. Greer's face turned very red, but he didn't try to talk over her because Phyre had always had one of those voices that was so quiet, but firm, that when she spoke everyone listened. "I meant we should wait until Rus wakes up. Forget what the board wants," she said in a tone that kind of sounded like, *Fuck 'em.*

"You don't mean that." Nesta leaned forward in their seat. For all that their words might say to the contrary, their face was a mask of delight with the idea of Phyre going against Brant Ironwood. Which was fair—most people hated the old bastard who had been a part of the board since before Azure had even been born. What little respect Azure might have once had for him had evaporated at the last Board of Magic meeting where he'd talked down to Rus like she was a child and tried to bully her into signing herself and her daughters over to the covens.

"I do." Phyre lifted her chin, her hands clutching more tightly around one another.

Nesta looked like they wanted to let out a delighted squeal, but a sharp kick under the table to the shin from Greer silenced them.

"Then it's settled." Cagney smiled sharply at all of them. "When sleeping beauty wakes up, we get to work. Greer, were you able to get into contact wi—"

"Get to work doing what?" Rus asked, her voice a scratchy reflection of what it might have been a week ago before all of this started. Her clothes were rumpled, and she had a crease on her cheek from the living room throw pillow Azure had rested her gently on, but she was so achingly beautiful that Azure's arms itched to wrap her up in them again.

"Finding Huaner," Meiling piped up from where she'd been mostly silent sitting between Greer and Nesta, watching the volley of conversation between the adults like it was a particularly boring tennis match.

"I was on my way to her." Rus scowled at them, her hands fisting at her sides. She didn't look grumpy and rumpled anymore, she looked pissed. Which was understandable, considering they had stopped her before she'd gotten to wherever she was going. "And you all got in the way!"

"We didn't get in the way. We saved you from killing yourself stumbling into the street and getting hit by a fucking car," Cagney snapped back, her green eyes narrowed in rage.

"Fuck you, Cagney."

"No. Fuck you, Rus! Fuck you for thinking you can just—"

Before she could finish, Rus spun on her heel and stomped down the hall, the front door opening and slamming behind her hard enough to rattle the windows.

"Well. That could have gone better." Nesta's voice was light, their eyes still staring at where Rus had disappeared in the doorframe.

"I'll talk to her." Cagney's shoulders slumped as she let out a long breath.

Azure shook her head, already walking across the kitchen to the door where Rus had been. "I think you've said enough for the moment. I'll speak to her. You all start getting everything ready for the ritual."

Cagney opened her mouth like she wanted to argue further. Funnily enough, it was a frown from Greer that stopped her. With a shrug, she nodded. "All right. Just don't let her leave the property. We can't trust her to—"

"I know. Not run off and get herself killed."

IT WAS EASIER TO BREATHE OUTSIDE, RUS REALIZED, IN spite of the chill that threatened to settle into her bones. Anything was better than being in the kitchen, suffocating under the weight of their pitiable stares. She didn't need their pity. She just needed to find her little girl. Aihuan must be so scared. So alone. What if they'd . . . No. No! She wouldn't think like that. She'd focus on the fact that she was going to get Aihuan back, whether the board wanted to help or not.

The door creaked loudly behind her, and Rus didn't have to turn around to know who it was. Az's soft steps were as engrained in her mind as Aihuan's delighted screams and Meiling's soft scoffs. They were a part of her. Likely always had been.

"I'm not going to apologize for what I said back there," Rus said, not even bothering to lift her face from where she'd pressed it into her knees. She had curled into herself on one of the wicker chairs on the front porch, hoping that no one would find her, and then she could escape to follow Jin. If she could *find* Jin again; the pixie's presence had been weirdly absent since she'd woken up, and Rus couldn't figure out where she'd gone.

"I'm not going to ask you to." Az shrugged, moving to sit in the chair beside Rus, her legs crossed neatly at the ankles. "I don't think Cagney will either. You're under a lot of stress right now, and we all understand that."

Rus clicked her tongue, turning her head to press her cheek into her knee so she could look at Az through the curtain of her unkempt pink hair. She looked just as tired as Rus felt, dark bags under her eyes, the weight of their situation making her shoulders slump. It was hard to be angry with her when she looked like that. Not at all put together and proper the way Rus had always known her. Rus swallowed down the urge to reach for Az, to run her fingers over the flyaways that had escaped her high bun and slick them back into place.

"I do think we need to talk about what happened back there, though." Az sat up a little straighter, lifting her chin to meet Rus's eyes.

"There's nothing to talk about." There wasn't, not as far as Rus was concerned. It was a standard possession. Nothing at all to write home about. Well, except for the way Jin had disappeared and been replaced by that gravelly voice. Rus shook herself mentally. She wouldn't think about that now, she'd worry about whatever *that* was later. Especially as getting in the car had clearly dispelled it.

"There is. And we're going to," Az pressed, because of fucking course she couldn't leave well enough alone. She never could. That'd been why Rus had had to leave. She couldn't stay knowing that if she did, she'd never be able to break up with Az and let Az move onto bigger and brighter things, because Az wouldn't let her. She was a stubborn bitch that way. Goddess, Rus had loved that about her once upon a time. She might still, if that stubbornness weren't aimed at her that very moment.

Rus let out an audible breath, her shoulders lifting and falling with it, as she turned to rest her chin on her knees, gazing into the middle distance. "Have you ever looked at yourself in the mirror and not recognized yourself? Almost like the you that was staring back at you wasn't the same you that people see on paper . . . or—or something?"

Rus didn't need to look at Az to know that she was shaking her head. They'd never really talked about what it was like for Rus to be possessed, mostly because Rus had only ever had minor possessions before leaving Moondale.

She'd only been dabbling in it in those days, just enough to get under the board's skin and not enough to get her driven out of town via torches and pitchforks. But out in the big wide world? Well, people cared less about shit like that out there. What was a little possession and necromancy compared to everything else?

"That's what it's like. That's what being a medium with a low possession threshold is like. It's like looking in the mirror and not recognizing the person on the other side of the glass. Except it's not recognizing the voice in your own head, and the way your hands move, and your own gait." Rus ducked her head so she could rub her chin against her torn black jeans when it started itching under Az's intense gaze.

"It didn't used to be —"

"That was before I did what I did to bring Huaner back." She shrugged again. "And besides, back then I wasn't really doing full possessions. I'd let them latch onto me a little. Dig their claws into me so they could use my voice if they needed it, and whisper in my ear. But . . . Well, that stopped working."

"Why?"

"I imagine it's because I'm too close to them —"

"No. I mean why did you do that? Let the pixie in, knowing what would happen to you?"

"Oh." A laugh crawled up her throat, strangled and uncomfortable. "Seemed like a good idea at the time." It *had* seemed like a good idea at the time, the best idea, the only idea. But she also hadn't been expecting something else to hitch a ride on Jin. She probably should have known better than that and taken precautions, but nothing had seemed as important as finding Aihuan. *Still*, nothing seemed as important. The need to hold her little girl in her arms again sat like an itch, threatening to make her very skin crawl off her body.

With an audible sigh, Az rose from her chair and stood in front of Rus, one hand extended out to her to help her up. "You don't have to do this alone anymore."

Rus stilled, staring down at Az's socked feet. Her socks looked brand new, too white and free of holes, like she kept several packs of fresh socks in her drawer and threw them out after she had worn them once. Rus knew that wasn't the case, that Az was just like that—clean, tidy, put together. Fuck. Rus had loved leaving her mussed, once upon a time. Loved watching as the tidy, tightly controlled woman came undone at her hands, and lips, and teeth.

When Rus didn't say anything, Az reached forward and unwound Rus's hand from where she was clasping her forearms to hold her knees to herself and gave it a little tug. "We've got a better idea. And you're not going after Huaner alone, not this time. Come on, let's go see if everything is ready for the ritual."

She let Az pull her to her feet and tug her back inside, the door creaking closed behind them again. Let herself be led back to the kitchen. Let Az thread their fingers together like they always used to, palm to palm. And all the while, all Rus could think was . . .

No, I suppose I'm not alone this time. I'm not alone at all.

The thought settled like something warm and full in her belly. They'd find Aihuan together.

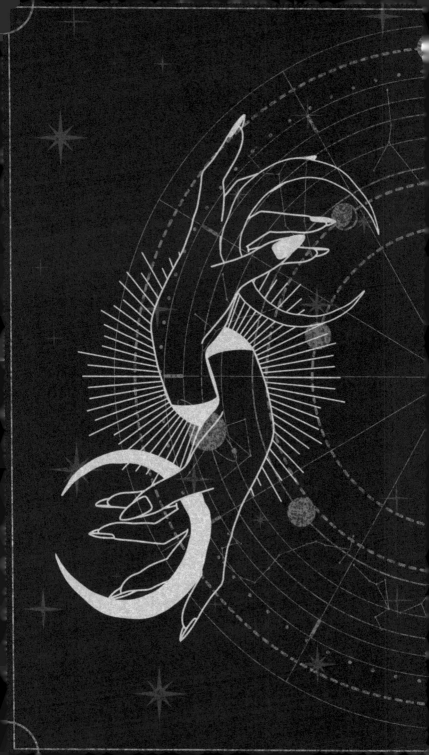

THE KITCHEN TABLE had disappeared by the time they returned, and a large summoning circle had been drawn on the hardwood with Meiling and the goblin sitting in the middle of it.

Greer held out a sharp looking athame made of black iron—Rus's athame, Azure would recognize it anywhere, with its black blade carved with crows—to a perturbed looking Meiling. "Why are you rolling up your sleeve? Just use your hand like—"

"The hands have too many nerve endings. Don't you know *anything*?" Meiling snorted, her words condescending and annoyed, and sounding so much like a young Icarus Ashthorne that Azure had to squeeze her eyes shut to keep the image of Rus with her dark hair pulled back into a crooked ponytail from supplanting itself over Meiling standing there, hands on her hips, staring down a witch more than twice her age.

Rus barked a laugh at Meiling's words and snatched the knife from Greer so she could press it into Meiling's waiting hand once she'd joined her in the summoning circle.

"Crimson Tide always uses animal blood for their rituals. Greer probably hasn't cut himself for magic since he officially joined his coven."

She sneered at Greer, the expression clearly baiting, and Greer opened his mouth, his face as sour as Azure had ever seen it, ready to rise to the challenge.

"Enough, you two," Cagney said, putting an end to the fight before it could even get started. "Rus, get out of the circle."

"No." Rus shook her head, pushing up the sleeve of her own hoodie and taking the knife from Meiling once she'd finished cutting herself. "You'll need me too. Huaner's my daughter, after all."

Cagney's eyes narrowed, her expression assessing and thoughtful, and Azure felt her own face mirroring the look. Rus was right. Aihuan was her daughter, in more ways than one. It wasn't just about words with Rus and Aihuan, or legal documents, it was also about blood. Rus had used her own to bring Aihuan back when everything had happened. Aihuan had been reborn with Rus's blood on her skin. That would mean something to the magic they were planning to use.

"Plus, I'm not letting Meiling stand here alone and open herself up to whatever might come for her on the other side of the veil. If we use my blood too, they're more likely to target me instead of her." Rus shrugged, the idea of using her own magic as a shield for Meiling not even a question in her mind as she drew the blade over skin that already had too many scars. She didn't even wince at the pain the way Meiling had, too used to it by now. Which was a thought that Azure didn't have the time to be upset over right this second.

"She's right," Azure said. She shifted from foot to foot in her spot between Nesta and Cagney. "The spell will have a better chance of working with three points of contact over two."

"The trinity," Nesta murmured, a soft reminder.

"Oh fine." Cagney rolled her eyes.

"Before we start." Rus leaned against the chair the goblin still sat in, and it looked like she might be using it to hold herself up against some dizzy feeling. Azure wanted to step into the circle and steady her, but it wouldn't help. All it would do was make Rus look weak in front of Greer and all the others. Rus would hate that. "I should tell you that Jin seemed to think we'd be heading to Ironport."

"We should all be able to fit in my van," Phyre volunteered. "I'll just have to move some of the car seats."

Rus nodded once, short and sharp, and then bent down to nick the goblin's fingers with the point of her blade while Cagney struggled with balancing Rus's tablet in her hands —it seemed to be vibrating as if it wanted out of her grip and back to its mistress, but Cagney wouldn't let go.

"You're sure this is going to work?" Cagney's hands slid against the smooth surface, nearly dropping the damn thing for the third time since they'd all been standing there. Rus cut it a warning look, and the tablet immediately stopped its struggling. "It might be easier if I just asked the—"

"It'll work." Rus took Meiling's hand, threading their fingers together.

Meiling frowned. "You said you'd never—"

"Hush, A-Ling." Rus narrowed her eyes on Meiling and waited a long moment until the wayward teen pressed her lips together and raised her brows in question. Then she nodded and looked back at Cagney. "It's too cold to ask the roots for help right now. We'll have to make do with this. Just remind me when we're done to take this spell to my workshop."

Cagney snorted, rolling her eyes. "Yeah. I'll get right on that. All right, everyone ready?"

Everyone around the circle nodded and then started murmuring the incantation, the magic building in a low hum in the air until Azure could feel it buzzing under her skin. It didn't take long at all for the droplets of blood that had been spilled to rise up, twisting and swirling like a tornado, until they fused together into one little bouncing ball that wasn't even really large enough to balance on the end of Azure's finger.

Cagney took a breath, her eyes lifting to meet Rus's across the space between them as if she were unsure. Rus nodded once, again, and then Cagney tapped something on the tablet with a decisive click and the ball shot through the air to smack against the back of it, smearing like jelly. A second later the humming stopped, and then they all fell silent.

"Not the neatest thing," Rus said, taking a Band-Aid that Phyre had pulled out of her oversized purse to cover Meiling's slowly weeping cut, ignoring her own in favor of tending to her daughter. "Once we get Huaner back, I'm running both hers and your blood through the sequencer and putting a tracker on you."

"That's so invasive, Auntie Rus," Meiling grumbled, tugging down the sleeve of her hoodie to hide the princess Band-Aid.

"But obviously necessary. I can't have my witchlings running all over Goddess-knows-where and not be able to keep track of them." Rus reached for the tablet, taking it from Cagney with the hand attached to her still-bleeding arm. "I'll make an app. It'll be called Find My Witchling." Rus grinned, her eyes glittering with the new idea in a way that made Azure's heart lurch in her chest.

"Sequencer?" Azure asked with some interest, moving

to peer over Rus's shoulders to watch her pinch and swipe at a map on the screen.

"A DNA sequencer." Her fingers stopped moving when Rus found the little blinking dot on the map she was looking for, and her shoulders relaxed. "There's my girl."

"Do I even want to know where you got a DNA sequencer from?" Greer muttered as he pushed the goblin from the center of the kitchen so the house could clear away the mess and return the table to its proper place.

"Oh, come on, Greer, a girl's got to have *some* secrets." Rus winked at him, and then held the tablet out to Azure for her to get a better look at it. "She's in Ironport, just like Jin said."

"I'll go get the van ready," Phyre volunteered before disappearing outside again, and the rest of them circled the kitchen table that Rus sat the tablet in the middle of.

"We should do recon," Greer said, his fingers tight on the back of one of the chairs. "We don't know how many people they have, what their wards are like, anything. I don't like going in blind."

"Then you don't have to go." Rus didn't look up at him to cut him with the expression of pert annoyance, but Azure could tell she wanted to. A headache was slowly building behind Azure's eyes, and she lifted her hand to rub at the bridge of her nose. It wouldn't do them any good to be at each other's throats about this, no matter what Rus might think.

"Evander is right," Azure said, before an argument could break out. "We need more information. We can't go running in underprepared." When it looked like Rus was going to turn her ire on Azure, she added, "That's likely to get Huaner killed."

Rus deflated from where she'd been sucking in air and power to clap back, "I hate it when you talk sensible."

"I'm aware." Azure felt her lips twitch in amusement, but she swallowed down the smile to press her face into a more serious expression. They'd have time for banter later.

"We should go in at night," Nesta said, pressing their shoulder in closer to Cagney's. "That way Rus and Meiling can speak to whatever spirits might be lingering around the group, get us information on their numbers and such."

"What if they lie?" Fernando's quiet voice asked. Those had been the first words he'd said since they'd found Rus wandering down the streets of Moondale looking strung out. Azure had almost forgotten he was there at all.

"What?" Azure frowned, looking up at him, confused.

"He's right." Rus scrubbed the palm of her hand down her face. "Being a medium is different than being a seer. Spirits, no matter how they seem, are just people, and people lie. It's up to the medium to know what's true and what isn't. Whatever information they give us, we'll have to take with a grain of salt."

"Oh." Nesta seemed to deflate.

"We'll use Az's abilities too." Rus met Azure's eyes, brows raised, questioning. "You can do that, right? You can go in and see what it looks like on the inside?"

"Provided they don't have wards blocking for that kind of thing, yes." Something swelled in her chest, rising in her voice. Pride, Azure realized perhaps belatedly. Pride, and elation at being able to do more than take a backseat to help Rus and her family. She could do something. Put her gift to use for something more than getting customers out of her store as quickly as fucking possible. Rus had always tried to tell her that there was more to her gift as a seer than Azure was seeing. That she had so much potential. But Azure had always denied it. Now—*now* she was seeing how true that could be.

"Good. Then we'll let Greer inspect the wards. He

should be able to tell us what they're for. That is Crimson Tide's area of expertise, isn't it?" Rus sneered at Greer, but he didn't bite back, he just nodded. "I'll contact whatever spirits linger around the place, see what they have to say. And if Az can get in, she'll give us a layout and numbers. Once we have information on what the inside looks like, we can formulate a plan."

"I'll stay here with Meiling and the goblin," Phyre said, her keys clattering on the table beside Nesta's hand. "I've already called Brenton. He said he'd meet you guys there. I'd go along myself, but the kids—"

"No. No." Rus shook her head, reaching for Phyre's hands and giving them a firm squeeze. "Your boys need you. I understand. You can't risk yourself and leave them alone."

Phyre smiled, returning the squeeze and leaning in to kiss Rus's cheek. She whispered something to Rus that made Rus's eyes widen and then water, but Azure couldn't hear it.

Rus's lower lip was still wobbling dangerously when she pulled back to address the group again. "Is there anyone else we should be expecting to join us?"

"I'm going to contact my aunts. Carmine probably can't help, given her position, but Maureen is always up for a little trouble." The phone was already in Azure's hand, even as she said the words.

"What about Violet and Indigo?" Cagney drummed her fingers on the table, her brow creased as she seemed to go down her mental list of their allies.

"Vi won't outwardly go against the board, and neither will Dillan." Nesta shook their head, frowning at the thought of their brother.

Greer coughed something that sounded like *cowards* but didn't say anything else.

"And Indie is too young," Rus said. "I'm not taking anyone under legal witching age into this. What about the druids?"

"They're all in hibernation already, except our elder, and you and I both know he's not going to be any help." Cagney rolled her eyes.

"Right. Then I guess it's just the eight of us, huh?" Rus's laugh was high and nervous, her gray eyes flicking around the group of them.

Azure took her shoulder, giving it a firm squeeze, and felt the tension bleed out of Rus under her hand. "We've done more with less."

"We have." Rus's smile turned into something genuine when she met Azure's gaze, gratitude shining from her eyes, and it took everything Azure had not to kiss her. "We certainly have."

"And besides," Greer said, breaking the moment quite soundly, "witch hunters don't tend to travel in big packs. That would mean sharing their power with too many people."

"Right." Azure nodded, pulled away, and went into the study to call Maureen.

21

MAUREEN BEECHER and Phyre's brother, Brenton Ironwood, were waiting for them when they reached the small industrial park on the outskirts of Ironport nearest Moondale and climbed out of Phyre's minivan like clowns out of a VW Bug. It looked like Maureen and Brenton had come on Brenton's motorcycle based on the wind-ruffled and annoyed expression on Aunt Maureen's face.

"Next time you call me out of the greenhouse for something, you will provide transportation, Icarus Ashthorne." Aunt Maureen shook her finger at Rus, who was holding up her hands, a wide grin on her face, not even trying to point out that it had been Azure who had called Maureen out of her precious greenhouse.

"I did provide transport." Rus nodded to Brenton, who had taken to leaning against one of the parking lot's light posts, his arms crossed as he surveyed their motley group.

"That . . . that *thing* is not transportation, it's a death trap!" Aunt Maureen flapped her arms through the air.

"Vi likes it," Brenton muttered, his voice more growl than anything else.

"Vi likes *you*," Aunt Maureen's incredulous look seemed to say, but before they could get into all of that Azure stepped between them. Because she was a good sister, unlike some people, and this wasn't the time or the place to discuss Violet's inability to see her nose for her face even though she was an empath. "Have you noticed anything since you arrived?"

"Nothing out of the usual for a place like this." Brenton shrugged, standing up from his casual lean. "Some pick-ups and deliveries."

Rus shifted uncomfortably beside Azure. Azure stuffed her hands farther into her pockets to keep from trying to comfort Rus. Aunt Maureen seemed to notice her unease too because she said, "Nothing from the specific address you gave us."

"Right. Just a tractor trailer parked with its back to the loading bay. But the bay is shut, and there are no other cars. If I didn't know better, I'd say no one was there." Brenton's dark blue eyes swept over their group again, his jaw tightening at whatever was going through his head. Azure was grateful when he kept his observations to himself and just nodded a "hello" to the others as they settled in behind Rus and Azure.

"Oh, they're there." Rus's hands were flexing at her sides, the brilliant green of her magic fluttering around her fingers like smoke as the whispers started up again. "This place is drenched in spirits."

"Anything useful?" Cagney asked, her eyes narrowing on the warehouse in question. It was tucked into the back corner of the little industrial park, the parking lot around it just busy enough to hide the group of magical folk on the outskirts holding an impromptu war council.

"Nothing yet. I might need to get closer." Rus tilted her

head to one side, like she was listening to someone whispering in her ear, her brows creased in concentration.

"Evander, the wards." Cagney turned back to where Greer had perched himself a little closer to Nesta than might otherwise be considered polite.

"Right." He gave a halfhearted salute and stepped away from the group to pace the perimeter of the industrial park. Azure watched him go for a moment before turning back to the others.

"It'll be nightfall soon," Cagney said. The whispers had gotten louder, but no one else seemed to hear them, and Azure wasn't sure why. "You'll have an easier time reaching out to anything here after that."

"That's also when they're more likely to try to move Aihuan," Nesta said. "With business hours over, there won't be any humans to see what they're up to."

Brenton grunted his begrudging agreement, his expression saying he wished he'd been the one to make that observation.

Maureen turned back to the group. "Cagney, you and I should go and get acquainted with the land and plants. I know it's cold but—"

"There are some scrubby bushes out front that might be cooperative." Cagney nodded to Maureen, walking past her to get a closer look at the plant life near the warehouse in question, with Maureen following behind her.

"Guess that just leaves us." Nesta laughed, clapping their hands first in front of them and then behind them as they rocked on their feet.

"Will the Ironport covens be upset when they find out we haven't checked in with them about this?" Fernando asked. He was looking around the parking lot, fidgeting, and jumping at even the smallest noises of traffic or squirrels.

"They'll be fine." Brenton snorted. "I've got some friends who are in leadership in Ironport. They'll just be happy we took care of this for them."

"Provided we don't make too much of a mess," Nesta piped up brightly. "But don't you worry about the politics, Nando, I've got it covered." They tapped their nose and winked at Fernando, which made the young man sputter and Brenton roll his eyes and mutter something that sounded like the word *flirt* under his breath.

Azure turned back to the too-quiet Rus, frowning. It wasn't like Rus to sit silent through a conversation. She always had something to say, whether it be snarky or playful, some witty anecdote to add. Her magic was swirling faster and faster around her wrists, creating a cyclone, her eyes glowing softly with the green light.

"Rus?" Azure asked. When no answer came, Azure reached for her wrist, only a little afraid that the magic would lash out at her in retaliation, but it didn't. It just wrapped up the length of her arm in greeting. "Icarus," she repeated.

Rus jerked, her fingers squeezing Azure's almost painfully, but she met Azure's eyes and looked to be listening for the first time in several minutes.

"Are you all right?"

"Uh, yeah, sorry. You were saying?" Rus offered her a hesitant smile.

"Are you all right?" Azure repeated, hoping to get an honest answer this time.

"Oh yeah, sure. Fit as a fiddle, me." Rus laughed, rubbing at the back of her neck. "It's just really umm . . . loud here. You know?" Azure didn't know. Only mediums knew how loud a place steeped in spirits could truly be, and after spending enough time with Rus, Azure had begun to thank the Goddess she too hadn't been born with the ability to speak to the dead. It was amazing Rus could concentrate at all with the constant noise. "I'm glad we didn't bring A-Ling with us; this would have been too much for her probably." She fiddled with the ends of her hoodie strings, her teeth biting at her bottom lip, clearly holding something back that Rus didn't think Azure should hear.

Just as Azure was about to open her mouth and press Rus to say whatever it was, Rus said, "Oh look, Sheriff Greer is back! What did you find, Sheriff Greer?" And the conversation was over.

Greer's eyebrow twitched at the use of his title, but he didn't say anything about it, just rejoined the group and gave his report. "Looks like they have catch-all wards for the most part. No surveillance magic would work in there. If any magical creature steps over the boundary, they hear about it. No offensive spells can be sent through the barrier. Yada, yada, yada. All standard fare."

"Except?" Nesta asked, seeming to sense that wasn't all.

"I was getting to it," Greer grumbled.

"Not quickly enough."

Greer scuffed his boots on the pavement and lifted his head just enough to fix Nesta with a glare through his lowered lids that made Nesta preen.

A knot had formed in Azure's stomach, and the only way it could escape was as an impatient "Well?"

"They've put up a warding circle against spirits." Greer shifted a little, his shoulders drawing up toward his ears.

"Motherfucker." Rus stomped her foot. The swirling cloud of green kicked up from a lazy spiral into a vicious tempest that threatened to engulf all of them in its fury. Brenton and Nesta took a step back. "Seriously?"

Greer nodded. He looked like he wanted to shrink away from the wave of Rus's magic too, but was too proud.

"What does that mean?" Nesta took another tentative

step from the swirling cyclone that had begun to lift Azure's hair and pick at the ends of Rus's hoodie strings.

"It means she can't use any corpses or spirits from outside to fight them. Unless we bring down the wards." It also meant they had essentially rendered Rus powerless. She was smart and resourceful, yes, but her greatest abilities had always come from asking the dead for help. And in a fight like the one they might be facing, she would want to fall back on it.

"They thought you'd be coming alone." Greer finally lifted his head, not looking at all bothered by the way Rus's magic seemed to be leaving stinging red marks on his cheeks as a slow, amused smirk tilted up one corner of his mouth.

"Well, they were wrong." Azure rubbed her thumb over Rus's knuckles, and the gentle pressure seemed to calm the raging magic as Rus let out a long, slow breath. "Show me where the edge of the boundary is so I can get a look inside, Evander."

Greer nodded, and she squeezed Rus's hand one more time before dropping it to follow him around the back of some of the buildings, through a patch of trees littered in beer bottles and plastic bags. Leftovers, very likely, from Ironport's teenage citizens looking for a place to drink and get high where their parents wouldn't find them.

"Should we try to take the wards down while we're here?" Greer moved almost silently through the underbrush, his steps practiced.

"No." Azure felt her lips twitch into something like a sneer. "I want them to know we're coming for them." She had little doubt Rus would feel the same way. She'd want to instill in Aihuan's captors the same fear and panic Aihuan probably felt.

A soft snort left Greer, and Azure could feel him watching her as they made their way to the invisible line of the wards. She felt it when they got close enough, her toes curling away from the foreign magic licking at her boots.

"You can't kill them for what they've done," Greer warned, crouching down to press his fingers into the dirt and browning pine needles. "Ironport might let us get away with coming here and taking care of this, but they won't let us get away with killing witches on their soil."

"Who said anything about killing them?" Azure closed her eyes, homing her focus on the softly thrumming magic. It wouldn't be easy to step over the line using her abilities; she'd have to concentrate.

"Please. I can tell how pissed you are about all this." Greer still wasn't looking at her, focusing all his attention on the wards. Likely to make sure they didn't react to Azure sending her consciousness through. But that was the thing about her magic—it was less about moving through the world, and more about moving in between the seconds. In between the tick and the tock. So long as she held her breath and let herself focus, no one would notice her. But he was right, she *was* pissed. She was fucking livid that someone had come onto Moondale soil, *her* family's land, and hurt someone she loved. How could she not be?

Azure didn't respond, just took in a deep breath in preparation for holding it.

"Anger can be useful, just don't—"

And then the whole world stopped. The soft hum of the wards on her skin, the buzz of insects in the trees, the sound of traffic from the street beyond . . . it all stopped. Azure turned to look at Greer, who was frozen in place, his mouth hanging open to say whatever inane bit of advice he was trying to impart.

She returned her attention to the wards. She could see it now, the barrier. It was a soft shimmer on the air, like a film had been put over the building in front of her, but it didn't stop her when she held her hand up to it and pushed through like a ghost. Rus had joked before that this was why they were so compatible—because Rus could talk to ghosts, and sometimes Azure was one. The memory brought a little smile to her lips, but she didn't let it break her focus.

Through the wall and into the big open warehouse space on the other side, Azure found a group of five witches frozen in their milling about. Two sitting at a card table, playing dominoes, another three on a couch that looked like they'd dragged it from the dumpster, watching a fuzzy TV screen. Azure frowned, her eyes narrowing when a couple of the faces came into sharper focus. Two of the people from Elwood & Co. who had been holding her up when Rus needed her most. They'd go first, she decided.

Aihuan was sitting in a chair off to the side of the couch, her little arms bound to the back of it, but she looked otherwise unharmed.

Azure must have made some noise, maybe a sigh of relief, because Aihuan's head jerked up, her lidded brown eyes widening. "Miss Az?"

Azure frowned, not sure how the little girl was seeing her. "Huaner, are you okay?"

Aihuan nodded, her eyes flicking around them for a moment in confusion when she realized that no one else in the room was moving. "What is this, Miss Az? What's happening?"

"I'm not exactly sure." There would be time to think about how Aihuan was seeing Azure later. "But I need you to be calm, all right, Huaner? Can you do that for me? Can you be calm?"

"Yeah, I can do that." Aihuan jerked her head in rapid agreement, her curly brown hair falling into her face. "Is Auntie Rus with you?"

"Not right now, but she's coming, sweetie, and so am I. We're going to be here soon, and when we get here, we're going to take you home. But I need you to be brave and calm for me. And I need you to try to stay out of the way when the magic starts flying."

"I can try. I'm not good at shield magic, not yet."

"That's okay. We'll have someone to help you with that." Azure offered her a kind smile, but already she could feel herself getting lightheaded from trying to speak while she held her breath. She was running out of air. If she didn't go soon, she'd drown. "I have to go now, Huaner. But I'll be back."

"Okay." Aihuan's face wrinkled up, but she didn't cry or scream or fight like so many children her age might, clearly used to following Rus's orders during scary situations. Azure sent up a silent prayer thanking the Goddess for that, and then she sucked in another breath, and she was back in her body.

"—do anything stupid," Greer finished whatever he'd been saying.

Azure took a step back from the barrier, brushing her sweating hands down the sides of her sweatpants as she sucked in another much-needed breath. Her lungs were screaming at her. She'd never gone in between time like that and spoken to someone. There had never been anyone to speak *to*.

"Are you even listening to me?"

"Let's go tell the others what we've found," Azure said, spinning on her heel to head back the way they'd come.

"Wait. Did you already—" Greer huffed. "Of course you did. You know I hate it when you do that."

Azure didn't answer him. She couldn't give less of a fuck that her ability annoyed him or anyone else. Not when she'd been able to use it to bring reassurance to Aihuan, and probably save all their asses.

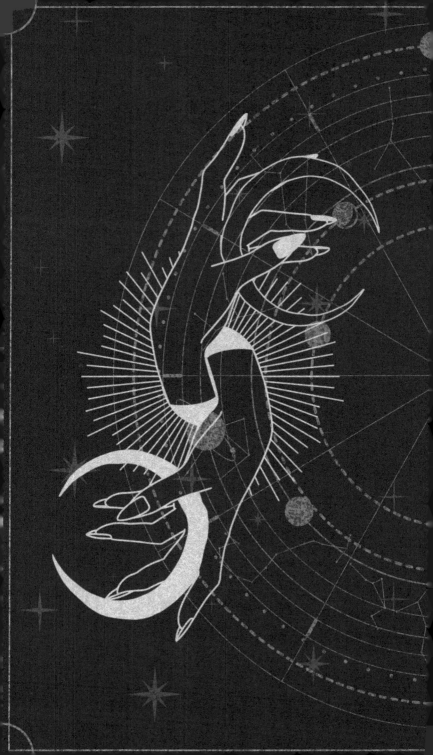

22

RUS DIDN'T LIKE this plan, not even a little bit. Logically, it was sound—and since it had come from Az's mouth, Rus was hard pressed to argue with it. Divide and conquer, as it were. The part where she went in the back entrance, the one closest to where they were holding Aihuan? Also very sound, she could see no fault in that. The bit she was struggling with—nay, hated—was the bit where she was separated from the people she actually *liked* in their motley crew—namely Az, Fernando, Nesta, and Cagney—and was instead teamed up with Brenton and Greer.

Az had dubbed them the retrieval team—which was arguably adorable, look at Az using her strategic know-how like a badass—and tasked them with exactly what the name said: retrieval. They were to go in, use the others as a distraction, get Aihuan, and get the fuck out of dodge. They were not to "engage"—whatever the fuck that meant—just get Aihuan out before hexes started flying. The question was, why? Was it because Rus couldn't use her magic the way she normally might? Unlikely. Az knew she was powerful in her own right, even without the dead to fall back on. Or was it because she was the one most apt to use deadly force? Probably. Not that Rus could blame Az for thinking that; she did kind of want to twist the witch hunters' heads off like bottle tops with her bare hands. But she could control herself, damn it! Or at least, she liked to *pretend* she could.

Az was under no such delusions, and thus Rus had been relegated to the retrieval team. She found herself creeping up to the door off the back where one too many people took their smoke breaks—seriously, why couldn't the cigarettes have killed these guys before they took her daughter?— with Brenton and Greer flanking her. They both were looking at her askance, their gazes a prickle on her skin, probably waiting on her to rip a corpse army out of the ground to take into battle with her. Joke's on them, there were no corpses, not for at least a five-mile radius around the shithole where the witch hunters had taken Aihuan. A fact that the witch hunters had probably taken into account when choosing their nefarious locale. Little did they know, Rus didn't *need bodies*.

"I'll go in first," Brenton said, bobbing on the toes of his well-worn boots.

Greer shot Rus a look that seemed to say, "Fire elementals, amirite?" and Rus had to nod in agreement for a moment before she realized she hated Greer's face, and then she promptly stopped.

They reached the edge of the wards a moment before the soft sheer wall of magic turned violent red and started to squeal like a car alarm. Energy surged from it, pushing them back a little, Rus's boots skidding in the dirt, before Greer could throw up a shield of his own to stop it.

"Fuck. They're early," Greer spat through the strain of

shoving back against their wards, and then they were all moving.

Brenton threw up a wall of flame that cut through the magic and barreled down the door with a heavy boot, Greer hot on his heels and Rus bringing up the rear.

Az had been right to want the witch hunters to know they were coming; what she hadn't been right about was the numbers. When Rus finally broke past the line of defense that was Brenton's fire and Greer's shield magic, she noticed not five but *seven* witch hunters in the room, making them almost even with the group she'd brought, and maybe more powerful as the witch hunters had the time and training to learn to fight with each other's magic, and her people did not. And they were already putting up a fight. Magic flew through the air, leaving it streaked with the smell of ozone, damp earth, and the metallic tang of blood.

But none of that mattered. Not a single bit of it mattered as someone shot what looked like a fucking lightning bolt right over her head and she had to duck to protect herself, because in the middle of the melee was Aihuan. Her eyes were wide and wild as she tried to look every direction at once, chubby little arms tied behind her back to a chair. She was so close and also so fucking far away. Rus wanted to run to her, to eat up the space between them, but she couldn't. There were people in the way, and magic flying the likes of which she'd never seen before.

"Greer, I need a shield," Rus said, her hands flexing at her sides. She wondered if there were any corpses buried *under* the industrial park that she might have missed. Probably not. But if there were, they'd have to rip themselves through concrete and cement to serve the witch who wanted them. It would take too long and would leave the bodies shredded. That was fine. There were other methods. *Worse* methods. Methods the witch hunters hadn't thought of.

Rus squinted, her eyes catching on the wisps of shadow and fog fluttering like a miasma over their heads. There was so much negative energy in the place, she was surprised it hadn't gone up like a powder keg as soon as Brenton fired the first shot.

"What are you talking about? You're behind a shield!" Greer grunted as another spell hit the barrier he'd thrown up between himself and Rus, and everyone else in the warehouse. Using Brenton like a battering ram, they were making slow progress across the big open space toward Aihuan. But they weren't moving fast enough, and for what Rus wanted to do, she couldn't take any chances with Aihuan getting caught in the crossfire.

"Not for me, you dipshit!" Rus hissed. The whispers were louder now; she knew a way to turn them into screams. But not before she knew Aihuan was safe. Not before she knew that the swirling vortex under her skin wouldn't suck Aihuan in too. It had the power to do that — she'd seen it rip the soul out of more than one living thing that had already been close to death. And since Aihuan had died once . . . well, she was closer to death than anything else in the room, except maybe Rus herself.

There was blood on the air already, metallic and sharp, the smell and energy of it feeding into the rage swirling around the witch hunters. They were running out of time. If Rus didn't control that energy, someone else might.

"Put one up around Huaner. You can do that, right? From here? You can put a ward up around her?" Was she pleading now? Was she that desperate that she would beg *Evander Greer* for a shield charm? Yes. Yes, she was. And she wasn't even ashamed to admit it. "That's what the Crimson Tide is good at, right?"

Greer frowned; his eyes flicked from her over to Aihuan still tied to the chair. The witch hunters had originally formed a wide circle around her to keep Rus and her squad from getting to her, but they were breaking ranks now, leaving gaps in the child's protection in an attempt to save their own asses. Rus's people would be careful, of course, but there was only so much they could do to pull their spells without completely succumbing to the witch hunters' magic. If Aihuan were behind a barrier, it would leave them open to attack without worrying about hurting her. "I won't be able to focus on trying to bring down their wards so you can use your magic."

"That's fine." Rus couldn't look at him, not for long stretches to see what he might be thinking, because her gaze was consistently drawn back to Aihuan looking scared and alone in a sea of unfamiliar faces. There were tears streaming down her cheeks, shimmering in the light. It was going to hurt more to do this without the use of corpses or outside, less personally invested spirits. But fuck it.

"I'll have to drop our shield," he warned further.

"Just do what the woman asked!" Brenton snapped, blocking a stray hex with a wall of fire that Rus distinctly remembered him not being able to conjure some ten years ago before she'd left Moondale. Fuck, things really had changed, hadn't they? No. No time to think about that. She needed to focus. Rus drew her athame from where she'd tucked it into her waistband at her back, the blade sharp and glinting in the low lights.

Greer looked between them again, unsure, but Rus wasn't paying him much mind. She was already pulling up the sleeve of her hoodie so the elastic pinched around her forearm.

"Well?" she asked, picking at the scab from the cut they'd used to track Aihuan with the point of the blade.

"Fine, but it's your head." Greer crouched to the ground, his hands pressing into the cement slab the warehouse was built upon, which had already started to crack under the weight of so much power. The shimmering wall of magic that separated them from the rest of the battle fell a moment after his knees hit the ground, but then there was a sound like air being pumped into a blow-up mattress, and a wall of light curved around Aihuan, cutting her off from everything else.

"How long do you need me to hold it?" Greer grunted under the pressure of the spell, sweat already forming on his temples. Brenton's wall of flame took another hit, pushing him backward till his heel braced itself on Greer's bent knee.

"Not long." Rus's voice went up with a smile as she finally pulled the scab loose and a small dribble of blood slid down her arm. It wouldn't be enough to raise an undead army from a cemetery, but it would be enough to stir up the restless spirits that surrounded the people of this room when added to the blood that was already beginning to coat the floor. "I'd suggest you two close your eyes."

"Close our eyes against what?" Brenton snapped, but he'd already squeezed his blue eyes shut, and Greer had followed suit without so much as a nod at the instruction.

"It's about to get really ugly in here." Rus chuckled darkly, and the whispers turned into screams. Voice upon voice shouting over one another, fighting to be heard, wanting to be acknowledged for their story. She'd have to do a cleansing ritual when all this was done—of the warehouse and herself to make sure nothing clung on—but for now she could give them what they wanted most: someone to listen. A conduit. "Yes. Yes. I hear you."

The voices swelled, so loud they blocked everything else out, and Rus slammed her own eyes shut in an attempt to limit the stimuli and maybe ward off the encroaching pressure of the spirits. It would do nothing for the headache that would follow that was sure to be killer, but it would help her focus for the moment. Taking in a deep breath, her nose already starting to bleed, she imagined the faces of the people she'd brought with her, whispering back to the spirits that they were not to be harmed. It was always a gamble—pissed off spirits were pissed off spirits and they didn't usually pull punches on any magical being in the vicinity, but a girl could hope.

"I'm not the one you want to yell at." Rus shook her head, clicking her tongue softly in reprimand. "Why don't you yell at *them*?" She opened her eyes just enough so she could point to the group of witch hunters the others had begun to corral into a corner away from Aihuan. They were trying to back themselves to a door, likely to escape to fight another day, *cowards*, but Cagney and Maureen had blocked it with some truly heinous-looking shrubs.

It took the spirits a moment to understand. Some of them were so old, and so long attached to the beings that had killed them, that they couldn't focus on what was being offered. But Rus pressed her thumb on the edge of the seeping cut on her arm, the blood swelling over a little more and dripping onto the cement, and then they came at her like a tidal wave.

She stumbled back under the tide, a dozen shrill voices, each clamoring to be heard over the others, each screaming to be louder than the next. There was nothing else besides the voices and the roiling undertow of spirits. Nothing but their anger, and their need for vengeance, and the betrayal that tasted like sour candy on her tongue.

When she opened her eyes a second later, after letting every single one of them into her veins, the room was still and silent, even as her vision swam like she was peering at everything through water. She took a moment to breathe through the strange buzz of too many minds in her head, and then she lifted her hand, let the magic that swam through her veins power the spirits, and sent them back from where they came, to the people who had taken their lives.

A hive of locusts descended on the witch hunters, and their faces distorted in terror. Rus had just enough time to see Az running toward her, shouting *something*, and then the world went black as her knees crumpled beneath her.

FOOLISH. Foolish and beautiful and brilliant. That's what Icarus Ashthorne was. Azure had always known it, but she didn't think she'd ever fully realized it until the moment she looked over and saw Rus glowing from the inside like she'd swallowed a galaxy, the light phosphorescent and seeping out of her every pore. And Goddess above, and below, Azure was so in love she felt as if she was drowning. Count that as another thing she'd always known but hadn't fully realized until that moment. Azure had spent years filling the void that was Icarus Ashthorne with other people, but no one could fill the Rus-shaped hole. Clearly, Violet was wrong, Azure would never be over *her*.

A spell whizzed past her, burning a hole into the sweatpants on her legs, and making her hiss where it landed against her thigh, but Azure hardly felt it.

"Rus!" The word crawled up her throat, a living, breathing thing, but it didn't reach Rus in time as the spirits feasted on what Rus offered them willingly. Her power. Her life force. Anything and everything they could ever need to manifest themselves and turn their ire on the people who had made them what they were. Rus was pointing a second later, giving them direction, and they rushed from her like a stampede and left the woman who had given them her power to crumple to the floor. Azure didn't know how she'd done it, but Rus had given the spirits enough direction, and enough force, to send them where she wanted them. To protect everyone else from their wrath. *That*. That was power. That was control. That was . . . Rus.

"Icarus!" Azure screamed again, and then she was running, her feet smacking against the floor, her heart pounding in her ears. A spell caught her in her arm, something sharp and nasty enough to leave her bleeding, but she was too busy skidding to her knees to catch Rus as she fell, cradling her head in her hands to keep it from smashing like a watermelon against the concrete floor.

"You fucking idiot," she rasped, pressing her forehead against Rus's. It took her a moment to hear anything past the slowing of her pulse now that she had Rus in her arms, but when she did, she heard the screams of horror from the witch hunters. Azure looked up from where she still cradled an unconscious Rus to see that the rest of their party had stopped in their attacks because the witch hunters were screaming and swiping at the phantoms, attacking each other in their attempts to get away. One of them smacked the other so hard that the man stumbled to the floor and knocked his head against it with a sickening crack. Another had pulled a knife from somewhere and was swiping wildly at the air, every now and again catching one of their comrades, the blood spurring the spirits into more of a frenzy.

"Call them off!" Brenton shouted where he'd ducked down to keep the spirits from turning on him. "Someone needs to call them off!"

"Where's Rus?" Nesta's voice trembled in horror as they

watched one of the female witch hunters begin to rip her own hair out in clumps, trying to get to the phantoms that had burrowed deep into her long tresses. "What the fuck happened to Rus?!"

"She passed out." Greer moved toward where Azure still knelt on the floor, holding one of the most precious things in the room to her chest, to look down on Rus.

"They're going to kill each other!" Cagney took a step toward the thrashing witch hunters but when one of the spirits turned to scream at her, she thought better of it and retreated.

Azure pulled Rus in closer to her chest, rocking a little, not sure what to do. She'd seen Rus stir up spirits countless times, but never like this. There was so much hatred and pain there, she didn't even know if Rus would be able to soothe them should she wake up. Even Fernando, who had been with Rus more recently, was hiding behind the others, seeming afraid for the spirits to see him.

"The cleansing verse," Rus croaked, her eyes still closed.

"What?" Azure leaned in closer, needing to be sure she heard her correctly.

"The Jade Waters cleansing verse. The one Carmine always made us sing while we were cleaning the kitchen after one of your baking sprees." Rus coughed. It sounded wet, but there would be time to worry about that later. "You know the one, Maureen."

Maureen frowned and her eyes flicked up to meet Azure's as if unsure. Azure nodded. She'd never heard of it being used that way, but if Rus said it would work, then it would. Rus had always sung it to the tune of the clean-up song they'd learned in elementary school, and just like then, Rus started humming the tune, the sound a little broken and choked, but it made Azure want to laugh.

Azure started singing to Rus's humming, and then

bobbed her head to it, encouraging Maureen to sing along. It took a couple of verses, but before long they had the whole room doing it, and the magic of a group of magical folks singing what was essentially a charm to ward off dust a little longer than was usual—along to the tune of a pre-school song—seemed to do the trick. The spirits slowed down, then stopped in their violence. The witch hunter's screams died into ragged sobs where they all collapsed onto the floor, magic spent, faces ashen. By the end of the second repeat, the spirits were dangling in the air, looking thoroughly dazed.

"There," Rus said with a little laugh, "that's the stuff. Greer, I believe you have some like . . . wibbly wobbly magic handcuffs." She spun her hands in the air above her chest, almost smacking Azure in the face with her erratic motions, and murmured a soft, "Sorry, love" before promptly passing out again.

"I can't believe we just sedated a bunch of ghosts with a housekeeping charm," Greer muttered sullenly as he held out a set of cuffs he'd pulled from his magic pocket to Brenton, and the two set about cuffing the witch hunters.

"Stranger things have happened." Nesta shrugged, but Azure had to agree with Greer—this was one of the strangest. Especially as she watched those ghosts drift closer to the ceiling like balloons let go of for just a second, never to be seen again.

"You should make the call in to Ironport's law enforcement," Maureen said, sitting down beside Azure so she could check Rus over, something Azure should probably have been doing. She was a little too distracted holding Rus close to her. She felt so *tiny*.

"Aye, aye, captain." Nesta gave a lazy salute and pulled their phone from their pocket as they stepped over the cracked cement and headed out the door to make the call.

"Let me have her." Maureen took the weight of Rus off of Azure's lap, in spite of Azure struggling to keep her there, and nodded over her shoulder to where Fernando was holding a sobbing Aihuan. "You should check on the little one. She's pretty shaken up."

"But Rus—"

"Will be fine in a bit. She's just drained herself. Let her rest, and check on her daughter. Huaner shouldn't see her like this." Maureen's words were gentle but firm, leaving no room for Azure to do anything other than rise and head over to where Fernando was whispering words of comfort to the sobbing child.

"Huaner?" Azure asked, crouching down in front of them.

The little girl startled, her head whipping around and her magic flaring up as if to protect her and Fernando. Strangely enough, it was the same color as Rus's, maybe a little paler, more toward pastel green than the glaring chartreuse of her mother's, but close enough. "Where's Auntie Rus?"

"She's just over there with my aunt." Azure tilted her head in their direction. "She'll be all right in a minute, Aunt Maureen says, we just have to let her rest."

Aihuan scrubbed at her face but bobbed her head in understanding. "Can I see her?"

"When she's awake again, of course you can see her. But right now, why don't you sit with me and your Uncle Nando and drink some water?" Azure took a bottle that Cagney had pulled from the vending machine, along with a chocolate bar, and cracked it open.

"And chocolate?" Aihuan perked up, taking a few hurried sips from the bottle of water, her eyes wide on the candy bar as Azure worked to unwrap it.

"And chocolate. This is a trick your Auntie Rus taught

me when we were little," Azure whispered, leaning in closer. "Whenever we had to face something big and scary, we always had a little chocolate to help us calm down and—"

"And to be brave!" Aihuan's little chest puffed out with pride, and she nearly spilled the water for how hard she was nodding her agreement. "Auntie Rus taught me that too. You knew Auntie Rus when she was little like me?" Aihuan had settled enough to sit down in Fernando's lap, taking the square of chocolate and biting off a piece to let it melt on her tongue as she talked around it. Azure didn't have it in her to chide her for speaking with her mouth full.

"Not quite as little as you." Azure smiled, taking another peek over at where Maureen seemed to be pushing some magic into Rus to speed along her recovery. "But pretty close. We were best friends when we were little."

"Can you see ghosts too?" Aihuan asked, her voice a whisper as her own gaze jerked nervously around at the gathered adults.

Azure frowned. Rus had said that Aihuan could see the future, not that she was a medium. But it made sense; Rus always said mediums were born with one foot in the grave —it was really beyond the veil, Azure had told her that multiple times, but Rus seemed to think *in the grave* sounded cooler—and Aihuan *had* died. So she'd stepped beyond the veil herself. Why wouldn't she have gotten some extra abilities for her trouble?

"Well?" Aihuan pressed, stuffing the rest of the square of chocolate into her mouth and smearing some of it on her cheek from where it had melted on her fingers before holding her hand out for more.

"No. I'm afraid I can't. I have the ability to see the present." Azure pulled a handkerchief out of what Rus called her "air pocket"—really just a temporal pocket of space where she was able to keep small things like hankies —and wiped Aihuan's face and hands.

"That's how you saw me!"

"Yes. That's how I saw you. You're very clever. Has anyone ever told you that?"

"Oh, all the time," Rus's voice still sounded like diamonds on glass, but when Azure turned around she was sitting up under her own power and had even let Maureen put a Band-Aid on her cut arm. "Right, little monster?"

"Auntie Rus!" Aihuan jumped up and ran past Azure, the candy forgotten, to fling herself at Rus. Rus caught her, nearly pitching them both to the floor if not for Maureen steadying her on her shoulder, but the smile that split her face was worth it.

"Thanks, Maureen." Rus buried her face in Aihuan's hair for a moment, breathing her in, seeming oblivious to everything else around them, and Azure felt like that weirdo peeping in through someone's living room windows from the sidewalk just watching them. So she turned away, rewrapped the candy bar, returned the hankie to the pocket, and stood to help finish cleaning up the mess they had made of the warehouse.

By the time what Rus had taken to calling "The Ironport Equivalent of Greer" showed up, the warehouse had been swept for lingering traces of magic, the witch hunters were lined up against one wall, and the only thing left to handle was the spirits still floating about on the ceiling.

"We're not doing anything about those, they're your problem," Sheriff Regan said, giving the phantoms a cursory glance. "We don't have a necromancer or a medium in Ironport."

"Not dealing with what?" Rus looked up to where she'd indicated and huffed so hard Azure could feel it through where their shoulders were pressed together. "Well"—she paused, looking down at the sleeping Aihuan in her arms, and shrugged—"fuck."

"We can deal with that," Greer volunteered, looking for all the world like a puppy who wanted a pat on the head. Azure glared at him until he turned to look at her with his brows raised.

"You shouldn't volunteer people's services without first consulting with them," Azure snarled.

Rus choked back a laugh at the reprimand. "Don't worry about it, Az, I can do it. I did stir them up, after all."

"You shouldn't have to."

Rus shrugged.

Azure resisted the urge to roll her eyes and turned back to Sheriff Regan. "It might take a couple of days. She's a little spent and needs some rest. Can you keep this area cordoned off until then?"

Greer scowled. "I'm sure that—Ouch! What the fuck, Cagney?"

"Yeah, we can do that." Sheriff Regan nodded, her lips pursed as she tried not to laugh at the now bickering Greer and Cagney. It sounded like Cagney had trod on his foot to get him to shut up, and Azure decided she was going to buy Cagney the best bulbs Maureen could find her come springtime. "Can I get your number though?" Sheriff Regan pulled out her phone and held it out to Rus. "We've got a few low-level hauntings in Ironport that could use some attention, and like I said, we don't have anyone."

"Sure. Az, would you get that? My hands are a little full." Rus held up Aihuan a little higher, laughing softly.

Azure took the phone, typed in Rus's number, and handed it back. She was tempted to give the sheriff her own instead—then at least she would be able to vet any jobs before they got to Rus—but she knew well enough not to overstep. She didn't want to push Rus away. Again.

"Right then, I think that's all from us. Did you have any questions for these guys?" Sheriff Regan gestured over her shoulder to where her men were marching the witch hunters out the front door.

Rus wavered for a minute, her brows creased, and then she shook her head. "No. I think I'm good."

Sheriff Regan nodded, and like that the witch hunters were towed away to be charged, and Azure and their little crew were left standing in an empty warehouse.

"Well, I'm fucking starved," Brenton said when the quiet stretched on for too long. "Who's up for pizza? I'm buying."

"Oh! Me!" Nesta jumped up from where they'd been slouched in one of the chairs.

Azure had just a second to ponder what pizza joints would be open this late before Rus freed one of her hands, moved it between them, and threaded their fingers together. She squeezed once, a silent *thank you* from when they were kids, and saying words like that were hard, then dropped it and turned to follow the others out the door like nothing at all had happened. Azure's palm tingled for the rest of the night.

24

THE CLEANSING RITUAL TO brush off any lingering traces of spirits required a bath (blessedly), and after what felt like weeks without one, Rus didn't have it in her to fight Az as she grabbed the basket that had mysteriously appeared on the floor of the pantry to start gathering ingredients. She could have done it herself. She wasn't that wrecked from what she'd done, especially not now that she had half of a pizza sitting heavy in her belly, but it was nice watching Az's long brown fingers flit over Rus's neatly organized stores. The pantry was perhaps the only organized place in the house, and that was only because she wanted the girls to be able to get to what they needed in case of an emergency.

Once the basket was loaded down with everything for the ritual—candles and herbs and flower petals—Az started up the steps without a word, not even giving Rus the option of taking the basket from her. With a shrug, Rus followed her up. The house was quiet around them, the girls staying across the street with Maureen and Carmine in case Rus accidentally brought something nasty home without realizing it. She doubted she had, but it wouldn't be the first time and after everything that had happened, she wasn't going to put the girls in danger like that.

When they reached the top of the steps, they found that the house had moved the clawfoot tub from Rus's bathroom to the middle of her bedroom. Rus took a moment to cock her head at it and then sighed a soft "thank you" to the house.

She tried not to think about the twisted hell that it had probably left her pipes in. The house could sort that out later.

"Does it always do things like that?" Az asked, setting down the basket next to the tub. She pulled the big piece of sidewalk chalk from the lot and started around the tub in a tight arc to draw out the protective circle.

"Yeah." Rus flopped unceremoniously onto the floor to begin sorting out the items they'd need, and she patted the floorboards affectionately. 157 Mourning Moore was a very good house, all things considered. It kept them safe. It told Rus when there was trouble. And it moved her bathtub without being prompted. So what if it occasionally grew a pastel coffee mug just to fuck with people? No place was perfect. "157 is a real peach like that."

"Will the water work here, or do I need to siphon it off from the sink in the other room?"

"Nah. If 157 put the tub there, the pipes'll work. Just remember to put a bit of—"

"Grave dirt in the bottom, yes, I remember, Rus." Az sounded annoyed. But then . . . when didn't she? And she was still there, helping Rus perform a ritual that she arguably could have done by herself without any real trouble. But Az had seemed to sense that Rus didn't want to be alone right now, not after everything, not when her magic was at its most vulnerable. It would have been better to have the girls within arm's reach, but again, she wasn't willing to risk their safety for her own comfort. There would be plenty of time for cuddles and reassurances after she was sure she was clean.

They worked in silence after that, marking out the four directional points and lighting candles at each, preparing the bath, burning incense . . . all the things that needed to be done before Rus got in. There was a moment of awkwardness as Az stared at the steaming tub, and Rus stared at her, before the house erected a screen in front of it that Rus could duck behind to maintain what limited modesty she had with a woman she'd been naked with every chance she got when they were younger. Az took the hint and turned her back on the screen, moving instead to lean up against one end of the trunk at the foot of the bed.

Shaking her head, Rus stepped behind the screen and stripped out of her clothes. The scent of ozone and rotting earth still clung to the material, and she wasn't sure if she'd ever get it out. No amount of Tide in the world could fight off the smell of vengeful spirits; Rus had learned that early on. Which was a real shame, because she'd loved that slightly tattered hoodie.

Once she was in the tub, she dunked herself under the water, holding her breath as she counted. One-one thousand, two-one thousand, three-one thousand . . . She waited for the feeling of her lungs screaming for air, and then a little beyond, before she came back up to suck in a deep breath that burned going down. Az had started humming something soft and soothing from where she sat on the other side of the screen, and it made the oil-slick sludge the dead left behind in her veins loosen all the more. It would take days to feel normal again, Rus knew that. But this was a good start. Maybe the best one she'd had in a while.

The water had cooled by the time she scrubbed the last traces from herself using the clean cotton-smelling soap, leaving her skin pink and her fingertips pruned. But Rus didn't want to get out, not yet, so she murmured a soft heating charm and turned to brace herself on the lip of the tub, looking out the window at Moondale in the distance.

"I hated it here, did you know that?" Rus asked into the quiet, half hoping Az wasn't still awake to hear it.

Az made a soft "Hm?" from the other side of the screen. *No such luck.*

"This place. Moondale," Rus clarified, dipping lower in the water till no more than her head was bobbing above the surface like a ghost. "It was never my home. My parents weren't from here, I know you know that, but I feel like you forget sometimes that I'm not from a Moondale family like you are. My blood doesn't run in the soil here like yours does." She didn't know why she was saying this. Was it meant to be an explanation for what she did? Was it meant to negate the fact that she'd left without so much as a goodbye? She knew it wouldn't.

"I don't forget," Az said, almost sounding offended at the insinuation that she could *ever* forget something about Icarus Ashthorne. And that—*that* broke her. Rus felt the tears running scorching trails down her cheeks into the tepid bath water.

"When I left"—she swallowed thickly to try to keep the sound of them out of her voice, but she knew Az would hear them, Az always heard them—"I spent the next decade or so trying to find one."

They were quiet for a moment, Rus scrubbing at her face and breathing through the choking sobs. She already knew where this conversation was headed; it might hurt more if she hadn't already made up her mind about what she needed to do. She'd come to the decision sitting in that fucking grease trap of a pizza joint Brenton picked out, Aihuan in her lap, Fernando and Cagney on either side of her, and Az sitting across from her. They'd had to push a bunch of the rickety two seaters together to make room for all of them, but the skeleton crew working the red-eye shift at Paul's Pizza Palace hadn't given a fuck.

"Did you?" Az's voice floated over the screen again, reminding Rus that they were having a conversation here — it was hard sometimes to stay in the present after letting that many passengers in — talking about the fact that Moondale wasn't home. That Rus had never really had a home. "Did you ever find it?"

"No." The word was a raw, jagged thing in her mouth for her to cut her teeth on. "I never did." She sucked in another breath, although by that point her lungs had started to burn again. "I don't think there's one out there for me."

And there it was: the truth. The thing Rus had never admitted to anyone else in her life, not even Az, not even when they'd been at their closest. That she didn't think she fit in this world. That she didn't think she ever would. That being born with one foot beyond the veil as she was had made her a stranger in her own life. Even still, she knew what she had to do next, and so she opened her mouth to do it. To seal her fate.

"But I —"

"That's why you have to make one," Az said at the same time, cutting off the words Rus had been prepared to stumble over with a tone so fervent and loaded with conviction that Rus felt the air hum with the magic of it. Because that had been the thing Az had never realized about herself and likely still hadn't — that Az held so much magic within herself. And not small magic either. Not housekeeping spells and temporal pockets; that was child's play. No. Az had the power to shape the world in her image with but a few words. If only she'd get out of her own fucking way long enough to do it. Maybe she finally was, Rus realized. "Build it, from the ground up. For yourself. For your girls."

Rus shifted, the water loud in the tub as the silt from the grave dirt at the bottom chafed her waterlogged skin. She grabbed the towel, getting ready to step from the tub, but then thought better of it. This wasn't a conversation she could have with Az when they were sitting face to face.

"It doesn't have to be in Moondale," Az mumbled, seeming suddenly cowed by Rus's silence, which was unforgivable. Rus let out a long breath, rubbing her wrinkled hands over her face. Fuck. She was in such deep shit if she stayed in Moondale, she could already tell. But . . . was there ever really a choice? No. There wasn't. Moondale wasn't going to give her one, as was her way. Just like the fucking Bermuda Triangle. "But you should let yourself—"

"It's going to be Moondale." *Where else could it be?* she didn't say. "The girls like it here." *I like it here.* "And we have the coffee shop, and the house now." *I'd miss you again, I missed you so much already, I don't want to miss you anymore.* "Plus, I can't think of any place safer for Huaner. She's a fucking lighthouse with that magic of hers."

"That's true." Az's tone had gone thoughtful. Rus could hear her clothing rustle as she nodded. They moved on from the heavy topics, letting Rus breathe for the first time since she'd made her choice hours, and a lifetime, ago. There would have to be more heavy discussions, an apology probably, but for now they could talk about logistics and avoid all that, like adults. "You'll have to start a coven, like we talked about, then the land will shield her like it does all Moondale witchlings."

"Right. You still got that paperwork?"

"It's downstairs on the kitchen table. We can look at it tomorrow after you've had some rest."

"Cool. Cool." Rus nodded, the water sloshing around her. Fuck, how many times was she going to wind up having serious discussions while she was in a bathtub? Two was already too many.

"What do you think you'll call it?"

"Fuck, I dunno. Something dramatic like Coven of the Dead or something."

"I think you should sleep on that."

Rus snorted a laugh. She might be a little punchy from exhaustion and magic strain. Az was right—she shouldn't look at the paperwork tonight. There was no telling what kind of bullshit she'd put down. "You're probably right."

"I usually am." Az sounded like she was smiling that smug bitch of a smile she tended to use when she wanted to rub her accomplishments in other people's faces. Rus loved that smile. She remembered kissing it off Az's face more than once when Az had won an argument and decided to be petty about it.

"Shut up and go get me some pajamas." Rus bent to unplug the tub, the water draining loudly in the too-quiet of a mostly empty house. "I'm going to sleep for a decade after all this shit is finally settled."

Az hummed her agreement, and Rus could hear her moving about the room, her steps light across the floorboards as she made her way over to the old wardrobe and pulled out clothes for Rus while Rus climbed out of the tub and started to dry off.

It was a nice sound. A homey sound.

Yup. She was royally fucked if she stayed in Moondale.

Too bad Moondale seemed unwilling to let Rus go now that she had her claws in her again.

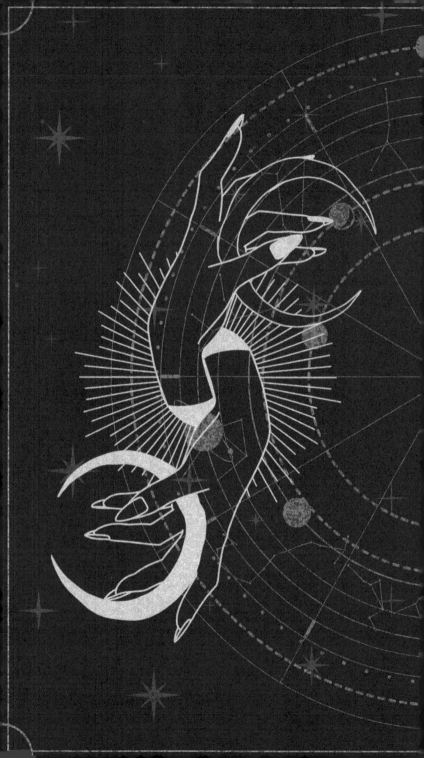

AZURE'S FINGERS tapped nervously at her sides. Rus's handwriting was abysmal. It hadn't gotten any better in the last decade, and Azure wanted nothing more than to reach out, snatch the pen away, and fill out the paperwork herself. Because of expedience and because of Rus's horrible handwriting, not because she was in a hurry to know that Rus wouldn't be going anywhere anytime soon. Certainly not that. She shook out her hands, loosening the ache that had started in her palms from holding herself too still for too long.

"There, that should do it," Rus said, straightening up with a proud tilt to her lips. She arched her back, stretching out her own aches and pains that Azure had begun to realize seemed to linger at all times. They'd have to do something about that later.

"What did you name it?" Meiling asked, reaching for the paperwork to get a look. "Not something stupid, I hope."

Rus snatched the packet away and fixed her daughter with a scowl. "I don't pick stupid names."

Meiling snorted. "Sure, you don't. Remember what you named your car in Hong Kong?"

"Cherry was a perfectly respectable name for a red car." Rus puffed her chest out in defense. "It's not my fault the car didn't seem to like it."

"I'm noticing that you aren't answering the question." One dark brow rose high on the teenager's face, her tone turning into something sassier than Azure thought she'd ever heard it.

It was funny how quickly the girls had settled back into normalcy. They showed up still wearing their pajamas from Carmine and Maureen's impromptu sleep over, and it was like the house let out a sigh, welcoming them back, and that was that. The girls didn't miss a beat going back to their rooms to make a mess of things and pulling too many dishes from the cabinets in the name of cooking breakfast. Rus hadn't said anything; she'd just smiled indulgently, watching Meiling overflow the pancake batter trying to make one enormous pancake out of all of it in the pan. Azure couldn't help but agree with the house. Things were better this way, even if she had enjoyed the quiet intimacy of the hours she'd had alone with Rus.

"I'm noticing you aren't answering the question," Rus repeated, her tone haughty and more than a little nasally.

Meiling huffed, crossing her arms over her chest in a truly impressive pout. "Well, if I'm going to be a part of it, it better be something cool."

"Who says you're invited? Hm?" Rus's eyes were alight with amusement. This was the most alive Azure had seen her in days, and Azure ached to be a part of their playful bickering, but she knew that wasn't her place. Not yet, at least. She and Rus had come to a careful truce the night before, and Azure felt they could build back up to where they'd been, given time. But right now, they were hardly even friends.

"Of course I'm invited! You can't have a coven with just you and Uncle Nando. Who ever heard of a coven with only two witches in it?" Meiling snatched the papers from Rus's suddenly slack grip to get a better look at them. But Azure wasn't really paying attention to what Meiling's expression said she thought about the name. She was looking at Rus instead, who had turned to look at her with a wide, worried gaze.

"Do you think it'll be a problem?" Rus's voice was tentative, her fingers twitching at her sides like she wished to reach out to Azure for reassurance. If she did, Azure would fall all over herself to give it to her, but Rus wouldn't. Not yet, anyway.

"I don't think Moondale will have a problem with it," Azure hedged. Moondale wanted Rus here. She wanted Rus and the girls to stay, and no matter what Rus had said into the dark morning quiet of her bedroom, Moondale had always been Rus's home. She belonged to this land as much was Azure did. Azure could feel it in her bones. She'd let Rus think otherwise, once upon a time, let her doubts fester without saying anything. She wouldn't make that same mistake again. "No matter what the board says, all that matters is if Moondale accepts your offering, and she will."

Rus's shoulders relaxed a little and she nodded, letting out a long, slow breath. "Right. I just have to get the board to sign off on the paperwork."

Azure wanted to say *fuck the board*. They could do the ritual without them. The ritual to start a coven and tie it to the land was older than Moondale herself, brought with the magical folk who had fled to Moondale to escape the oppression of the magical world in other places. The paperwork was just bureaucratic bullshit. In the end, it was the land that would decide.

"Coven of the Forgotten," Meiling read from the page she'd just reached toward the back of the packet.

"Yeah." Rus turned her attention back to her daughter, her smile falsely bright, covering up whatever nerves Azure had been unable to dispel with her words. "What do you think?"

"It's okay, I guess." Meiling shrugged, dropping the papers back onto the kitchen table. "It's not the worst name you've ever come up with."

"Oh, that's it!" Rus squawked, and that was the only warning Meiling got before her mother was lunging at her, fingers extended, reaching for her ribs and all those ticklish spots only a mother knows. Meiling squealed, skidding out of the kitchen on socked feet. Azure smiled, and she felt 157 Mourning Moore smile with her.

There would be time to repair what she and Rus had broken, now that Rus was staying in Moondale. If there was one thing Azure Elwood was, it was patient. She could wait.

THE CLEANSING RITUAL TO CLEAR OUT THE WAREHOUSE was easy enough; Rus could have done it in her sleep. But Az had insisted on going along, and it took too much energy to try to talk a stubborn Az out of something once she'd put her mind to it, so Rus had promptly given up. All she could hope was that Az had wanted to go along to spend more time with her, not to keep tabs on whatever nefarious thing she might do with the spirits still floating around the rafters like three-day-old birthday balloons. They'd even begun to look a little shriveled like the latex ones tended to get. Bobbing listlessly, but ultimately going nowhere.

After Az had dropped her back home, Rus had quickly changed back into her soft sweatpants and hoodie and gone to make herself some coffee. Dispelling spirits always left her with an all-over chill, and nothing helped quite like a big mug of coffee, a fuzzy blanket, and a snuggle on the couch with her girls to watch whatever movie they were currently obsessed with. The first time she'd done a job while they were living with her, it had been *Frozen*. And Rus still found herself humming that snowman's song sometimes while she waited for her body to heat back up to a temperature that would be deemed normal by medical standards.

With her mug finally chasing the blue away from her fingers, Rus headed through to the living room. She was just stepping onto the rug, her socked feet sinking into plush fibers, when she noticed it, her mug paused halfway to her lips. "A-Ling!"

"What?" Meiling called from where Rus had just seen her in the study. She was pretending to do her homework, but Rus had noticed the distinct shine of a phone screen reflecting glassily off her eyes. Normally, she'd have called Meiling out for such foolishness, but Meiling was ahead in her classes in spite of everything, and the last couple of weeks had been stressful enough without a fight with a teenager over her cell phone. None of them needed that bullshit right now.

"Why in the name of the three Goddesses do I have a lavender accent wall in my living room?" Rus lifted one hand to rub at the slowly forming headache behind her eyes. Fuck, she was too tired for this shit.

"A what?" Meiling poked her head around the corner to get a better look at what Rus was talking about. When she saw it, she grinned the grin of a teenager who thought they knew absolutely *everything* and was very amused by the adults who didn't seem to know *anything*. Goddess help her, Rus hated that grin. "Well. It's not the whole living room."

"Of course, it's not the whole living room. What do you think an accent wall is?"

Meiling shrugged, leaning against the doorframe.

Rus clicked her tongue then swiveled to eye the toddler sitting in the middle of the rug surrounded by dolls in various stages of undress. "Did you do this?" she asked, gesturing to the wall.

"Nope!" Aihuan said, popping the *p* before descending into a giggle fit.

Rubbing at her suddenly throbbing right eye, Rus let out another long sigh before narrowing her gaze on Meiling. "You?"

"Ew. No." Meiling scoffed. "I don't even like purple."

"Well, it wasn't Fernando!" Rus huffed, shuffling her feet over to the couch where she promptly sagged into the lush velvet cushions. It felt good to sit down, even if she had been riding in the car for hours already that day. "So who else could it be? No one else lives here!"

"Might just be the house," Meiling offered, turning on her heel to head back to the study. "Remember the mug?"

Rus glared after her, wondering when Fernando had told Meiling about the damn mug. Once the teenager had well and truly disappeared back into the office, Rus turned to kick her feet up onto the coffee table, sipping her coffee as she studied the wall. It wasn't really her vibe, but it did lend a homey quality to the room that it hadn't had before, and something about the color had her relaxing further into the cushions.

She supposed she'd just have to get used to the house on 157 Mourning Moore making decisions without consulting her. Maybe one day she'd understand why.

Today was not that day.

Tomorrow wasn't looking so good either.

glossary

While not required, this glossary is intended to offer further context to the world of Moondale.

pronunciation guide

- **Aihuan:** Aye-hoo-wahn
- **Meiling:** May-lee-ng
- **Jiejie:** Gee-ay-gee-ay

terms guide

Witch Terms

- **Athame:** A ceremonial blade used in ritual magic.
- **Aura:** An emanation surrounding the body of a living creature , regarded as an essential part of the individual.
- **Covenless:** A witch who does not belong to a formal coven.

- **Familiars:** A living creature (traditionally a cat) attending and obeying a witch.
- **Moonmother:** A witch assigned by a child's parents to take responsibility for the child in the event the parents are unable.
- **Poppet:** A small figure or doll used in sorcery or witchcraft.

Chinese Terms Guide

- **Jiejie:** A familiar way to refer to an older sister or older female friend, used by someone substantially younger.
- **Niang:** Mama
- **Baba:** Papa
- **A-:** Familiar diminunitive
- **-Er:** A word for "child", added to a name to express affection.

board of magic files

Circle of Jade Waters
WITCHES

best known for being scholars

Elder: Carmine Elwood

Members:

- Carmine Elwood
- Maureen Beecher
- Violet Elwood
- Taryn Elwood
- Azure Elwood
- Indigo Elwood

Circle of the Silver Flame
WITCHES

best known for being weapons & wand makers

Elder: Brant Ironwood

Members:

- Brant Ironwood
- Brenton Ironwood
- Phyre Ironwood

Circle of the Crimson Tide
WITCHES
best known for security & ward work

Elder: Cliantha Greer

Members:

- Cliantha Greer
- Evander Greer

Clan of Crescentia
FAIRIES - Cupids
best known for their skills in matchmaking

Elder: Enfys Snowthorn

Members:

- Nesta Holyore
- Dillan Holyore

<u>Grove of Elderwood</u>
DRUIDS
best known for their agricultural skills

Elder: Gilroy Herne

Members:

- Gilroy Herne
- Cagney Cashel

about lou wilham

Born and raised in a small town near the Chesapeake Bay, Lou Wilham grew up on a steady diet of fiction, arts and crafts, and Old Bay. After years of absorbing everything, there was to absorb of fiction, fantasy, and sci-fi she's left with a serious writing/drawing habit that just won't quit. These days, she spends much of her time writing, drawing, and chasing a very short Basset Hound named Sherlock.

When not, daydreaming up new characters to write and draw she can be found crocheting, making cute bookmarks, and binge-watching whatever happens to catch her eye.

Learn more about Lou and her future projects on her website: http://louinprogress.com/ or join her mailing list at: http://subscribepage.com/mailermailer

facebook.com/LouWilham
instagram.com/lou.wilham

also by lou wilham

Sneak Peek!

continue reading for a sneak peek of Witches of Moondale
Book Two, The Ghost of Hexes Past

The Hanged Man

the Ghost of Hexes Past

Witches of Moondale: Book Two

Lou Wilham

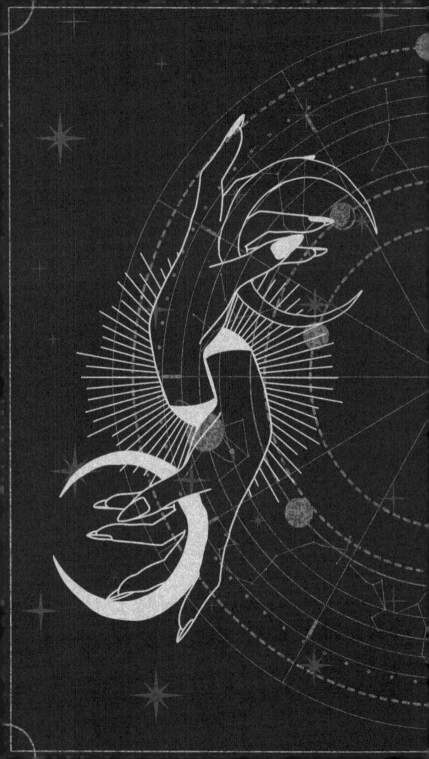

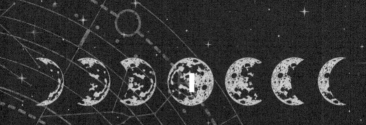

1

IT HAD BEEN a month and a half.

Six long weeks of petitioning and politicking and ass kissing.

Forty-two days of Azure racking her brain to get what they needed out of the Board of Magic. Of doing everything she'd always vowed she wouldn't, everything she hated, all for the woman that she loved. Because Rus deserved to have a home for herself and for her girls. She deserved to be happy, whole, and complete. And because this was the only way to keep Aihuan safe. Azure would be damned if she'd let a little thing like the fact that she hated talking to people ruin what Rus and her girls could have in Moondale.

So she'd swallowed down all of the bitchy things she wanted to say to the Board of Magic, pulled on a semi-neutral expression, and gotten things done.

The paperwork had been the easy part. Anyone could petition for the right to start their own coven in Moondale, Rus had joked about it once or twice when she'd been not more than ten. Laughing, and saying that when she grew up, she was going to marry Azure, and they would form their own coven, with their own rules. Azure supposed not much had changed really, she had been fool enough to want that—even then, even now.

The hard part had come when the Board of Magic had started to quote unquote *consider*, Rus's proposal. There hadn't been so much in-fighting amongst the elders, aunt Carmine said, since before her own father had been the Jade Waters elder. Many wanted to dismiss the application out of hand, but Azure had shown up to every meeting—closed door or not—and made a nuisance of herself until they had at least agreed to meet with Rus about it. It wasn't much, but she considered it a win. A tiny victory in a battle that might be otherwise full of defeats.

So that evening, Azure had dressed appropriately for the meeting, a long pale pink skirt with a crisp white button down tucked into it, and a felt pointed hat perched firmly on her head. Then she'd gone off to the board building, fully expecting to meet Rus there.

A mistake, she realized some minutes later, when the meeting had begun and she was sitting in her seat, listening to Brant Ironwood drone on and on through the minutes from the last meeting, with an empty chair beside her. The watch on her wrist ticked away, and a quick glance down at it told her that Rus was quickly approaching the fifteen-minute mark of being late.

Fuck.

Rus was notorious for being tardy to *everything*. But this was important, and Azure had convinced herself that Rus knew that, would respect that. Goddess, she was such an idiot. One would think that she would know better by now. One would be wrong. Still, she wasn't going to let all of her hard work go to waste. The girls needed the land of

Moondale to protect them, and while simply joining a coven would be easier, Azure knew that was a non-option. For more reasons than one. So, if Rus wasn't there to state her case, Azure would simply have to do it for her.

"The board will now hear the case for the *Coven of the Forgotten*," Brant said in a nasally, knowing tone, his eyes almost gleaming beneath the yellowed fluorescents, as he sneered around the name Rus had chosen for her coven. His gaze flicked back down to the piece of paper in front of him, as if checking to make sure that he was reading it correctly. An act that made Azure grind her teeth. "We call upon the petitioner, Icarus Ashthorne."

Everyone there could see that Rus was not in attendance. Brant had likely planned this. Made sure that it was the first thing on the agenda, so the woman who tended to be late for things would miss it. Maybe he — and the others against Rus — had thought that no one else would fight for her. One glance at Aunt Carmine who was looking thoroughly annoyed with Brant's antics told Azure all she needed to know of that. If he weren't an elder, and Azure wasn't trying to get him to do what she wanted, she likely would have called him out on it. But she needed the elders in a somewhat amiable mood, and getting into a shouting match with Brant Ironwood wouldn't ensure that.

"Icarus Ashthorne? Is Icarus Ashthorne in attendance?" Brant looked around, his dark eyes slightly lidded, a twitch of his lips betraying him, the absolute bastard. The crowd of Moondale folk collectively shifted in their creaking fold-up chairs, either uncomfortable with the obvious ploy, or looking for Rus. Azure wondered idly if she could get away with hexing Brant. Not a big one. Just a teeny tiny hex. One of inconvenience. Like he would forevermore forget about his freshly brewed coffee until it was lukewarm and thus disgusting to drink. *No sense in chancing it.*

Greer shifted beside Azure, his posture rigid. If Azure didn't know any better, she'd say he looked like he wanted to stall for Rus. Rus would get a kick out of that. Her own nemesis trying to help her. Silliness, in Azure's mind, because Greer hadn't been able to hide from *her* how he adored Rus's daughters. How he took every excuse given to stop by and make sure they were doing all right, how Aihuan had taken to calling him *Uncle Vander*. He was a softy, when a person got right down to it, but Azure wasn't going to say as much out loud, lest it draw too much attention to it and make him change. Or, Goddess forbid, make Rus realize what an absolute nitwit she was half the time.

Azure wiped her sweating palms on her skirt, and willed her heart to stop leaping into her throat. She needed to be calm when she did this. She needed to have a level head. She needed to not leap to her feet like an over-eager witchling.

"Well," Brant said, victory lining his tone, "since Icarus Ashthorne has not seen fit to join us, I suppose we can just—"

"I will speak for the Coven of the Forgotten." Azure leaped to her feet *exactly* like an over-eager witchling. Fucking damn it. Would Icarus Ashthorne ever cease to make her look like an idiot? Probably not. Anger simmered low under Azure's skin. She shouldn't have to do this for Rus. Rus knew how important this was, what was at stake here. Rus had promised she would do everything she could to make this work. Rus should *be* here. Inhaling deeply, Azure willed the oxygen to slow the racing of her pulse, and hopefully keep her voice even. Brant would look for any weakness he could find, and Azure needed to offer none.

"You?" Brant asked. He had leaned back in his chair, a king on his throne surveying a particularly lowly subject.

Azure prayed to the Goddess that his familiar threw up a hairball in his shoes next time it had the chance. Maybe she'd have a chat with Lizzie about how best to make that happen. That thought alone was enough to calm her to a point. Make the heat recede from where it had threatened to darken her cheeks in something that might be mistaken as shame. "As a member of the Elwood family, and the Circle of Jade Waters, I don't think that—"

"There is no rule that states that a witch from a more established coven can't sponsor a fledgling clan or coven." Her heart pounded in her throat, threatening to choke off her words, she swallowed around it, sucking down another breath. *Slow and steady, Azure. You've got this.* Or at least she hoped so. She'd been practicing it enough. So much so that Indigo was quite sick of hearing this little speech. Not that he'd ever say as much, he was too good for that. But Azure had seen it on his face the last time she had rehearsed it, her baby brother was reaching his limit.

"In fact," she continued, licking her lips and resisting the urge to blanch at the feel of waxy lipstick coating them. This was the absolute last time she let Aunt Maureen help her get ready for a stressful day. "In the year 1789, a fledgling coven known as The Silver Flame was established under the sponsorship of one Irving Elwood of the Circle of Jade Waters."

Brant's eye started to twitch with annoyance, but he pursed his lips to hold back whatever words crossed his mind. Probably for the best. Azure's skin prickled with every gaze in the room. Greer cleared his throat behind her, and she wondered if it were to fill the sucking void of silence left behind while everyone in the room waited for the other shoe to drop, or if he were simply hiding a laugh. She'd have to ask later.

"So, it would seem to me, that an Elwood of the Circle

of Jade Waters is the perfect person to sponsor an up and coming coven." Azure's fingers tapped at her sides, and she resisted the urge to tighten them into fists around the fabric of her skirt. All it would do was wrinkle it. Brant's gaze jerked down to the subtle movement, clocking it for the fidgeting that it was, but Azure lifted her chin, daring him to say anything. When another minute ticked away loudly on the clock on the wall, Azure realized that he was going to save that weakness for later, and all she could hope was that her next words would be the nail in the coffin of his limited arguments. "After all, where would Elder Ironwood and his coven be if not for the sponsorship of the Elwoods?"

The twitching of Brant's eye increased in speed and strength to a satisfying degree that almost had Azure smirking. She thought she heard Greer choking back another chortle, but she couldn't rip her gaze away from Brant. It was like staring down a beast, if she looked away first, she'd be considered lesser, vulnerable. And Azure was neither.

"Very eloquently put," Cliantha Greer said, breaking the stalemate and drawing everyone's attention to her. A smile had split her slightly wrinkled face, making her crows-feet more pronounced, but she didn't look happy about this. None of them would be, Azure wasn't fool enough to think that just because she'd leaped over this particular hurdle the race was done. For appearance's sake, they would hold the hearing. They would let her and Rus state their case, dig their own graves. But Azure knew until she had thought of something to use as leverage, it would mostly be a farce. She was hopeful, not stupid. "As that is the case, you are welcome to act as sponsor and spokesperson for the Coven of the Forgotten once you have filled out the required paperwork. Until that time, I motion that we table this disc—"

"I have already submitted the paperwork. If you will turn to page five of the submission packet you will see that under sponsor, I'm listed. My sponsorship approved by my coven's elders." Was it wise to continue to cut off the elders? No. Azure knew that. But they couldn't wait another month for the probationary period to begin. Another month and they would be in the depths of winter, approaching the solstice. They could do rituals, of course, to protect against the ever shortening days and the thinning veil, but nothing would protect Rus and her girls quite like Moondale herself. Azure wasn't taking any chances. "As that is the case, I think we can move forward."

"I see," Cliantha practically huffed the words, annoyed by Azure's foresight. Good. Let them be annoyed. Let them realize that they weren't going to get one over on Azure or Rus.

Azure ducked her head, hoping to hide the smug twitch of her lips. "Do I have your permission to continue, Elder Greer?"

"Please do." Cliantha flapped her wrist at Azure, dismissive, and irritated. Let her. All Azure had to convince them of today was that there was no reason beyond their own biases that they could cite to dismiss Rus's application out of hand. It sounded easy. It would be anything but.

"Thank you." Biting at the corner of her lip, Azure lifted her head again to look at the Board of Magic as a whole. They weren't all in attendance, the elder from the Grove of Elderwood was missing due to the druid hibernation season, but the remaining nine looked far from moved by her pleas. They would not be easy to convince. The werewolf elder from the Chesapeake Pack looked particularly grumpy to be giving up her hunting time for this conversation. There was nothing Azure could do about that. "Icarus Ashthorne and I would like to petition for the right to start a new coven in Moondale. A place for the folk like herself, who find themselves outside of the usual clans, packs, and covens of Moondale."

"A place for necromancers, you mean." The elder from the Clan of the Emerald Forge, a slight man named Dhiren leaned forward, his glowing eyes cutting into Azure like a knife. It had always been amazing to Rus, Azure knew, how ten beings so different in power, and temperament could agree on one thing to the point of blind ignorance: necromancy was evil. Even a Djinni like Dhiren who had arguably done far worse before settling in Moondale, couldn't think beyond his prejudices.

"That is not what I said." Her tone was impassive, but Azure could feel a growl growing in her chest. She cleared her throat to push it away if just for the moment.

"But that is what you *meant*," Dhiren hissed, leaning further forward onto the table, his fingers heating so much that Azure could hear the laminate of the table sizzling, leaving behind a mark of his anger that would be permanent.

"No. It's not." Azure squared her shoulders. "If you review the packet again, you will see that the only necromancer listed under the coven roster is Icarus Asthorne. Fernando Perez's specialty is kitchen magic, while the two children have not chosen their designations yet."

"We have not accepted a new clan or coven into the Moondale system since 1790, as you so kindly pointed out," an elven woman named Yaereene, the elder of the Clan of the Unseen Moon, pointed out, and Azure almost winced. She knew that would be a sticking point for them, it always was with the Board of Magic. They liked to say that this is how things had always been done, and thus saw no reason to change them now. It was why Rus had met so much push back when she'd begun experimenting with technology back in the late 90s. *Old goats, stuck in their ways.* "Why should we accept a new one now? It seems to me that ten clans is more than plenty for our little town."

It was an excellent point, one that Azure hadn't really come up with an argument against just yet, other than the fact that Rus didn't want to join one of the existing covens, *couldn't* join one of the existing covens. She didn't feel safe with them, and she knew that their old ways would limit her abilities, and the growth of her girls who shared those abilities. Azure licked her lips again, her mouth suddenly dry. "Times have changed, Elder Yaereene. The traditional covens can be stifling in the way that they see the world. Icarus brings a fresh perspective to magic and the way it interacts with technology, and other such advancements. Her insight will only benefit the magical community of Moondale."

The hall fell silent for a moment, all of the elders processing the implications of this statement. Likely all thinking of how their particular clan could benefit from Rus's unique genius. Azure had been counting on that. Their greed had reared its head when Aihuan's power had been exposed, why not use it against them now?

"That being the case," a thready voice said, and all eyes shifted to the Elder of the Ladies of Nimue. She was the oldest being on the board of magic. Old enough that there was some rumor that maybe she had been one of the founding women of Moondale, but there was little proof of that. Nixie Virnan was a tiny woman of unknown origin. Some people thought she was a selkie, others a water sprite, but one thing was for sure, no one had done more to keep the delicate ecosystem of the bay from collapsing than Nixie

Virnan had. Azure had always respected her, wanted to be like her one day. Now, with those keen eyes boring into her, Azure felt her stomach fall out through her feet. Something was coming. Something bad. "If Miss Ashthorne is so very serious about starting her own coven, then where is she?"

Fuck.

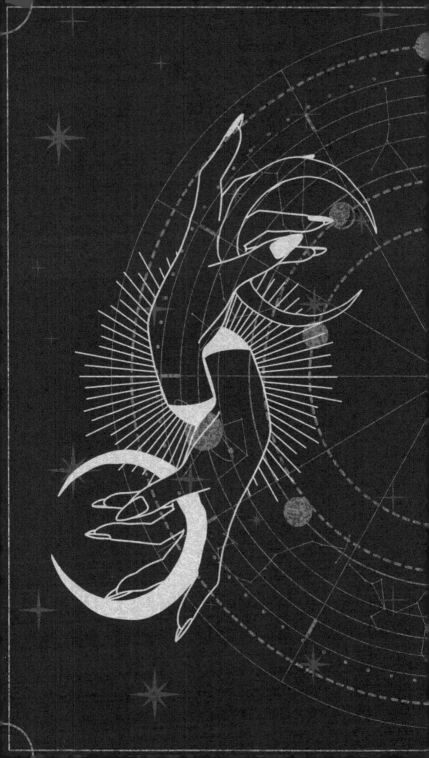

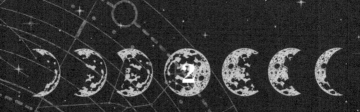

2

RUS HITCHED her bag further up her shoulder and checked the address Sheriff Regan had sent her for the fifth time. The light of her phone burned her eyes in the dark of a dead streetlight. It had been on before she'd walked up the sidewalk to it, but had flickered off almost immediately after she'd stepped beneath it. Usually a bad sign when one was approaching a building that was supposedly haunted.

Huffing out a breath, Rus scrubbed at her face. The surly woman had said nothing about an entire fucking apartment building. Rus's fingers twitched around the scuffed case of her phone, the urge to text back and tell Sheriff Regan that this was the last job she'd be doing for her so strong that Rus had to physically shove her phone into the bottom of her bag to keep from sending the message. It wasn't that she needed the money, although Aihuan went through clothes faster than a crow through bird seed—the perks of a growing toddler. It was just that Rus didn't have it in her to let a spirit languish, and languishing the spirits of Mirror Lake Park Apartments were.

Spirits plural.

Rus inhaled deeply, the cold November air getting caught in her lungs and threatening to send her into a coughing fit as she focused on the energy emanating from the building at the end of the sidewalk.

Three, at the minimum would be her guess.

Sheriff Regan had said it was haunted, but she hadn't done a headcount. Likely because she couldn't, not without a medium present or the use of some other apparatus to speak to spirits. And even those weren't always accurate as very often the spirits wound up trying to talk over each other and just mucking up the works. Pinching the bridge of her nose, Rus nodded to herself, and took the last few steps up to the front door without so much as a glance over her shoulder.

With one final prayer to the Goddess that none of the spirits inside would be combative, Rus turned the key in the lock, and pushed through. The front door squealed on its hinges, letting anyone within a mile of the place know that someone had entered. Not that it would have mattered, Rus wasn't exactly trying to hide. The spirits would know she was there whether she wanted them to or not, trying to be sneaky would just waste time.

"If anyone is here," Rus called into the cavernous dark of the empty building, "show yourselves."

Her voice echoed back to her with no furniture or carpeting to muffle the sound in the main lobby. It wasn't a terribly large apartment building, only about ten units. But that didn't mean it would make for a quick clean up. Not if the spirits proved reluctant.

A chill ran up Rus's spine, and something small and glowing shifted out of the corner of her eye. When she turned her head to look, it was gone.

"Of course they wouldn't make it that easy," Rus huffed,

tucking her chin down into her scarf to hide her neck from the cool air of the empty building. She wondered idly if it were because they had turned the heat off, or if it were the shades that lingered, and made a note to ask Sheriff Regan. The owner didn't need burst pipes on top of the ghosts.

Another quick glance around the empty lobby turned up nothing. Rus shook out her hands, and pulled a jar of salt from her bag. Then turned to crouch and sprinkle a thin line across the threshold of the front door. Not that she actually thought the spirits would try to leave the building, but it paid to be prepared. She didn't exactly have time to be chasing them all around the grounds, so if she could corner them in one room or apartment, that's what she'd do.

"I wish I'd brought Nando with me." Things would be easier if she had. He at least understood the process of all of this, and having another set of hands to block off potential exits would definitely make things go faster. But someone needed to watch the kids, and everyone else was either working or planning to be at the board meeting later.

With that done, Rus sat down her bag, and dug around in it until she pulled a little pendant from one of the pockets. It shone bright in the security lights of the building, reflecting their yellow glare in a golden sheen. Rus weighed it in her hand for a moment, considering her options. Az would be absolutely livid if she found out Rus hadn't used it, especially after she'd put so much effort into designing it for Rus. It was silver, forged in Phyre's workshop, and inscribed with the tidy characters of one of Az's protective talismans. There had been a small tiff over whether Rus needed it or not before Az had obstinately put it in with the rest of her exorcism kit, all while maintaining eye contact with Rus and not saying a single fucking word. Because that's the kind of bitch Az was. Goddess she was hot when she had a mind to be. She was also hot when she didn't have a mind to be, but that was neither here nor there.

Focus. Rus huffed a breath. *Fuck it*. She didn't have time to jump through all the extra hoops that wearing the talisman would incur. She was already probably going to be late for the Board of Magic meeting, and that was unacceptable. Stuffing the pendant back down into the pocket, she rose to her feet, squared her shoulders, and did the one thing she knew Az didn't want her to do. Stepped through the veil for the first time since they'd saved Aihuan.

The world on the other side was colder, and darker. All sounds and colors dull and muted by the barrier between the living and the dead. Like slipping under the surface of murky bay water, and listening to the sounds of life from above. It took her eyes a moment to adjust, but once they had she could see the trails left behind by the spirits that lingered in the space. Their lines thin, and fading, a wake from a boat, but there just the same.

Her bag rattled against her side as she took the stairs two at a time, following the thin blue line left behind by whatever Rus had seen out of the corner of her eye. If she had to guess, it was a relatively young spirit, both in length of time it had been attached to the property, and in age of the being before it had passed—a thought that made her heart squeeze a little in her chest. Human, probably.

"Come out come out wherever you are," Rus whispered into the murky darkness as she pushed through the door into the corridor of the second floor. A name would make this whole thing much easier, but as Sheriff Regan hadn't even known there were three spirits, and Rus hadn't had time to do her own research because she'd been so busy dealing with the Board of Magic. . . Well, she'd just have to make due with her other methods.

Bright green magic lingered around her wrists, whispering into the dark, and lighting the way as she stepped into an apartment down the end of the hall. In the corner of the front room she found the spirit from the lobby, a slight little thing made all the smaller by the fact that they were curled around their knees, shaking like a leaf.

"Hey," Rus murmured soft, and soothing, holding up her hands to show that she was unarmed.

The little spirit squeaked, jerking at the sound, and their trembling intensified. They peeked up at Rus from behind their knobby knees with wide, glassy eyes. Rus crouched to set her bag down, the weight of it making no sound on the floor in the space beyond the veil. Then she pressed forward, her hands still held in front of her, palms out.

"It's all right. I'm not here to hurt you. You don't need to be scared of me." The tone of her words remained a calm rumble in her chest, the same tone she used with Aihuan or Meiling when they got scared.

"You— You can see me?" There was a hopeful note to those words as they floated through the air. Like they were used to not being seen. Like maybe they had tried to make their presence known, and been ignored. Poor kid.

"I can see you." Rus nodded slowly, taking another careful step toward where the little spirit was huddled on the floor. "My name's Rus. And I'm here to help you."

"Help me how?" The spirit cocked its head, bird like and confused. Poor thing might not even know they were dead. They didn't sometimes. Sometimes that was the source of a haunting. It was sad, but also usually easy enough to correct, and get them to leave. Oh, to have them all be that simple.

"Help you move on, I suppose." Rus stopped just in

front of the spirit, and sat down, crossing her legs into a lotus pose in front of her. "You know you can't stay here, right?"

"Why not?"

"Because you don't belong here anymore." Rus'd had this conversation enough times to know that it could go one of a handful of ways. The truth was never something people wanted to face, especially when it didn't fit a person's internal narrative. And spirits, whether the living wanted to believe it or not, were just people. Lost. Distressed. Sad. Dead. But people nonetheless. "Why don't you tell me what happened to you?"

"I don't remember." The spirit frowned, but they were starting to unfurl. Their small hands no longer as tight around their forearms where they used them to hold their knees to their chest. Now that they had untucked their face, Rus could get a better gauge on how old they were. Late teens, early twenties. Likely this had been their first time away from home, their first place all their own. They had so much life ahead of them, no wonder they had clung to this place. She hoped they decided to reincarnate, for another go at it.

"All right." That would make things harder, but not impossible. "Can you tell me your name?"

The spirit opened its mouth, a black hole that looked like a scream and a swirling vortex of nothingness all rolled into one. Their eyes became the same nothingness, mirroring its mouth, and if Rus hadn't seen this a million times she might have screamed from the sight of it. A normal person probably would have. Good thing Rus wasn't normal. A moment later the spirit's face was back to looking like a scared human, and they shook their head, pouting a little.

"That's okay too." Rus offered the spirit a soft smile, and a wink. "What would you like to be called?"

"I always liked the name Holly." They grinned, their eyes glittering a little more in the softness of the security lights filtering in through the veil. "Like holly jolly Christmas."

"That's a pretty name," Rus murmured. "Do you know you're dead, Holly?"

"I—" Holly stopped, their cheeks puffing out in annoyance for a moment as they thought about Rus's words. They looked like they wanted to argue, tell her that she was wrong, and to leave them alone. But then they deflated, and nodded. "Yes, I do know that."

A relieved breath left Rus, her shoulders relaxing a little. "Good. That's good. Now let's try again, can you tell me what happened to you?"

"I can't. I don't remember. I just . . . I woke up like this." *Oof, that's the worst.* Holly's legs fell to the sides, revealing more of them. They had a stain on their torso that might have been blood, or something else, but Rus didn't let her eyes linger on it. She didn't want to upset Holly any more than she had to.

"Let's try a different question." Brushing at the tip of her nose, Rus tilted her head to one side, and went for a different tactic. "Do you know why you stayed?"

This had Holly blinking for a moment, their mouth going wide and hollow again, their face shifting into the terrifying rictus once more. Goddess, Rus wished they'd stop doing that. It wasn't scary so much as it was annoying as the seconds slipped away. Az was going to kill her for being late. And there were still two more spirits to contend with. She wondered how pissed Sheriff Regan would be if Rus told her she'd have to come back to finish the job.

Probably very pissed. Rus didn't think she wanted to see that side of Sheriff Regan.

The minutes ticked by in a crawl.

One.

Two.

Five whole minutes before Holly's face cleared again, and they shook their head. "No. I don't know why I stayed."

"Then don't you think maybe it's time you left?" Rus asked. She sent up a silent prayer to the Goddess that this would be enough to convince Holly to leave. It wasn't usually that simple, but sometimes Rus got lucky. She held out her hand, her magic flittering around it in a soft, throbbing light.

"Will it hurt?" Holly stared down at the outstretched palm, their own fisting in their lap.

"No, sweetie, it won't hurt." Rus shook her head. She didn't know for sure, of course, because she'd never been on the receiving end, but she'd never had any complaints. And she had had a spirit from time to time who returned as a gesture of gratitude to help her when she needed it.

"What do I need to do?" Holly looked up at Rus again, their eyes wide and so achingly young. But they had lifted one of their own hands to their chest, clearly tempted to reach back.

"Just take my hand, and my magic will do the rest." Rus sucked in a breath, readying herself for the sensation of sending a spirit through to the other side. Holly still didn't look convinced, they were holding their hand close to their chest, their eyes flickering between wide and glassy, and the deep pits of a spirit left to languish too long. "You can come back, and visit, if you like," Rus said, trying to ease some of their worries. "I have spirits do it all the time."

"How?" A frown pursed Holly's lips, and Rus resisted the urge to sigh.

Pinching the bridge of her nose, Rus shifted around on the cold hard floor. Her back was starting to ache from sitting there, but she wasn't about to move, not until she'd gotten Holly to move on. Something passed them in the hall, a whisper of material, and boots, that told Rus the other spirit or spirits were close. She needed to get Holly out of there before the others scared them off.

"You just have to use my name," Rus explained, patient in spite of the rushed feeling nipping at her limbs. "Because I helped you move on, I can act as a direct line to come back whenever you'd like to check in. It's temporary, of course, but many of the spirits I help come back every once in a while. Unless of course they choose to reincarnate."

"Rus." Holly repeated the name, and the wrinkle between their brow eased a fraction.

"Icarus Ashthorne." Rus held out her hand again, this time like she meant to shake Holly's hand.

Holly blinked at it another moment before lurching forward and grabbing onto Rus's hand to give it a hard shake. A shudder ran up Rus's arm, lifting every hair in its wake, a bone deep chill that ached on a cellular level followed. But she held firm, clasping onto the freezing, insubstantial palm clasped around her own. One second. Two. Then the light from her magic, and from Holly faded, and Rus was left alone in the dark of the empty apartment.

Her breath was loud in her ears, her heart slamming against her chest as if trying to make up for the fact that it had stuttered the second Rus had helped Holly over to the After. A side effect of Rus's abilities that she recognized was probably worrisome and unhealthy, but didn't ever really have time to contemplate. Especially not now as there was a soft shushing sound, and she felt the cold breath of someone or something on her face.

The chill twisted around her throat, as if it were trying to choke her, or maybe look for a pulse. Fuck. She really should have just worn the damn talisman shouldn't she have? And her bag was all the way by the door. There was no time to get to it and pull from it what she needed. She'd have to wing it.

"What I wouldn't give for names," Rus mumbled lifting her lids just enough to see the blurry shapes of two figures through her lashes. They were drifting around each other, tangled together.

They cackled, the sound echoing, and chilling. The grip around her throat tightened enough that Rus was gasping for breath, and slammed her onto her back on the ground. Coughing, the breath knocked from her, Rus twisted, her eyes flying open as she scrambled at the hand locked around her throat. It had a dark vine running up it, thick, and dense enough that it looked to be absorbing what little light there was coming in through the window from the outside. It twisted round and round the first spirit's arm like a snake, before ending at a face that peeked over its shoulder. The face, what Rus could see of it through its long dark hair, was sharp, and angular, that of an older woman where the first spirit's was a young man.

"Creepy," Rus choked around the tightness at her throat, and the man's spirit snarled in her face, breath misting her cheeks in ice before he lifted her head and slammed it into the floor beneath again causing her to see stars. The floor creaked with the impact. *Fuck, I hope that doesn't give out.* Pain lanced through her skull as he grabbed her by the hair, lifting her head in preparation for another hard slam against the floor which may very well render her unconscious.

Her phone started ringing right then, distracting the spirit with the bright tones of some K-pop song Az had chosen as her ringtone. Rus thanked the Goddess that her phone wasn't on vibrate, gathered her magic to herself in the brief moment of respite, and slammed it into the spirit's chest.

He flailed back onto his ass, legs kicking out like an upturned turtle, giving Rus just enough time to scramble to her bag and yank out the little spirit box she'd brought along. Thunking it hard against the old floor, she pressed the latch and it popped open like a flower bud. A faint sucking noise followed, a vacuum cleaner with a sock stuck in it, then it ripped the spirits from where they were still trying to get its bearings. The box shut with a click, leaving Rus panting in the aftermath.

She sat for a moment, just trying to get control over her upset magic again, the green light lashing out around her, leaving tiny burn marks in the floor. When her heart had finally stopped pounding in her chest, she let herself slip back through the veil, pulled her hood up over her head, and reached for her phone at the bottom of her bag as a chill crawled up her spine, something lingering from beyond the veil that would probably slough off after she'd crossed the salt line. Still, she hated the way its eyes followed her, a feathery caress that made the hairs on the back of her neck stand on end.

A quick glance around showed no lingering spirits, but that didn't mean there wasn't something there. Rus shook herself, looked down at her too-bright phone screen to check her messages, and got a look at the time instead.

"Fuck me. I'm late," Rus hissed, clambering to her unsteady legs to haul ass back to Moondale. "Az is going to skin me alive!"

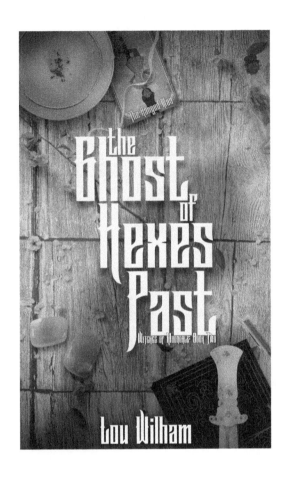

Pre-order your copy today!

acknowledgments

I always start these things by thanking the reader, and this book is no different. I want to thank *you*—whether you're a returning reader or Lou is new to you—for picking up my little indie published book, supporting my dream, and following along with Rus and Az on their journey. Without readers, I can't do what I do, so I greatly appreciate the support.

If you loved every moment of Rus and Az's story (as I hope you did) please leave a review, follow me on social media, or give me a shout out on your blog. I love hearing from you guys, it's really the best part of writing.

Next I'd like to thank my family who supports me in this weird journey I'm on to become an established author. They show up to my signings, they listen to my rants about my characters, they look at my covers and tell me when they're complete shit (I design my covers FYI), and they're the best people to have in my corner, no joke.

Then there is the small hoard of beta readers I had look at this bugger to tell me if any of it actually made sense, and if I'm as funny as I think I am (turns out I am). Thanks Tanya, Meg, Val, and Steph! You guys provided so much helpful feedback you don't even know.

And of course my editor, Brenna. Who I have only worked with on one small project before, but who gave this story all of her love, just as I did.

And last but certainly not least, thank you to my publishing family at MTP.

more books you'll love

If you enjoyed this story, please consider leaving a review.

Then check out more books from Midnight Tide
Publishing!

come true

Come True by Brindi Quinn

A jaded girl. A persistent genie. A contest of souls.

Recent college graduate Dolly Jones has spent the last year stubbornly trying to atone for a mistake that cost her everything. She doesn't go out, she doesn't make new friends and she sure as hell doesn't treat herself to things she hasn't earned, but when her most recent thrift store purchase proves home to a hot, magical genie determined to draw out her darkest desires in exchange for a taste of her soul, Dolly's restraint, and patience, will be put to the test.

Newbie genie Velis Reilhander will do anything to beat his older half-brothers in a soul-collecting contest that will determine the next heir to their family estate, even if it means coaxing desire out of the least palatable human he's ever contracted. As a djinn from a 'polluted' bloodline, Velis knows what it's like to work twice as hard as everyone else, and he won't let anyone—not even Dolly f*cking Jones—

stand in the way of his birthright. He just needs to figure out her heart's greatest desire before his asshole brothers can get to her first.

COME TRUE: A BOMB-ASS GENIE ROMANCE is the romantic, fantastic second-coming-of-age story of two flawed twenty-somethings from different realms battling their inner demons, and each other, one wish at a time.

Available Now

the devil you know

Burnout by Devon Thiele

Her boss would call it a 'strongly encouraged leave of absence.' Quinn Brennan would call it her last chance.

Quinn, as the leading magical analyst for the Arcanum —a renowned organization advancing the world's knowledge and use of magic, as well as defending against its darker forces—, is no stranger to life-or-death decisions on the front lines in the battle against magic. Driven to advance her career in the Arcanum to fulfill a promise to her parents, Quinn has always put work first. When one decision goes awry, it costs Quinn her career, two of her closest friends, and her self-confidence. Now placed on leave from the job she once loved above all else, she is determined to prove that she still has what it takes to be number one.

Her interest piqued by reports filed by the town of Beteville located in magic's hot zone, Quinn uses her leave of absence to conduct an investigation of her own. What she finds is a mystery that was decades in the making.

When townspeople begin disappearing without a trace, eerily like those thirty years prior, Quinn must use her Arcanum experience. Assisted by the lone survivor of her last botched mission, Quinn must put a stop to the Beteville Beast for once and for all or lose her last chance at redemption.

Preorder Now

beneath the willow

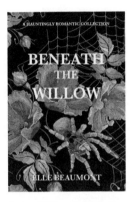

Beneath the Willow by Elle Beaumont

Love deserves a second chance.

Something lurks deep within the mysterious inn, and when a paranormal expert arrives, so does an unexpected visitor.

A woman pores over letters she discovered in an old bookstore, and every time she reads them, she can feel the presence of the man who wrote them, making her uncertain of her sanity.

A spirit plagues the owner of an inn, but when a paranormal investigator arrives, he requires the aid of the anomaly, or the owner risks losing everything.

After a tragic loss, a man leaves his old life behind. Beginning a new adventure should be easy, but when a friendly ghost appears, he realizes nothing ever is. But with memories of his past haunting him, will he ever be truly ready?

Beneath the Willow is a romantic collection of ghost stories that will haunt you long after reading. From newfound love to rekindled flames, and even healing after loss, these contents are dark, beautiful, and tragic, surely inspiring heart-pounding moments and tears.

Available Now